DOUBLE BLUFF

I am sorry I have not learnt to play at cards. It is very useful in life: it generates kindness, and consolidates society.

Dr. Samuel Johnson, as quoted in *The Journal of a Tour to the Hebrides*

DELL SHANNON

Double Bluff

WILLIAM MORROW & COMPANY

New York, 1963

DOUBLE BLUFF

CHAPTER ONE

"You're going to be late," said Alison, pouring Mendoza's coffee as he came into the kitchen. "I've finished the paper—you're all over the front page." She plucked El Señor off the table for the fifth time, and he lashed his blond-tipped tail sulkily. Bast got up on Mendoza's lap.

"Damn," said Mendoza. "And Holmes will never believe I didn't angle for it." He looked at the front page resignedly. If he was not exactly all over it—space was also devoted to the Russians, the newest satellite, and the arrival of some V.I.P. from Norway—he occupied a prominent spot in the upper left-hand column. KILLER CAPTURED AFTER ASSAULT ON POLICE, said the headline; and the cut showed a somewhat disheveled but recognizable Mendoza in the foreground, with a couple of much bigger men behind him grimly handcuffed together. "And if I didn't know," he added, "I wouldn't like to guess which one was the honest man. Art looks much more the criminal type. Talk about a tempest in a teapot. A very ordinary thug—only a question of time before we dropped on him. You'd think they'd have enough news without building it up like this. And it was Art who got assaulted, not me."

The story started out, *"Lt. Luis Mendoza, star veteran of Headquarters Homicide, today arrested and charged Fred W. Myers, no fixed address, as the brutal mugger who for six weeks has terrorized lone women and murdered two in the course of robbery."*

"I don't know that I care for that 'veteran.' I'm not senile yet, am I? . . . Well?"

"What?" said Alison, looking up. "Oh, certainly not, *amante*. . . . Athelstane, now there's a nice name, don't you think? Athelstane Mendoza. It means 'noble stone.'"

Mendoza looked at her, getting out a cigarette. "This low humor I don't appreciate, especially at breakfast. And the doctor said you ought to have more than just toast and coffee."

"Pot calling the kettle black. I never want much breakfast. . . . And if it's twins, which is quite likely, you know—twins on both sides of my family——"

"*¡Ay de mí!* Don't hold the thought, damn it!"

"—we could call the other one Aspasia. Or Aubrey. Or," said Alison, turning a page in the Oxford Dictionary of Christian Names, "Augustus."

"In fact," said Mendoza, lifting Sheba off the table, "a new low level of humor. Of course it's my own fault for marrying a Scots-Irish girl, and a redheaded one at that. When I think of what the combination might produce——"

"It would be rather funny," agreed Alison, "if it—or

10

they—got that. Redheaded Mendozas. You know what it comes down to, Luis—we'll have to go all the way in one direction or the other. The only thing to do. Of course I always thought I'd like to call a boy for my father."

"I don't think I remember——"

"Angus Andrew," said Alison.

Mendoza set down his coffee cup and said, *"¡Carape, que Dios te envie a otra parte!* Over my dead body!"

"Well, of course it'd sound odd. But that's just what I say, we'll have to go one way or the other. Either Angus Andrew or something like—like Rodolfo Diego. Of course we've still got seven and a half months to decide."

"It should be obvious by now that it's what's called an impasse," said Mendoza, pushing Nefertite's nose out of his coffee. "And I thought we'd agreed——"

"On Teresa, if it's a girl, for your grandmother. Yes, that's all right. But it *is* apt to be twins——"

"There you go again, just inviting trouble," said Mendoza.

"Well, it's past praying for now, idiot," said Alison.

"There's a properly respectful wife. And I will be late now." Mendoza swallowed half of his second cup of coffee and went to get his jacket and hat. Shrugging into the beautifully cut new silver-gray herringbone, he added, "It should also be obvious that there's only one possible solution: John. Unless you want him to go through life explaining his peculiar ancestry to every chance acquaintance."

"Well——" said Alison.

11

He put a hand under her chin, bent to kiss her. "See you at six, *querida*, unless something comes up. And if you go out, *not* the high heels. The doctor said——"

"Oh, bother the doctor!" said Alison. "I'm feeling fine, it's a perfectly natural process after all. . . . Boniface, Botolf, Brendan—my grandmother's maiden name was Brendan—— Yes, all right, good-by, *amado.*"

"*¿Porvida, donde irá a parar todo esto*—what will be the end of this indeed?" wondered Mendoza, kissed her again, patted all four cats, and went out to the garage for his Ferrari.

He fully expected to take a little kidding about his publicity over the ordinary thug, and he was not disappointed. Sergeant Arthur Hackett, who had sustained a wrenched shoulder and several bruises in the actual capture, said rude things to him. But Captain Edward Holmes really meant the rude things he said.

Inadvertently, Mendoza had managed to get his name in the papers on several occasions in the last year or so, and if it didn't matter to him one way or the other, it did to his immediate superior. Not that Holmes would ever admit it, but he'd have enjoyed being featured in the papers, and saved clippings secretly. Possibly what annoyed him more than the mere fact that Mendoza received the attention was that he was indifferent to it. And that was to have certain unfortunate results.

But a more immediate result of this latest publicity came at a little after ten o'clock.

Mendoza had gone over the new cases that had turned up overnight—all routine; discussed the Hammersmith business with Hackett and agreed on what to do about it; and was now going over the Shane case with Sergeant Palliser, and approving his handling of it. Palliser, who had made rank less than a year ago, was turning out to be a bright boy; Mendoza liked him.

"O.K., then, you go on handling it that way and we'll see what——" He looked up as the office door opened.

"Excuse me, Lieutenant," said Sergeant Lake, "but" —he shut the door behind him—"I can't get rid of this nut. He says he's got to see you. Says it's about a murder. I think he's just a crank of some kind, but he won't leave. He gave me a card."

Mendoza took it. "Lawrence S. Winthrop III. Well, well, how impressive. All right, I'll give him ten minutes, Jimmy. If I buzz you, come and help me toss him out. O.K., John, you carry on and keep me up to date." Palliser went out, and Sergeant Lake held the door open for Mr. Lawrence S. Winthrop III.

Mr. Winthrop was in his late fifties, tall, lean, and scraggly, with a hatchet profile, thin gray hair, and weak china-blue eyes behind horn-rimmed glasses. He came in in a rush, hat in hand, already talking.

"Lieutenant Mendoza? You are the same—yes, I see you are—the picture! It appears, sir, that *you* are an efficient police officer. I said to Janet at once, we must have *you*, when I saw what this morning's *Times*—— You have my card, sir? It is a most urgent matter, Lieutenant, and I am quite put out at those fools of policemen! But an experienced officer like yourself——"

"Sit down, Mr. Winthrop," said Mendoza, "and tell me what this is all about, won't you?"

"Thank you, thank you—yes, I must be calm and

orderly, I must—— But there, you see how inefficient they are, when they have not informed their own headquarters! This *is* the headquarters of the Los Angeles Police Department, is it not?" Mendoza admitted it. "You see! I must tell you—something must be done at once! It's my sister—my older sister Arabella—I tell you, Lieutenant, she has been made away with—murdered! Murdered in cold blood by her villain of a husband! On," said Mr. Winthrop anticlimactically, "last Tuesday evening. New Year's Day, in fact."

"Just a moment," said Mendoza. "You said something about police, Mr. Winthrop. Which police? Where did this crime occur, if—mmh—it did occur?"

"I swear to you—this vulgar upstart from heaven knows where—Bella is dead in some terrible way, perhaps he has buried her, or even dismembered—one reads of such things—— Where? Of course you must ask for relevant facts. Yes. My own address is the Trevelyan Arms, 4766 Wilshire Boulevard. Bella's name and address is—*was,* I should say!—Mrs. Francis Ingram—and I always thought it was a made-up name, doubtless the fellow has a police record somewhere— Mrs. Francis Ingram, 296 Sycamore Terrace in Hollywood. I——"

"Yes, thank you. But neither of these addresses is in the Headquarters jurisdiction, Mr. Winthrop. You should——"

"I am telling you, sir, I have gone to the—um, ah, the precinct is the correct term, is it not?—but had absolutely no satisfaction! The officer I spoke to has taken no action in the matter at all—disgraceful—he appeared to believe the lies Ingram told him. He had the

14

effrontery to say—— But when I noticed the article in the paper this morning, I said to Janet—that is my other sister, Lieutenant, my younger sister, Mrs. Janet Barron—I said, 'We must go to higher authority for any result.' I am convinced——"

"But I'm afraid Headquarters can't interfere," said Mendoza, "unless we're officially requested, you see. You went to which precinct station, Mr. Winthrop, Wilcox Avenue or Pico Boulevard? Wilcox, yes. Who did you see? . . . Lieutenant Ames, yes. Well, we can't take over unless Lieutenant Ames or his superior asks us—— Yes, certainly it's all the same police force, but—— The Headquarters jurisdiction takes in only —— Yes, I understand, Mr. Winthrop, but——" After five minutes of this he despaired of getting through to Winthrop, buzzed Sergeant Lake, and stood up. "I'm very sorry, but you must understand it's outside my jurisdiction. And we're rather busy this morning, I'll have to ask you to excuse me."

They got rid of him with some difficulty. "Just a nut," said Sergeant Lake, when Winthrop had finally stalked off down the hall in what he'd probably call a huff.

"Maybe," said Mendoza. "Never knew anybody really talked like that." He went back to his desk, picked up the outside phone, and requested the Wilcox Avenue station in Hollywood. Was Lieutenant Ames there? He was; who wanted him? . . . Just a minute, sir.

Lieutenant Ames had a rough bass voice and sounded tired and elderly. "Winthrop?" he said. "Yeah?"

"I just had him here, telling me how inefficient you boys are. I thought you'd like to know, he's hell-bent for making trouble, this kind or that. When he left he was muttering something about seeing the editor of the *Times* to Demand Action."

"Oh, fine," said Ames. "That's all we need."

"I don't want to butt in on your business, which is what I told him. We've got quite enough to keep us busy down here."

"I bet," said Ames. "I suppose it could be he's right, but there's nothing to go on. We went and looked, what else? We have to investigate complaints. But it looks like just nothing, see? These Ingrams are Money. Big new house in an exclusive section, two Caddies, the works. Both in the sixties, married just a couple of years—she was a widow. Ingram, he's annoyed, and I don't blame him. He says her family never did like him, resented her getting married at all, to anybody, you know? And now they're telling nasty lies about him and jumping to wild conclusions. He seems like a nice fellow, perfectly O.K."

"Yes? What about Mrs. Ingram?"

"Well, she's gone off somewhere, but what's that say? Since last Tuesday, Ingram says. He's perfectly frank about it, says she got a little miffed at him about something and decided to go off alone for a few days. Says she's done it before. She packed a bag and drove off in her own car. Well, I ask you, Mendoza. I'm not justified in sending out an eight-state alarm, or digging up the damn yard for a body, on that. Chances are Ingram's telling the exact truth and she's in some classy motel down at La Jolla or up at Santa Barbara."

"How right you are. You told Winthrop if she didn't

show up after a reasonable time to go to Missing Persons."

"Well, hell," said Ames, "it's not as if we'd found bloodstains all over, or something like that. The woman's competent, she can do what she wants, and Winthrop admitted he's known her to go off for a weekend alone before. He's just imagining things, because he doesn't like the husband. But, my God, if he goes to the newspapers——"

"Uses in publicity," Mendoza consoled him. "It might turn up the miffed wife right away. Well, it's none of my business, I just thought you ought to know."

"Sure, thanks," said Ames gloomily. "And talking about publicity, congratulations on Myers."

"Oh, that. It wasn't really me at all," said Mendoza, as Hackett loomed in the doorway, "but my gallant senior sergeant. O.K., Ames, luck." He put the phone down.

"Soft soap," said Hackett. "I should be taking the day off, with this shoulder. And no sleep, or none to speak of. I don't understand it—Angel says it's perfectly natural, but *she* can stay home and sleep in the afternoon. Why the hell don't babies sleep at night like normal human beings?"

"One subject I know nothing about."

"You will, *hermano*—oh, brother, you will!" said Hackett, grimly pleased. "Like a time bomb. Two-forty on the dot every night, he goes off. And keeps it up steady until five o'clock. I'm just looking forward to August, misery loving company like they say. I hear Alison might have twins. She told Angel——"

"*¡Anda, Dios me libre!* From you too? *¡Basta!* I refuse to think about it. Any man's a fool to get married and involved in these domesticities."

"About two forty-five every morning," said Hackett. "I agree with you, in spades. Who were you talking to, about what?"

"Nothing important," said Mendoza. And there, unwittingly, he told a lie.

Apparently neither the *Times*, the *Citizen-News*, nor the *Herald-Examiner* thought much of Lawrence Winthrop's suspicions as a news story, but (as might have been expected) he was welcomed with open arms by the *Telegraph*. It was the kind of story the *Telegraph* loved; and the *Telegraph* knew exactly how to stop short of libel—just short of it. The allegedly missing Mrs. Ingram occupied half of the second page of the *Telegraph* next morning; and the accompanying column bristled with "alleged," "implied," "stated as personal opinion," and all the other indicated circumlocutions.

Glancing over it, out of curiosity, when Sergeant Lake drew his attention to it, Mendoza thought that if Francis Ingram couldn't sue the *Telegraph* he had a nice little case for libel on Winthrop. Who, surprisingly, was identified as "formerly active on local political committees," an occupation that ought to have taught him something about tact.

Both Winthrop and the *Telegraph* joined in baiting the stupid cops who refused to take action, and there was, of course, a dramatic appeal for Mrs. Ingram—if, after all, she was alive—to return home.

Which she didn't do.

That was the first indication that there might be something funny somewhere. Unless the woman had amnesia, she must have seen some paper (after a few days the others had carried the story too, more discreetly) or heard a radio news broadcast. And if she did have amnesia she'd probably have ended in a hospital somewhere, and been identified.

After a week, with no Mrs. Ingram turning up dead or alive, the papers lost interest and relegated the topic to an occasional mention on the back pages. But presumably all the furor started Lieutenant Ames doing his homework over.

Meanwhile, other less ephemeral cases came Mendoza's way to be dealt with; he didn't as a rule read any paper but the *Times*, which took a poor view of sensationalism, and he didn't follow the case of the missing widow.

Until, nearly three weeks after Winthrop had invaded his office, he had the widow handed to him.

On Wednesday morning, January eighth, Sylvia Glass had cleaned the hearth in the Ingram living room. And she found Mrs. Ingram's upper denture plate among the ashes. No attempt had been made to burn it; there hadn't been a fire laid for several weeks. It was just there. She was, not unnaturally, very surprised; and, Winthrop arriving at the house just then, she showed the plate to him. The discovery would have constituted a fairly good reason for his agitated charge of murder; but he'd been talking about murder the week before, to the police. . . . Ingram had nothing at all to say about the plate. "But it shook him," said Ames to Mendoza later, "anybody could see that."

There were also Mrs. Ingram's glasses, discovered on the first routine search of the house—lying on the dressing table in her bedroom. She was very short-sighted and wore glasses every waking moment. Ingram said she had two pairs of glasses; everybody else said they had never seen her wear a different pair, and her optometrist said he had never made her a second pair. No other optometrist, so far, had claimed her as a patient.

Which just sufficiently bore out Winthrop's charges that the Hollywood boys thought now that it ought to be investigated more deeply. But after a couple of weeks' vain work on it they decided they wanted no part of such an ephemeral business, and handed it over to Headquarters with relief. "And I wish you joy of it," said Ames.

Holmes didn't think there was much in it, that was obvious. If he'd had any idea of the publicity in store, he'd have taken the case on himself. As it was, it was also obvious that Ames was passing the buck. "And I can't say I blame him," said Holmes. "It's one of those things where there's nothing to get hold of. We could work on it for a year and never get any more, and I don't think, on what there is, we'll ever get to a prosecution. But there's just enough there so it's got to be worked on, you know."

Mendoza said he knew. On the way back to his own office, with an armful of typed statements, he did a little swearing. He had enough unfinished work on his desk now; and a thing like this, all up in the air, was always irritating.

He spent an hour digesting all the statements and transcribed notes, sent for Hackett, handed the pile over to him, picked up the phone, and called Ames to set up a meeting in his office. Statements and notes were all very well as far as they went, but personal impressions were often more valuable.

"All this," said Hackett, reading, "is just a handful of nothing. Mostly—— What the hell is this about calling an inquest? You can't have an inquest without a body."

"It's been done," said Mendoza. "There's this and that—have you come to the maid's statement yet? Well, it's our baby now, we'll have to do what we can on it."

CHAPTER TWO

"WELL, Ingram could have killed her," said Ames. "But I don't see why he'd want to. Not that that means much, I know——"

"No. They might have had a fight—he might have lost his temper and gone for her, something like that. A cynic might say," said Mendoza, "that the mere fact that they were man and wife—— How did he strike you, Ames?" He was getting all he could out of Ames before taking over officially.

Lieutenant Robert Ames chewed his cigar a moment before answering. He wouldn't be far off retirement, Mendoza thought: maybe in his early sixties. He'd joined the force a long while before it had demanded its present high requirements of I.Q., temperament, and education; but he was a long way from being a fool, and he'd had a lot of experience with human nature. He was a big paunchy man, bald and red-faced.

"Ingram's a nice guy, I liked him. Easy and friendly, you know. I tell you, in his place I'd have taken a punch at this Winthrop, but he just makes out he's kind of amused at Winthrop's suspicions——"

"Yes, that's one of the things that looks just a little funny to me," said Mendoza.

"For a fact, it does," said Ames. "I liked the guy, but I've been wondering if that doesn't maybe say he's trying to play down all the fuss."

"Mmh," said Mendoza, thinking of what all the statements and notes said about Francis James Ingram. In the last ten days a lot of routine work had been done on these people. Just in case.

The reports listed Francis Ingram as sixty-two. There had been a candid shot in the *Telegraph* a couple of weeks ago: he was a good-looking fellow. Looked younger than he was. Tall, and he'd kept his figure and his hair, which was either white or gray; he looked distinguished. Like a retired ambassador. He described himself as a former businessman, but said he'd retired since inheriting a modest legacy. He had met Mrs. Ingram—then Mrs. Simon—in January of 1961 in Mexico City, where they were both on a guided tour. They had been married in May of that year, and settled down in the house Mrs. Ingram owned in Hollywood.

Mrs. Ingram. Yes, thought Mendoza, a little something there. A picture of her too—a studio portrait, probably flattering; and of course a physical description according to police rules, since there was now a call out on her. She was sixty-one, and not very attractive; she had a characterful face, with a large aquiline nose and a little too much jaw, gray hair uncompromisingly short and straight, squarish plastic-framed

23

glasses. Five-seven, one eighty-five—she'd been a little overweight—eyes blue, complexion fair. She'd had diabetes and was taking insulin daily. She gave the shots to herself.

Her first husband, Rudolf Simon, had been an eminently successful real-estate promoter and dabbler in securities. He had left his widow somewhere around two million in capital. They'd never had children.

"But," said Hackett, still brooding over the maid's statement, "if Ingram married her for the money, that doesn't say he murdered her. So they had a quarrel once in a while—by what a couple of people say. She was strait-laced and didn't like his taking a drink now and then, and so on. They also say that Ingram never lost his temper, and the quarrels always got patched up."

"Well, what I thought," said Ames, "it could be it was a kind of accident, he did get mad for once and knocked her down or something, killed her without meaning to."

"Or I suppose," said Hackett, "he could have decided that life would be a lot easier with the money and without her. The will——"

Mrs. Ingram's lawyer had, reluctantly, parted with information to the police. Mrs. Ingram had made a will before her marriage in May 1961; she was a shrewd businesswoman and understood legal and financial terms. As was allowable (and, said the lawyer, an excellent idea) under California law (which acknowledged a general communal-property law in regard to married couples), Mrs. Ingram had signed a form claiming her listed capital holdings as her exclusive property, thus preventing this capital from passing into joint tenancy upon her marriage. She had then made a will. To Ingram she had left five hundred thousand dollars, the residue to be shared equally by her brother and sister—Winthrop and Mrs. Janet Barron —with the exception of a hundred thousand to her nephew. However, three months ago, in early October, she had revoked this will and made a new one. By this the brother and sister shared a half million and Ingram got the rest, except for a sum of fifty thousand, tax free, left to her nephew Hugh Barron.

The lawyer said austerely that he had no idea what had prompted her to make the new will. He really could not say whether its terms indicated that she had had a disagreement with her family.

There had, it seemed, been a loud family quarrel over the new will. The maid, Sylvia Glass, had overheard most of it. It appeared that Mrs. Ingram had been annoyed at some extravagance of her sister's, and told her relatives what she had done: whereupon such terms as "upstart," "confidence man," and "fortune hunter" had been bandied around freely.

Between the lines of the formally worded statement, Mendoza caught a faint true echo of Sylvia, eager-eyed: "An' then *she* said . . . an' then he comes right back with . . . An' then Mis' Barron, she said——"

The argument had taken place at a party given by Mrs. Ingram on Monday, New Year's Eve. Present had been Lawrence Winthrop, Mrs. Barron, Hugh Barron (twenty-six, employed as a salesman at an automobile agency), Linda Barron (described as a model, age twenty-four), and Hugh Barron's fiancée, Marcia Wills.

On New Year's Day, Winthrop said, he had gone to

the Sycamore Terrace house to "patch things up with Bella and try to make her see reason." He had seen her, but very briefly; she was just leaving the house to attend some woman's club party. But by what she said— or what Winthrop reported her as saying—she had then been very angry at Ingram. Her last words to her husband as she left were, "When I get home, we'll have this out and I'll have the truth!" Winthrop had left immediately after her, "not wishing to talk with Ingram, whom I have always regarded as a vulgar fortune hunter." That was about noon.

Mrs. Ingram had attended her party, at the home of a friend in Bel Air, and played bridge all afternoon, winning three dollars and sixty-five cents. There was no way to check the time of her return since the maid had the holiday off. Ingram said his wife came home about five-thirty and that they had had "a little fuss." What about? Nothing much; he liked a cocktail or two about then, and Mrs. Ingram was a strict teetotaler. In the end, she'd gone into the bedroom and packed an overnight bag and left, saying something about a few peaceful days alone. This she had done before. How often? Maybe three or four times since they'd been married. She got angry, and then after a little while she got over it, and everything was fine again. That was all. No, she hadn't said where she was going, not to him.

Her car was a 1961 Cadillac two-door, white. She'd had the tank filled, at the station she regularly went to, on the way to her party. No other station, apparently, had serviced the car since; nobody owned to seeing it. After she left the party at five o'clock on New Year's Day, nobody but Ingram admitted seeing her. Since the discovery of the teeth, Ames had set up a wide routine hunt. No hotel or motel within two hundred miles had knowledge of Mrs. Bella Ingram under that or another name. No hospital or morgue had received her. Nobody had seen the Caddy, license such-and-such. And that in itself suggested something funny.

Another point was that nobody could say how much cash she'd had with her. She had not cashed any checks since her disappearance. Even if she were staying away deliberately to make trouble for Ingram, she would need funds.

The second half of the maid's statement also indicated something a little funny.

The maid had a room and bath at the end of one wing of the house, off the kitchen. The two master bedrooms were in the other wing, and the Ingrams shared the largest. Sylvia said she'd come home about nine-thirty that night, and "gone along to the living room" to see if there was anything the Ingrams wanted. Ingram had been alone there, sitting over a book and a drink. He had told her that Mrs. Ingram had gone away for a few days. He said he wasn't feeling well, he thought he was coming down with a cold, and would go to bed early and sleep late. She wasn't to disturb him until he called in the morning. She didn't think much about that; but she did notice that the little hooked rug that had been in front of the hearth was gone, and asked him about it. He had seemed startled, and then said something had been spilled on it that wouldn't clean, and Mrs. Ingram had thrown it out. Sylvia had then gone to her room; but about twenty minutes later she had gone out to the garage. She wanted some solvent, from the big can on the shelf there, to clean a spot off the suit she'd been wearing. She also had carried the refuse can out to the street. That had been about nine-twenty; and she said that the two cars were in the garage then. Both Mrs. Ingram's white one and Mr. Ingram's blue one. That she was positive of, because she'd wondered how Mrs. Ingram had left and then thought she had probably been picked up by some friend.

Mendoza stabbed out his cigarette irritably. "So all right, Ingram killed her—either by accident or design. Why the hell did he dispose of the body? And so cunningly that it can't be found? As long as nobody can prove she's dead, nobody gets anything from that will. The obvious thing for him to have done, if he killed her, was to try to pass it off as an accident—a fall or something. Why didn't he?"

Ames looked at his cigar. "Not everything that maid said got into her formal statement, Lieutenant. She was awful interested in the family row, and thrilled to pieces at the idea of murder—but she doesn't think Ingram ever did such a thing. She went on to tell us he's an awful nice gentleman, put up with Mrs. Ingram's tantrums like an angel, and if you ask *her*, if the woman's dead she did herself in or one of her own family killed her."

"Like that?" said Mendoza. "Simultaneously causing her dead body and her car to vanish into thin air? What about the family?"

"Well, they're not exactly my kind of people," said Ames wryly. "I guess the right word for them is snobs. I don't gather any of 'em's got much money, except

Winthrop. Living in that classy apartment on Wilshire, I guess he's got some. But they fancy themselves all right. The Barron woman—well, maybe she's just an ordinary silly society female, but that young fella— kind you feel like kicking in the pants. Smarty. And the girl looks like a cold little piece. The maid says, and I go along with her, the whole family had their tongues hanging out for Auntie Bella's dough, and were mad as hell when she got married the second time. They never did like Ingram from the first, because he'd be due to get some of the money, they figured. It's on the cards they'd tried to turn her against him before."

"Natural, yes. What about this maid? Bright girl?"

"Not very. Tell you the truth, I think she was excited and blurted out all this about the car and the rug without intending to. Nearly as soon as she signed the statement she was going back on it. . . . I'd say she likes Ingram because he's good-looking and has nice manners. And didn't like the rest of the family because they're the kind of people don't treat servants very human. I gather Bella wasn't the easiest woman in the world to get along with."

"Mmh. You get the impression there's any involvement between Ingram and the maid?"

"Between—— I did not. He's—well, say he's not that kind. And her—well, to show you how dumb she is, she didn't realize that what she had to say was anything against him, until she'd said it and thought it over. You know? *Then,* she's very damn positive that if the car had gone out that night she'd have heard it, and she didn't. And Mr. Ingram's a nice man and wouldn't

29

do anything awful like that. So I says to her, well, if Mrs. Ingram's car was in the garage at ten o'clock on Tuesday night, and not there next day, it must have been taken out overnight. Whoever did it. So she says all in a hurry, oh well, now she thinks about it she can't positively say the car was there on Tuesday night. Maybe she was just so used to seeing it there, she took it for granted—— No, she thinks now the car wasn't there after all. But, like you see, we'd already got it down in her statement."

Hackett was flicking over the sheaf of papers. "When do we know for sure the car was gone?"

"Wednesday afternoon," said Mendoza. He was leaning back, eyes shut, smoking a new cigarette lazily. "Wednesday afternoon, about two o'clock, Mrs. Barron called on her sister and saw the garage open, and only the blue Caddy inside. As far as we know that was the first time the garage door was opened. The maid is vague about Wednesday morning, says she didn't notice what time Ingram came downstairs and had breakfast, maybe around ten o'clock. . . . One of the interesting things about all this is why Winthrop jumped the gun and got so suspicious right away. He says, and Mrs. Barron says, that Bella Ingram had made a luncheon appointment with Mrs. Barron for Wednesday. It was when she didn't show up that Mrs. Barron came looking. All right. But why jump to the conclusion that Bella's been murdered? Winthrop says something about 'the murderous expression on Ingram's face' when Bella was leaving for her party. But—— What kind of garage door is it, Ames?"

"What?" Ames looked surprised. "Why—oh, I get it,

the noise, sure—you won't get anything there. It's one of those electric-eye things. They say money isn't everything, but it sure as hell makes life easier. You know, coming in, you push a button on the dash, and going to get the car, you push a button set in the wall. It——"

"If it's the same installation I've got," said Mendoza, "it's an aluminum door on a counterbalance and makes almost no noise going up or down."

"You got one?" Ames wasn't aware that Mendoza had considerably more money than Mrs. Ingram, though he still occupied a lieutenant's desk at eight hundred-odd bucks a month. As he said, he'd never cured himself of earning an honest living, even after the old man died and they found all the safety-deposit boxes. "I thought they ran pretty high."

"About four hundred. But, as you say, convenient. How far is the maid's room from the garage?"

"Call it fifty feet. He could've shoved the car out by hand, it's a straight drive. No trouble."

"Yes." Mendoza sat up and opened his eyes. "What odds do you give she's dead?"

"Well, the D.A. seems to think we've got enough to hold an inquest on. There's her teeth—and her glasses —and the insulin. She hasn't bought any anywhere and she'd need it by now."

"Yes," said Mendoza again, sounding dissatisfied. He reached for the sheets in Hackett's hand, shuffled them for the one he wanted. "But still up in the air. I don't like it."

"I'm damn happy to turn it over to you," said Ames frankly. "I don't like it either. It's the kind of thing, you're damned if you do and damned if you don't."

"An inquest, on an upper plate and a pair of glasses!" said Mendoza. "*¿De cuándo acá*—since when do we operate this way?"

"There's the rug," said Hackett, taking back the sheaf of papers.

"To hell with the rug," said Mendoza. It had turned up, in rather odd circumstances. A Mr. Michael Underwood, of 207 Sycamore Terrace, had brought it in to them. Rubbish collection along Sycamore Terrace was made early on Wednesday mornings; residents put out their refuse at the curb on Tuesday nights. Mr. Underwood, who was a T.V. script writer, had accumulated two wastebaskets full of scribbled notes overnight on Tuesday, and rising early, had taken them out to empty into the refuse can. He had been surprised to find on top of everything else there a hooked throw rug which he'd never seen before. It was in quite good condition, looked clean except for a small dark stain in one corner, and he had rescued it for his den. His wife had scrubbed off the small stain.

Mr. Underwood had turned up with his tale of the hooked rug only three days ago; after mature thought, he had realized that the rug might be relevant to what the newspapers had been calling the Ingram Case. No, he'd never known the Ingrams at all. Well, he'd just thought some fool had thrown away a perfectly good rug, maybe a kid or . . .

Mrs. Underwood had used detergent and elbow grease on the rug; but the chemical lab of the L.A.P.D. is acknowledged to be the best in the world. The small stain had turned out to be human blood, type O. The maid reluctantly identified the rug.

Bella Ingram had worked as a volunteer for the Red Cross during the war, and had donated blood for the armed services. Her blood was type O.

"You can have the rug," said Mendoza, brushing tobacco flakes off the desk. "So Ingram is also type O. The commonest type, after all. He says once, a couple of months ago, he cut his finger opening a bottle and bled on the rug. Who's to prove he didn't? He says his wife decided she didn't like the rug, on the Saturday or Sunday before she disappeared, and got rid of it, he didn't know how or where. By his account, the maid just didn't notice it was gone until Tuesday night. He told the story about something being spilled because it was—*¡caray!*—easier. His wife took sudden unreasonable likes and dislikes, and he was just making it look 'more plausible.' He can't say at all how the rug ended up on top of Mr. Underwood's refuse can, but suggests kids. His wife sometimes did odd things, he says. So, prove it—prove she didn't."

"Well, but it adds up," said Hackett. "And when you put in the insulin—it seems she took the supply she had on hand, but that was only enough for about a week, and no pharmacist we can locate has refilled the prescription. She'd have needed more by at least two weeks ago. By what the D.A.'s office says——"

"I still don't like it," said Mendoza. "All up in the air."

Hackett laid down the pile of papers. "This one you'll need your crystal ball for, Luis."

CHAPTER THREE

MENDOZA was late coming home to the new, sprawling Spanish stucco house on Rayo Grande Avenue in the Hollywood Hills. He drove slowly up the left-hand side of the circular drive, alert for cats, garaged the Ferrari beside Alison's Facel-Vega, and walked around to the front door.

Past the wide tiled entrance hall, he turned into the large living room, and stopped short. It was a pleasant if slightly unexpected room. There were windows overlooking the side patio, and the tiled floor, walls, and curtains were all the same shade of cool aquarium green. There was an immense off-white sectional on two walls, and an antique mahogany table Alison had found somewhere and had cut down for a coffee table. There were two large leather armchairs, one dark green and one black, with matching ottomans. There was no hearth at all; the house was centrally heated and Alison said hearths were just habit and wasted wall space. But as a substitute of sorts there was a long, low credenza between two windows, bearing a lamp on one end; above it hung Alison's own portrait of El Señor elegantly posed beside a witch's crystal. On the opposite wall Mendoza had allowed her to hang one of her seascapes—pictures without people in them bored him; but on the rear wall hung one of his own choice, an excellent reproduction of Rembrandt's *Syndics of the Cloth Guild.*

At the moment, an extraneous object stood in the middle of the room: an open card table with a pack of cards scattered on it.

Alison came in from the second, rear doorway, surrounded by cats. She bore a newspaper and a jar of catnip. "Hello, darling—just a minute, I promised them——" She spread out the paper, emptied catnip onto it, and the cats pounced.

"Don't tell me," said Mendoza with misgiving, "that you're taking up cards. I forbid it." He loathed playing cards with women, who *would* chatter irrelevancies over the play. He kissed her and gave her a little shake.

"Heavens, no," said Alison, reaching up to smooth his mustache. "One of your interests I won't attempt to share. It was Bertha, she was telling my fortune. She says it *is* tw——"

"*¡Basta!* But I'll forgive you if it is. On the whole, you're a very satisfactory wife." He kissed her again. "Even a superlative one."

"*¡Cómo, oyé!*" said Alison. "What prompts the flattery? Not that it isn't appreciated——"

"I've been hearing about somebody else's wife who wasn't nearly so nice. Or, come to think, nearly so beautiful. At least," he added to himself, "I think the past

35

tense is the right one. And I don't think anybody's really mourning Mrs. Bella Ingram."

"Oh, are you on that now? Do you think she's really dead? *Did* the husband kill her?"

"Early to say," said Mendoza. He was watching the cats rolling in the catnip. El Señor was doing a complicated sort of ballet, using his sister Sheba as a prop. For no reason Bast suddenly stalked over and cuffed him hard. Mendoza laughed, hugged Alison again, and said, "Tell you about it at dinner. Which you should be seeing about now."

"I am, it's nearly ready. What's the husband like, as handsome as his pictures?"

"Maybe I'm prejudiced. Yes and no. Go and see to dinner, I'm starving." Mendoza stripped off his jacket and went down the hall to the bedroom to hang it up tidily. He wandered back into the living room, watched the cats' antics, drifted over to the card table and sat down. Automatically he gathered up the deck and began to shuffle it. He was thinking about Mr. Francis James Ingram, and he was smiling faintly to himself. He cut the deck and turned up the king of spades. Shuffled and cut again, and turned up the same card. And again. Just a trick; and he didn't exhibit card tricks in public any more. Sleight of hand was not an accomplishment for a police officer to show in public. It put ideas in people's heads, when he later came out a pretty consistent winner—at any game except bridge, which he detested.

He fanned the cards and stared at them absently, whistling softly.

> You jack o' di'monds, you jack o' di'monds,
> I knows you of old, boy, I knows you of old——

"And I really think I do," he added to himself. "I think so. Now I wonder——"

He laid down the cards; and Nefertite landed in the middle of the table in one flying leap, tail fluffed and eyes wild. The cards scattered in all directions and Mendoza laughed as Alison called him to dinner.

Ingram was even handsomer than his photograph. He topped Mendoza's five-ten by a good four inches and carried his lean figure erectly. He had a long, regular-profiled face, very blue eyes, and a genuinely charming smile, with something oddly shy about it. His still thick hair was a beautiful silver, and slightly curly. He was very natty in charcoal slacks and a lighter gray jacket, both excellent quality; his shirt was immaculate, his dark tie discreet.

He had been nervous, and that wasn't surprising. But he was putting up a good front; he had shaken hands with Mendoza firmly, asked him to come in.

The house on Sycamore Terrace was conventional, if expensive: a long low ranch house painted white, its yard manicured and neat. Inside, it was furnished in early American. Ingram had hesitated at the door of the living room and then said, "I think we'll be more comfortable back in my den. Bella let me fix that up the way I wanted—not fond of early American myself. Chairs without padding, and all those cast-iron whatchamacallems." He gestured vaguely.

The den was certainly comfortable. There was a big

table-desk in modern design, two deep armchairs, plenty of ashtrays. A window overlooked a pleasant strip of garden. Above the desk hung the only picture in the room, a good reproduction of Cézanne's *Card Players*. Mendoza recognized it; his education in art had been improved lately. Ingram noticed the direction of his glance and said hurriedly, "Sit down, won't you, er, did you say Lieutenant? Here—can I offer you a drink? No? Sure? Well . . ." He sat at the desk, in the big swivel chair, turned to face Mendoza. He had a very pleasant deep baritone voice; both his inflection and his grammar betrayed some education—or a lot of practice. Not native Western, thought Mendoza; not Middle Western either, the *r* was too soft. Possibly borderline Southern?

Ingram leaned forward. "I—I was very pleased that someone other than Ames is taking over the investigation, I might say. I suppose he's an honest enough fellow, but I can't say I was impressed with his brains. Have you found out anything new?" He sounded earnest and anxious.

Mendoza smiled at him. "Well, I'm supposed to be asking the questions, Mr. Ingram, if you don't mind." He got out a cigarette. Ingram sat back and lit one of his own, flicking the table lighter quickly. "Tell me, do you have any theory to offer, as against Mr. Winthrop's, to explain your wife's disappearance?"

"I can't understand why nobody's found her," said Ingram. "Winthrop? Winthrop's a nut, Lieutenant, that's all. God knows he's annoyed me enough in the past, but to accuse me of—— The whole thing's crazy. Just crazy. . . . Of course I've got an idea what happened. It seems obvious to me—or perhaps I'd better say it did seem obvious—that after Bella left, either she had an accident in some wild spot where she wasn't found, or some ̣-up punk jumped the car and forced her to——"

"That kind of thing happens," agreed Mendoza. "But the car hasn't shown up, you see. Even if it had been stolen, and disguised in new plates and so on, it probably would have ̣urned up by now. And even if a punk like that had killed your wife, the body——"

"Yes, I can't understand that. Though there are plenty of wild places around here—ravines and——" Ingram was nervous all right; he kept fiddling with things on the desk. He snapped the lighter on and off, ran one finger down the blade ̣f the letter opener.

"Mr. Ingram, let's no ̣ ̣aste time on improbable theories," said Mendoza gently. "You can see as well as we can that the fact that Mrs. Ingram's denture was found here in the house clearly indicates that something happened to her here."

Ingram sat motionless, head down. "Yes," he said. "Yes, I suppose it does."

"She was a fastidious woman? She didn't go around even at home without her teeth?"

"No. No, she never took them out except to clean them."

"Yes. She certainly wouldn't have gone off for the weekend without them."

"No, but——"

"Do you think your wife is dead?"

Ingram sat up, passed one hand across his eyes. "She must be. She must be. I hoped for a while—but when

you found out she hadn't bought any insulin anywhere—. Yes, I'm afraid she must be dead." He turned
the lighter round and round. "But—you see, I've
thought—she could have come back, that night. I
wouldn't have known, I—— After she left, I went out
for dinner. Sylvia had the day off, you know." He looked
up, gave Mendoza his unexpected shy smile. "It's so difficult to make you people understand how Bella was.
Look, Lieutenant—all of us have odd little ways that
would sound very damn peculiar, just told about to
somebody who doesn't know us. Do you see what I'm
trying to say? Bella—she was a naturally domineering
sort of person, but she really wanted to be stood up to,
that pleased her. Most of her life she'd been able to
have things just the way she wanted them, and when
any little thing went wrong, or wasn't exactly the way
she wanted, she'd lose her temper. She—all her opinions were very decided, and she could be impulsive.
She did peculiar things sometimes, but, hell, don't we
all? That rug—if I could explain her to you—she'd
done things like that before. There was a Wedgwood
vase, quite a nice thing—she took a sudden dislike to it
and out it went, in the refuse. Well, she could have sold
it or given it to somebody." He leaned forward again.
"That was why I made up that story about the rug. Because when Bella threw out the vase—it was worth a
little something, you know—her sister Janet said
openly she was crazy and ought to see a head doctor,
hinted that the family could get Bella tucked away. I
was just—this time—covering up a little. I don't know
what she did with the rug, I don't remember whether
it was that Sunday or Monday that I noticed it was gone.

All I do remember is Bella saying she meant to get rid of it. And if you ask me, that's what she did—put it out in the refuse can. Sylvia just didn't notice it there when she carried the refuse out on Tuesday night. Maybe some kids fooling around, for some reason, transferred it to Underwood's. . . . Well, I don't know, you'll think I'm prejudiced and maybe I am, but none of Bella's family gave a damn for her. All they were interested in was her money. Janet Barron's always been at her to give that young bastard Hugh an allowance—Linda too. Winthrop's got enough money of his own, but he's a miser. None of them much enjoyed coming here for dinner and so on—Bella was strait-laced, never served drinks, for instance—but they kept hanging around, just on account of the folding stuff. And that's why they didn't—don't—like me."

"All very natural," said Mendoza, watching him.

"Yes, sure, I'm just telling you my side. I'll tell you one thing," said Ingram, putting out his cigarette, "I wish to God Almighty she'd never left me a dime in that damn will! *I* never asked her to—never expected it. When all's said and done, damn it, they were the only relatives she had, only fair it should go to them. And I never expected to outlive her. I've got a kind of shaky ticker."

"Mmh," said Mendoza. "You went out to dinner after she left?"

"She left all right. I saw her drive off. So nobody else did, but look, Lieutenant—in a way, that shows I could be right. The way I think it must have happened, now, is that she decided to come back—as suddenly as she'd decided to leave. Maybe she'd forgot something——"

41

Irrelevantly Mendoza thought, Not Southern, or that would have been *forgotten*. Possibly British originally? "—came back to get it, and met somebody here. It could be that Winthrop had come back to see her—he hadn't had a chance to talk with her that noon. I don't know. What I do know," said Ingram with sudden violence, "is that several people had reasons to—well, at least dislike Bella, and I hadn't a reason in God's world —not a real reason. Her family—well, Winthrop was always arguing with her about her investments, other things. I don't know much about that kind of thing, but she took chances on wild stuff, you know, and it worried the hell out of Winthrop. As if it was his own money, and maybe he thought of it that way. He never did like me, not from the first—maybe that was natural —but he needn't have gone on needling at Bella, trying to turn her against me.

"As for her sister Janet—one of these would-be helpless females. You know, poor little me. No reason she shouldn't be out doing a job of work, she's not fifty yet. She's going through what capital her husband left her, complaining every step of the way because it's not more, and she always had a hand out for donations. She took the line that Bella owed it to her, you know? Well, Bella didn't like the extravagant way Janet's living and told her so. But Janet couldn't argue back, not while there was all that money in the offing. Bella wasn't backward in criticizing the kids either—Hugh and Linda. That Hugh, sure, he pretends to work at a job, but he'd the hell of a lot rather be the playboy-around-town. Champagne taste, you know? Bella didn't like the girl he's engaged to—cheap little piece, she looks like—*and* said so. But she liked Hugh, he was good at getting around her. Come to that, I don't suppose the girl liked Bella much—not after Bella called her down for swearing. Well, I don't like to hear a woman swear myself. . . . But you see what I mean, Lieutenant. Somebody could have been here when Bella came back——"

"And why do you suppose anyone, after killing her either accidentally or deliberately, would go to the trouble of concealing the body and her car?"

Ingram said flatly, "I don't know. I just don't know. I suppose—it might have been a burglar. Even a couple of burglars. And then they—— All right, that's far-fetched, isn't it? . . . All I know is, *I* didn't murder her. Why the hell should I want to? My God, we had little spats now and then, the way most couples do——" He swiveled around in his chair, running one hand along the desk; there was a pack of cards lying on the blotter, and he picked it up. "Well, if you're married, you know what I mean—some people flare up at each other once in a while."

"Seeing that I've got a redheaded Scots-Irish wife, I do know what you mean," said Mendoza.

Ingram laughed, relaxing. He had fine, even white teeth that looked like his own. "Well—Molly and I never were like that, but some people . . . And it doesn't really mean a thing. I'm not telling you Bella was the easiest woman in the world to get along with. You've probably heard she was a teetotaler and while I'm not a man to tie one on every night—I can't take more than a couple on account of my heart—I like a drink now and then. She'd rant at me about it, but it was more or less automatic, if you see what I mean."

"Mmh," said Mendoza. He was watching Ingram's hands. As he talked, Ingram was shuffling the cards, very rapidly. It was a well-worn deck, with a geometric design in dark blue on the backs of the cards. They flashed between his fingers. He was not looking at the cards. It was as if his hands constituted a separate entity and moved of themselves. And they were beautiful hands; very masculine, but long, well cared for, with square-tipped fingers and manicured nails. He wore two rings; on his right fourth finger, a gold ring set with a flashing white stone which could have been a diamond but was more likely a spinel or zircon, and on his left little finger a smaller gold ring set with a square dark stone which looked like a bloodstone. The cards passed between his hands with a little soft whirring sound; he squared the deck, cut it, and looked absently at the card he had turned up.

"Ace of spades, Mr. Ingram?" asked Mendoza.

Ingram started, laughed nervously, and turned his hand to expose the card. "Oh—of course that's supposed to be an unlucky card, isn't it?" He had cut the nine of diamonds.

Mendoza regarded him with meditative amusement. "But that's almost as bad, you know," he said softly. "Ingram . . . I believe that's a Scottish name, and the nine of diamonds is often called the Curse of Scotland."

"Oh?" said Ingram. He put the cards down. "Is it? I wonder why. . . . Well, look, Lieutenant, all I'm trying to explain to you—I don't pretend it was any great romance between Bella and me. After all, people our age—— But we got along all right. I will say, Bella

44

never listened to her damn family when they tried to run me down—which they did plenty of." He brooded a moment over his clasped hands. "If she's dead," he said, "and I think she must be—I tell you no lie, I'd give a year of what life I've got left to bring her back. And at my age, that's something. . . . This is a terrible situation for an innocent man to be in. I quite see that you have to ask questions and so on———"

"Which I haven't been doing, have I?" smiled Mendoza. "Had you been married before, Mr. Ingram?"

"I—why, yes, of course. My first wife died nearly twenty years ago. We had no family. But why———"

"You were in business, I think you told Lieutenant Ames. What business?"

"Several businesses," said Ingram shortly. "I can't see what this has to do—— Well, I was a traveling representative, wholesale, for several different firms—mostly in the foundry line. Then, after my wife died, I inherited some money from an old uncle, and as I'd been told my heart was a bit shaky, I———"

"Uncle's name, please?" said Mendoza, uncapping his fountain pen.

"What the *hell?*" said Ingram. Fine sweat suddenly beaded his hairline. "This is completely irrelevant, I don't see why—oh well. Thomas J. Bailey. He died in Persia—he was an archaeologist—August 1947. . . . I don't know what he died of, presumably old age, damn it. I don't see———"

"Detectives ask all sorts of funny questions," said Mendoza. Ingram's hands were on the cards again; as if with an effort he folded them in his lap. "So you went out, after your wife left that afternoon?"

45

"Yes, I—it was too much bother to rustle up a meal for myself. I went down to Chino's on Hollywood Boulevard. . . . I don't know what time I came out, it'd have been about six o'clock when I got there. And, well, it was a pleasant night—I didn't feel like going home— I just strolled along the boulevard, looking at windows and so on. . . . Oh, I'm not sure how far up I went, but I remember crossing La Brea. . . . Chino's, it's just a little place, near Vine."

"Well, well," said Mendoza. "Quite a little stroll, Mr. Ingram—around fourteen blocks."

"Yes, well, it was a nice night—I hadn't anything particular to do. I took it easy."

"You don't find walking hard on your weak heart? Where'd you leave your car?"

"In a parking lot around on Vine. I strolled back on the other side of the street, collected the car, and drove home. I hadn't been back ten minutes when Sylvia came in."

"You knew about what time Miss Glass would be back?"

For some reason that question flustered Ingram. "What d'you mean? No, I didn't know—or care—it was her day off, a holiday——"

"And you didn't meet anyone you knew on your evening stroll. Well, Mr. Ingram——" Mendoza stood up leisurely.

"But haven't you found anything new? Anything at all? Look, my God," said Ingram passionately, "why should you listen to Winthrop and not me? If Bella's dead, I didn't kill her—I hadn't any reason in God's

46

world to kill her—but her family was all damn mad at her, and——"

"And knew," said Mendoza, "that most of her money would come to you, Mr. Ingram, by the latest will she'd made."

"My good God above," said Ingram, "I never wanted it or expected it. Damn it, I wish to God she'd never—— What can I say to convince you?"

"You don't have to convince me," said Mendoza. "We'll be looking into everything, Mr. Ingram, and if you're innocent we'll find it out." He hoped he was telling the truth; this was a tough one.

"I can't understand why the body hasn't been found," said Ingram distractedly. "Lieutenant, I know it's no use just saying it, but I swear to you I don't know one damn thing about it. I——"

"We don't do much boasting, Mr. Ingram, but this is a very efficient police force, you know. We'll find out all about it." He hoped he was telling the truth there too. He smiled at Ingram. "Sometimes we get dealt a damn low hand, you know—like the sucker sitting in with a sure-thing man. But sooner or later we usually take the jackpot."

Ingram, who had risen with him, stepped back; his eyes flickered. "I—yes," he said. "Yes, I hope so. Because I never had anything to do—— If there's any way I can co-operate further, Lieutenant, I'll be happy to."

CHAPTER FOUR

"OF COURSE Bella was a fool to have married again, at her age," said Janet Barron. "But the man flattered her. Just after her money. Probably, if the truth were known, he's lived off women all his life! And for all we know murdered them before too! As soon as he'd persuaded her to leave most of her money to him——"

"Then there hadn't been any quarrel," said Hackett, "that turned Mrs. Ingram against all of you?"

"No, no, certainly not!" said Mrs. Barron hurriedly. "It was all him! Well, I won't say that dear Bella wasn't a little *sharp* sometimes. She was very decided in her opinions, especially to me, but Lawrence is just the same of course. I'm the baby of the family, you see, both of them so much older, and according to them I've got no sense at all." Mrs. Barron tittered, turning her pale blue eyes to him earnestly. It was, Hackett reflected, a common enough type, and maybe the adjective was right in another sense too. The predatory woman, the stupid woman. Shrewd only in little ways, and very much self-centered. She might be fifty, trying desperately to look younger; bleached hair, clever make-up job, high-fashion clothes but, he could guess, cheap copies of the real thing. This middle-aged apartment on a shabby street in east Hollywood didn't say money. The late Barron had left her a modest capital in insurance and savings, but nothing spectacular.

"If only she hadn't *told,* about the will—he'd never have known——"

"Do you remember how that came about?" asked Hackett, watching her. She was restless, nervous, but he thought that was probably a normal state for her. Now smoothing down her skirt, now frowning at a jagged nail and scrabbling for a file in the jumble of objects on the table beside her, next drumming on the chair arm. Her eyes roamed around the room more often than they turned to him or her daughter. A pretty woman, a very feminine woman in the derogatory sense of the word, who had once been "cute" and was keeping up the act; and automatically she was half flirting with him as she would with anything in pants.

"Oh, that was partly me," said Linda Barron with a brittle little laugh. "As long as we must wash our dirty linen in public, as they say . . ." She slouched across the room, staring amusedly at him. Hackett, who looked remarkably like the big stupid cop of fiction, read her mind accurately. *This dumb lout of a cop, out of his depth with people like us.* "It's no good pretending, Mother. Dear Aunt Bella was an awful prude. She simply hadn't kept up with modern ideas. And you see, Sergeant, I happened to mention that evening, never dreaming what a fuss it'd make, that I'd been up at Lake Arrowhead the weekend before with my young man and another couple. It was really all quite proper, but Aunt Bella lost her temper, wound up by saying that her suspicions were confirmed, and she had better sense than to leave her money to be thrown away by immoral——"

"Don't try to make it sound funny, dear," said her mother fretfully. "Of course you're not *immoral,* but——"

Linda was a type he knew too, thought Hackett. Or did he? "Common" might also apply to her. Not the kind of looks he admired personally, but she'd make a good model. Flagpole-thin, tall, dead-white skin, dark hair in the latest cut, and deliberately odd clothes— tight scarlet slacks and a pink sleeveless sweater. But the agency where her name was on file said she wasn't often asked for; she was "difficult." That might figure. A hair-trigger temper, he could guess.

"And of course Aunt Bella didn't much approve of you and Mr. Harley Stevens," said Linda spitefully.

"Only a good friend," said Mrs. Barron vaguely. "I can have *friends,* I suppose? Do stop wandering around and sit down, dear, my head's aching so—— Really, I don't see how we can help you at all, Officer, we've *told* all you people all the little we know, and made statements——"

"Just a few questions," said Hackett noncommittally. He took her through the quarrel on Monday evening, to her telephone call to Mrs. Ingram on Tuesday morn- ing—"I felt I simply must get things right again, and Bella never stayed angry long. She agreed at once to have lunch with me next day. We were going to meet at the London Grill——"

"Yes. And where were you on Tuesday evening?"

"Where was *I*? Well, really, it's some time ago, I—— That's when he killed her, it must have been. Well! All I can say is, the police certainly seem to be investigating this in a very odd way. That man's the only person who had any *reason*—— Oh, very well, if you're so persistent! Let me think—well, I was simply here. Alone. Until about twelve-thirty when Linda came home."

"And you, Miss Barron?" asked Hackett pleasantly.

She was smoking in quick nervous puffs. "I? I was out, Sergeant. With my young man. His name is Bruce Lauderdale, he works in a sporting-goods store, and lives with his brother on Normandie Avenue. You'll find him in the phone book. We went to the Cha-Cha Club on the Strip."

"Thanks very much," said Hackett, ignoring her mocking tone. He stood up. "You heard your daughter come in at twelve-thirty, Mrs. Barron?"

She looked vague. "You *said* you got home about that time, didn't you, dear?"

The girl just looked at her. Not lovingly.

"Thanks very much," said Hackett again, and left them thankfully. Not very nice people, these. Not a very easy case any way you looked at it.

Behind the wheel of his old Ford, he looked up addresses. Catch Hugh Barron where he worked—better take a look at this Lauderdale—Mendoza had said he'd see the maid after Ingram; it was her day off again.

Hugh Barron was closest. Hackett started the engine.

Mendoza had missed the maid by half an hour; she'd gone shopping with a girl friend, said her mother. The house was a shabby old bungalow on a shabby street. The mother had no idea when Sylvia would be back. "She don't stay at the Ingrams' house now, see, she just goes by the day. We figured it wasn't exactly respectable, Sylvia just a young girl and all, and him alone there now. But she says he'd never do such a thing, he's a nice gentleman. Anything she can tell you, mister, she'd be glad to help an' show how he never done it. Way it looks to me, the woman just had a brainstorm and walked out. No telling where. Why, when I lived in White Plains before I got married, there was a fellow lived right acrost the street—Barnes his name was, he worked for the post office—and he up and disappeared one day and they never *did* find him. Not ever. So it does happen. Well, I'll tell Sylvia you was here."

Mendoza went back to his office and read all the statements over again. Several ideas had occurred to him, but on all but one of them he didn't see any immediate way to prove or disprove them. It was four o'clock. He went out to the sergeants' room, met Hackett just coming in, and beckoned to Palliser.

"How near are you to winding up that business? Well, let Rolf or somebody take it over. We're going to need all the best brains we have on this thing. I want you now, in my office. We'll kick it around a little. Art, do we have any photographs of Ingram?"

"Not that I know of, why?"

"A little idea, and the only one we can do anything about right now. I want some——" He swung on Sergeant Lake. "You see to it. Send somebody to borrow one of the newspaper shots—a good one. I want half a dozen prints by tomorrow morning. O.K." He shepherded Hackett and Palliser into his office, sat down at his desk, squared up the letter file and desk box, brushed ashes away, got out cigarettes. "First of all, what's the rest of the family like, Art?"

"Wrong side of the tracks with veneer," said Hackett. "I'd lay a small bet that both Janet Barron and the girl are tramps at heart. For one thing, and a kind of funny thing too, the girl said she was out with a boy friend that night. Gave me his name. I went and took a look at him. And if I ever saw a typical pro lout—he's got an invisible *Wanted* across his chest."

"My Arturo, the human electric eye. You don't say so. Maybe she has a low taste in men?"

"That wouldn't surprise me. He's a muscle man— looks like a 1930-type gangster. I want to have a look for him in Records. And seems the mother's got a boy friend too. One Harley Stevens. I caught the name and looked him up. He lives in the same apartment building. Retired railroad man, with a nice little pension— I figure that's what Mrs. Barron's got her eye on. Then the boy, Hugh. He's straight out of Noel Coward, or likes to think so. Brash young sophisticate. Calculated rudeness to shock you. He was the only one who said, all cool and open, that all they really liked about Aunt Bella was the long green. Said he could 'usually get around her.' He also said he rather likes Ingram, and doesn't think he'd have the guts to kill anybody."

"Mmh. Where was he?"

"He's no fool. He said right off, 'Oh, you're checking up on the family, are you?' No argument—he told me he was with an old girl friend. Gave a little smirk and said the girl he's engaged to is 'kind of prudish about what they call premarital behavior.' I've got the girl's name and address, but she wasn't home. I didn't get a chance to talk to the Wills girl, the fiancée. She's a file clerk in a brokerage downtown."

"Yes. So maybe the old girl friend will say Hugh was with her whether he was or not. Well——" Mendoza looked at Palliser. "This is the Ingram thing, as you've gathered. Have you followed it at all?"

"The gist of it, I guess." Palliser's long dark face wore an interested look. "It's all pretty much up in the air, from what I know."

"How right you are. You can look over all the documents later. Right now, we're going to go over it and try to sort out a few elementary facts. If I say anything you don't agree with, stop me and say why. . . . Now, it seems about ninety-nine per cent sure that Bella Ingram is dead. If she wasn't killed that Tuesday night, she's dead now, because of the lack of insulin. If she was murdered, either Ingram did it or somebody else did it. If Ingram killed her, he could have done it any time between her arrival home after her party and nine-thirty when the maid came in. Mrs. Ingram left the party at five and so far as anybody knows she meant to come straight home. She probably did, getting there about five-thirty as Ingram says. If Ingram isn't guilty, the time limit is even tighter, because anyone else would have been worried that Ingram would come in unexpectedly. And everything had to be cleared up by about nine, or a few minutes later. If he did come in then, and not earlier. And if it was somebody else, they'd have no way of knowing when Ingram would come home. All right. Now if the maid was wrong about the car being in the garage at ten-twenty, somebody must have taken the body and car away before Ingram came in, or he'd have seen the car. Of course, if the car was there, that puts the finger on Ingram. Take your choice." Mendoza put out one cigarette and immediately lit another. "It seems to me that the biggest mystery we've got here is why, why the *hell*, were the body and the car taken away and concealed? It's of no benefit to anybody, damn who killed the woman. Nobody could be sure there'd be an inquest and death presumed. I think the intention was total disappearance, and those teeth and the glasses were slip-ups. If they'd been taken away, we'd have no evidence to presume death, except the negative one of the insulin. The heirs would probably have to wait the usual seven years to get death presumed. Why would anybody want that?"

"Maybe," said Palliser, "there was something about the body—type of wound or something—to show who killed her. There'd be no choice then. I know it's far-fetched."

"It is. We've got so damn little to go on! Evidently neither of the Ingrams mixed much with the neighbors —some people in that block didn't even know them by sight. And nobody saw Mrs. Ingram come home or drive away again that afternoon. So we've only got Ingram's word. But there's a good deal of circumstantial evidence against Ingram. I don't need Winthrop to tell me."

"One thing that struck me," said Hackett, "was the last thing she said to Ingram when Winthrop was there that day. If Winthrop isn't lying. Something like, 'When I get home we'll have this out and I'll have the truth.' Maybe she'd found out something about him? He already had one reason to kill her, if he's that kind —about a million and a half. If she'd found out, say, he was two-timing her, or had a prison record, something like that, she might not only have changed her will but kicked him out. You saw him today, Luis, what's he like?"

Mendoza smiled down at his cigarette. "A little inspiration came to me about Mr. Ingram. We'll try to check it out. He's a very nice fellow, Art. I think he's acquired his gentlemanly polish by self-education, but just naturally he's a likable, nice guy. *Eso no quiere decir nada* —that doesn't say anything. . . . I think, you know, that this murder happened almost by accident, on impulse. Because, suppose it was Ingram, he'd be inviting suspicion to stage a fake accident the very day after he heard he was her principal heir. And suppose it was one of the family, they'd be fools to kill her while there was any chance she might change her mind and make another will more favorable to them. Half a million is a nice round sum, but two million is even nicer and rounder. Of course, maybe Hugh Barron wanted his fifty thousand right away, and felt like old Omar— take the cash, et cetera. But just on the surface, Ingram's our prize suspect, isn't he?"

Hackett and Palliser made affirmative noises.

"You really think so?" said Mendoza. "Well, well. Maybe I'm as smart as I think I am sometimes. So you think Ingram's the likeliest. Then tell me how he managed it."

"Well, that's obvious enough," said Hackett. "Say they had a quarrel—she'd found out something about

56

his past, say, and was going to kick him out. He knocked her down, not meaning to kill her, or decided the only way out was to kill her. Anyway, there she is, dead, and the stain on the rug. I suppose it's possible that her upper plate fell out when she was struck and he didn't notice it. The blood on the rug says she was near the hearth."

"Yes, I think that's the way that happened."

"Well, then for some reason—God knows why—he decided to hide the body. He probably carried it out to her car, to be ready. He couldn't drive off right then, he had to be there to put up a front for the maid when she came home—and tell the story about Mrs. Ingram going off for the weekend. He waited until the maid was asleep, and pushed the car down the drive by hand, and drove off to stash the body somewhere. And———"

"And the car," said Mendoza.

"Yes. And then———" Hackett stopped suddenly.

"Yes?" said Mendoza. "And then he grew wings and flew back home? Because, you know, wherever he put the body and the car, it was some distance away. Just conceivably, the car may have been repainted, fitted up with new plates and sold, and be in New York or Alabama by now. Which would argue some connection with pro crooks, of course. There are, as Mr. Ingram suggested to me, a lot of wild places where a body could lie for years, not too far away. But too far to walk, and I don't think Ingram's so big a fool that he'd order a Yellow cab to meet him at the foot of the Mount Wilson Highway, to drive him home. He'd know we'd ask."

"I'm a fool," said Hackett slowly. "Of course. Nobody could do it alone. But wait a minute, Luis. All right, say Ingram has a record, that he's still in touch with some pros. Maybe that was what she'd found out. The murder happens just the way I said, and then Ingram gets a pal to help him dispose of the body. He——"

"Why? Why should he want to? I'll tell you one thing," said Mendoza, pointing his cigarette at Hackett. "Maybe he went to Chino's on Hollywood Boulevard for dinner that night, but I don't think he took that long leisurely stroll afterward. Because he told the maid he wasn't feeling well, he was coming down with a cold——"

"But that was just an excuse so she wouldn't expect him up early next morning. So he could spend most of the night getting rid of the body."

"Pues no. Details, *amigo,* details! Just think it through logically. It wouldn't do him much good to have an excuse for ostensibly sleeping late, when the maid would be up at the usual time and almost certainly would see him arriving home. And he *had* a cold. I asked Ames. Ames saw Ingram first on that Wednesday afternoon, after Winthrop had made the complaint. And Ingram had the cold then—runny nose, sneezes, and so on. If he wasn't feeling well Tuesday, the likeliest thing is that he came right home. And if so, that's something else to say it was Ingram who killed her, because she'd only have been alone in the house, available to somebody else, for a very short time. The waiter at Chino's identified Ingram as a fairly frequent customer but can't say definitely whether he was there that evening or not. Well, we'll try to dig up Ingram's past history. That interests me quite a lot. There'll be

some information on the application for a marriage license—they were married here, weren't they? One of you look that up in the morning, and I've got another ace up my sleeve in this line, too. Also, we'll look for Ingram's uncle and his will—hell of a job, but there should be something to get, American citizen dying in Persia. Of course—well, we'll see. And then we'll have another hunt for the body."

"How? There's no telling where——"

Mendoza swiveled around and picked a soft-cover book from the low shelves behind his desk—the new Los Angeles County guide. "We can make some informed guesses," he said. "Come on, boy, use your head! Obviously nobody buried her in the back yard—lawn nice and smooth, no disturbance. Most probably the body, and/or the car, is in some wild spot in the hills, thrown off a cliff or somewhere like that. So——"

"Listen, there must be ten thousand places like that, and the Rangers are looking——"

"Yes. But there's a time limit, and therefore a distance limit," said Mendoza patiently. "*¿Cómo no?* If it was Ingram, he had to be back in the house by the time the maid got up, or she'd have seen him coming home. If it was any of the family, much the same limit applies, unless it was Mrs. Barron and Linda in collusion——"

"No," said Hackett. "They wouldn't pull the same way. They don't like each other much." He made a grimace. "Not much to choose between."

"Oh? Well, Hugh Barron has his own apartment, true. Nobody there might notice what hours he keeps. But he'd have to be at work by about nine the next morning, wouldn't he? And either Mrs. Barron or Linda would notice if the other one was out all night——"

"Not necessarily. They have separate bedrooms," said Hackett. "As long as they were there at the usual time next morning——"

"Granted. O.K. Winthrop has a Filipino houseboy living in. The same thing applies there. So we've got two timetables. If it was Ingram, he couldn't have got started until after the maid went to bed or at least to her room. Call it ten-thirty to six the next morning. If it was somebody else, then whoever it was could have started operations before Ingram got home—would have had to, of course—any time between six o'clock when Ingram says he left the house and nine-twenty when he says he got back. And had until about the same time Wednesday morning. O.K.? X had to get there— wherever 'there' is—and back. Say it's Ingram—he'd have had about seven and a half hours. About the longest distance he could cover in that time—call it an average of thirty an hour, because a lot of it would be in traffic—would be somewhere around a hundred miles, a hundred and ten. Give him a quarter of an hour to do whatever he did with the body and car. He'd have the same distance to do back home."

"Yes, I'm with you," said Hackett, "but in that range, my God, there's a thousand square miles of wild country! The Santa Monica hills, and even places in Griffith Park—the whole valley range——"

"I don't think it'd be anywhere toward the beach," said Mendoza. "Not really so wild, you know. New tracts, up most of the little canyons. No, I think X would have headed for the hills the other side of the valley—Angeles Crest way, or out Santa Susanna Canyon. Which puts another limit on it, because going in that direction he'd have to go through a lot of towns first—Glendale, Burbank, Eagle Rock, Pasadena—or the other way, Sunland, Tujunga, all the upper valley towns, depending on which way he was going. He'd have used up mileage. Ten, twelve miles over to the valley in any direction, and then across town there to the foothills, another fifteen miles at least. And if it wasn't Ingram, add on another two hours, even three—another thirty or forty miles." Mendoza flicked the book of maps shut. "Seventy to a hundred miles up in the Sierra Madre range—that's where Bella will be."

"You and your crystal ball," said Hackett. "You make it sound so easy! But why? Why in God's name go to all that trouble?"

"You tell me. Right now, I'm damned if I know. And," added Mendoza, looking at his watch, "I'm now going home. Maybe I'll have another inspiration in my dreams."

"What's your idea about Ingram?"

Mendoza smiled. "A funny one. We'll see. And if it's so, on the one hand it says he could be X indeed—and on the other, it says, very unlikely. . . . I like him, you know. He's a nice guy."

CHAPTER FIVE

WHEN Palliser came in the next morning, Sergeant Lake jerked a thumb toward Mendoza's office and said, "Straight in." Palliser obeyed him, and found Hackett already there, listening to Mendoza at the telephone. Mendoza, discreetly elegant as ever in charcoal Italian silk, was being rather formal.

"Captain—I beg your pardon—oh, Walslowsky, yes. I thought I'd better let you know that I'll have some men down on your beat, if that's all right with you. . . . Just some general questions. Rather than ask your men to spend time on our business. . . . That's very good of you, thanks. I'd also like a little information, if you'd be so good. What with one thing and another, I suppose you have to keep pretty close tabs down there on who's doing what. . . . Yes. Well, can you give me any idea which establishments might be likeliest to—mmh—turn a blind eye on the pros? . . . Yes. Yes, I know that, but——" He groped for his fountain pen, drew the scratch pad toward him, began to scribble. "Yes,

O.K. . . . Yes, I've got that. . . . Thanks very much, Captain." He put the phone down, lit a cigarette, and looked at the notes he'd made.

"And what's this all about?" asked Hackett.

"My little brainstorm." Mendoza was copying addresses; he glanced up as Dwyer came in.

"Jimmy said you wanted me, Lieutenant."

"Yes. Here are some pretty pictures for you." The glossy prints were blown up from one of the best candid shots the *Telegraph* had run of Ingram. "And here are some addresses. You and Higgins and John divide them up as you please. I want you to ask around at these places if anyone knows this man—under any name. When you've covered these, try the other houses down there too. It'll make a day's work."

Hackett peered over his shoulder at the list, and his eyebrows shot up. "What set you off in this direction?"

"Experience gained from youthful sins," said Mendoza. "You'll find some people who'll recognize him, but they won't know much about him. What I'm after are the ones who recognize him but deny it. I think all of you are smart enough to guess when a man's lying. Make up a list of the ones you think might be, when they say, 'Never laid eyes on him.' You won't be able to get all the names, of course. Try the proprietors too. O.K., off you go. Art, I want you to have a good look at the Hall of Records for anything on Ingram——"

Palliser took his list of addresses and started down toward the elevator, Dwyer turning into the sergeants' room after Higgins. Waiting for the elevator, Palliser looked at the list and exclaimed under his breath. One Hundred and Fifty-eighth Street, Redondo Boulevard, the 16000 block on Western—— He was being sent to invade territory which didn't belong to the L.A.P.D.

When the Congress of the State of California drew up its bill outlawing all games of chance, by some strange collective blindness every such game was specifically mentioned except draw poker. Consequently it is technically permissible in California to play draw poker, and nothing else; providing that city ordinances conform, public gambling houses may be operated for the purpose. Only one incorporated town within the sprawling metropolis that is Los Angeles allows public houses to flourish, and that is Gardena, a little town within the big town, population 36,000, some thirteen miles through town from downtown L.A. and Headquarters.

Palliser collected his almost new Rambler from the lot and started for Gardena. He didn't know what Mendoza's idea was, but he had no doubt at all that he'd find exactly what Mendoza had said he would find. The younger officers in Homicide tended to feel a little superstitious about Mendoza and his hunches. Palliser wouldn't be at all surprised to learn that Mendoza had second sight.

So he wasn't as gratified as he might have been to spot two liars at the first place he hit. This was Benny's Poker Palace on Redondo Boulevard. Even at nine-thirty in the morning its neon sign blinked on and off in three colors, and there were already men at the tables in the main room; not a woman in the place. Recognizing a new face, the manager, or the man in charge, hastened up to welcome him. Palliser produced the photograph and asked his question.

"No, I don't know him," said the man promptly. "You're police?" His eyes flickered away. "No, I've never seen him at all."

"D'you mind if I ask around a little? And, excuse me, are you the proprietor here?"

"Yes. And yes, I do mind, but I guess there's nothing I can do about it." Benny, if that was his name, turned abruptly and walked away. He was a little fat man in his forties, going bald, well dressed.

Palliser drifted around the big room, showing his photograph. Everybody denied recognizing Ingram, with varying degrees of suspicion, but Palliser thought he spotted recognition in the eyes of an enormous fat man about sixty, flamboyantly dressed, who wheezed when he spoke. One of the other men at the table called him Eddy.

Palliser jotted down the salient information and started for the next place. Where he would probably find another liar. Mendoza had said so.

He wondered how it was all related to Bella Ingram.

Mendoza got out and about that day. He admitted to himself that he didn't much enjoy sitting at a desk waiting to have facts laid before him; he trusted his own leg work far more than even Hackett's or Palliser's.

He went to see Winthrop first. The Trevelyan Arms was class and money, all right. Mendoza knew a little more about Winthrop now. The family hadn't been wealthy to start with; Winthrop had both married and made money, the latter by shrewd real-estate investments. His wife was ten years dead; they'd had no children.

An elderly white-jacketed Filipino admitted Mendoza to a large, starkly modern living room. Sounds from beyond an archway indicated that Winthrop was still breakfasting. He came in at once, bearing a cup of coffee; he looked even grayer and more scraggly in a black silk dressing gown over pajamas.

"Oh, Lieutenant, I am extremely happy that you have at last been put in charge! The *Times* this morning— my sister Janet was telling me—— Have you found more evidence? Have you found poor Bella? I cannot help feeling——"

"We're just starting work, Mr. Winthrop. I'd like to——"

"But can't I offer you a cup of coffee? No? I'd be happy——" Winthrop collapsed suddenly into a chair, folding up like a concertina. "What may I do for you?"

"Why, I've been wondering," said Mendoza with a smile, "whether you're psychic, Mr. Winthrop. We now have some evidence indicating that Mrs. Ingram is dead, but before it turned up, you were trying to convince Lieutenant Ames that she'd been murdered. What made you think so?"

Winthrop drew his chin into his collar. "I don't understand your meaning, sir. I knew that scoundrel was capable of anything—I had warned Bella time and again——"

"All you actually knew, on that Wednesday, was that your sister wasn't home. She had gone off alone before, and on impulse too. Yet this time you were sure she had been murdered. Why? What put that in your mind?"

"I stated my reasons, sir! When I saw Bella that Tuesday morning—or noon, rather, as she was leaving

—obviously she and Ingram had been quarreling—he looked quite murderous, I assure you! And then, of course, his threats—I overheard him as I came up the front walk—they were quarreling——" Winthrop patted his forehead with a folded handkerchief. "It was a warm day, the windows were open——"

"You overheard Ingram threaten his wife? This is the first we've heard of that. What did he say exactly?"

"But I'm sure I must have mentioned it in my statement! I was agitated, of course—upset—I distinctly heard him say, 'Bella, if you do that I'll kill you!' I'm positive——"

"Mr. Winthrop," said Mendoza, "this is the first time you have mentioned this threat. Why didn't you tell Ames about it, include it in your statement? You made that statement nearly three weeks ago, two days after you had first gone to the police. Are you asking me to believe that you were so agitated you forgot to mention this very important piece of evidence?"

"I don't care what you believe," said Winthrop stiffly. "That is the fact. I overheard him utter those words. And I will so swear to any authority, sir. You'd be better occupied in looking for more evidence of his guilt—though it seems to be sufficiently clear."

Mendoza looked at him in silence for a moment. Winthrop was nervous, his long bony hands restless, fidgeting. "I cannot understand," he burst out, "why the police are so dilatory! It is obvious——"

"Well, there are rules of evidence," said Mendoza. "Where were you, Mr. Winthrop, on the evening of New Year's Day?"

"Where was—— What on earth can that signify? Do

you mean to insult me by implying that *I*—— My own sister! Bella! No one except Ingram——"

"Had an obvious motive. No. Where were you, Mr. Winthrop?"

"Janet did say that the officer who saw her asked some strange personal questions. Very stupid—very stupid!" gabbled Winthrop. "In fact, outrageous. To set your ridiculous suspicions at rest, Lieutenant, I had a simple meal here alone, prepared by my servant, and spent the evening reading. I——"

"And your servant was here too?"

"Most certainly, and he was in and out of the room, he can testify to that. I must say, Lieutenant—I should dislike to think that our police force is corrupt, but——"

Mendoza stood up. "It'll be some time before Mr. Ingram comes into his inheritance and can offer bribes," he said mildly. "Would you make a formal statement about that overheard threat?"

"I will, sir, gladly—I cannot understand how I failed to mention—I was upset, of course——"

Mendoza left him still gabbling. He liked this setup less and less. He hoped to God they'd find the body; the D.A.'s boys were still arguing as to whether they had enough to hold an inquest. If it was up to him, he'd say no; he could imagine circumstances in which Bella Ingram might still be alive. Farfetched, but . . .

He didn't like any part of it.

He drove up to Sycamore Terrace in Hollywood. The maid opened the door to him, and looked immediately frightened when he introduced himself and said he wanted to ask her a few questions.

"I told all I knew to the other———"

"Yes, but I've taken over the case now and we have to go over the same routine, more or less." Mendoza laid out conscious charm, easy and friendly; she relaxed a little. "Is Mr. Ingram here?"

"Yes, sir, back in his den."

"Well, I'm sure he wouldn't mind if we just sat down in the living room for a few minutes."

She followed him unwillingly. Sylvia Glass was a generously built blonde; Scandinavian blood, he thought. She had a round, rather foolish face, shallow agate-colored eyes, a breathless high voice.

"He never did such a terrible thing," she said. "Besides, she might not be dead at all. People do funny things and—and she was funny. Awful high blood pressure she had, she was doctoring for it. Liable to go off her head, she was, way she acted sometimes."

"Sit down, Miss Glass." She sat down reluctantly on the edge of a chair, twisting her hands together. "If Mr. Ingram's innocent, you know," said Mendoza, "we'll find out."

"I'm sure I do hope so, sir. It's an awful thing for him, just not knowing what happened to her. Bad enough without that family of hers saying he murdered her. Of all things! I'd never've stayed here this long, but for him. He's nice and kind. He gave me five dollars on my birthday once, when I happened to mention it. And he'd try to smooth things over, times *she* was sharp about something I'd done. Her, she was as bossy as they come. And never a pleasant word with it, like 'how are you' or 'good morning.' Like you was a machine or something. Not real class, she wasn't. Just money.

You know. And funny, like I say—I guess that was her high blood pressure, way she'd take sudden notions, like about that rug. I do remember now her saying she was going to throw it out."

"Oh, do you? I'd just like to ask you a few questions——" He took her through the main points of her statement. Yes, she was sure about the time she came in that night. And she was now denying firmly that she had seen Mrs. Ingram's car. "I dunno why I said it was, it wasn't—I remember clear now." One witness adding to a statement, one retracting. *Qué molesto,* thought Mendoza irritably, what a business! "That's all I know," she finished defiantly. She was twisting a piece of her blue print house dress between her fingers; her eyes slid away from his. "After I went to the garage I come in and went straight to my room and I never saw or heard nothing else that night. That's all."

Mendoza's interest quickened slightly. "When you came back from the garage, Mr. Ingram was still in the living room?"

"Yes," she said too quickly. "I already said, I told you all I know."

"But how did you know that, Miss Glass? You went out the back door, and coming in, to go to your room, you wouldn't have been able to see into the living room at all—no occasion to go down the hall."

"Well, I did, that's all! I remember now, I did go down the hall to see if he wanted anything."

"Miss Glass," said Mendoza, "sometimes in cases like this people tell little lies because they're afraid the truth would sound damaging. Do you understand what

70

I mean? It's not a good idea. We don't like to arrest innocent people, you know, and we're pretty good at finding out the truth. Are you sure——"

"I've told you the truth! Why d'you think I haven't? I don't t-tell lies—I——"

He got her calmed down; he asked her random questions. Yes, both the Ingrams had been out most days; Mrs. Ingram belonged to a couple of women's clubs, and Sylvia guessed Mr. Ingram had friends and so on. If Mrs. Ingram was going out she would usually leave early, but he got up later and would go out somewheres in the afternoons. They didn't entertain much. No, she'd never heard them quarrel; Mrs. Ingram could speak up awful sharp sometimes, but he never answered her back. No, she'd never seen Mrs. Ingram give him money. What an idea! He had money of his own.

And she couldn't say, now, but what that hooked rug *had* been gone for a couple days; she hadn't noticed until that Tuesday night, that was all.

Mendoza met her stubborn eyes resignedly. There was something she hadn't told, and it might not be worth a damn, but he'd like to know what it was. Something she thought would be against Ingram; but she wasn't a very bright girl.

He stood up, thanked her, and said he'd go back for a word with Ingram. He walked down the carpeted hall, Sylvia padding quietly behind him.

The long desk in the den stood at right angles to the door; Ingram sat there, shuffling the cards. His handsome, boyish face wore a troubled, preoccupied look. ,The cards fluttered between his hands; he squared the deck, cut it, looked at the upturned card; shuffled and cut again, and began to lay out a game of solitaire, placing the cards rapidly, neatly.

"Good morning, Mr. Ingram," said Mendoza.

Ingram looked up quickly and put down the cards. "Lieutenant——" He rose. "Come in. Is there anything I can do for you? Have you any—news?"

"Nothing yet." Mendoza walked over and stood above the desk, looking down at Ingram, who had subsided into his chair again. "I just said something to Miss Glass, Mr. Ingram, that I'll repeat to you. Sometimes in a business like this, with police asking questions, people get nervous. They suppress the truth, or they tell a little lie—or a big one—because they're nervous about the interpretation that might be made of the truth. That isn't smart, Mr. Ingram. We're not ogres and we're not fools. We can even understand and sympathize with the reasons somebody might have and make allowances."

"Oh yes, I expect you do run into that," said Ingram, smiling up at him. "But I assure you, Lieutenant, you needn't fix me with your gimlet eye! I've been perfectly frank with you."

"There isn't any detail of your story you'd like to change?"

"My story," said Ingram, "happens to be the truth."

"It may interest you to know," said Mendoza abruptly, "that Winthrop has added a little something to his story. He is now eager and willing to swear that as he came up to the house that Tuesday noon he overheard you and your wife quarreling, and heard you specifically threaten to kill her."

Ingram went dead white, and then a curious sickly

green; sweat sprang out on his face. He lay back in his chair, gasping; raised a hand feebly to his shirt pocket, and painfully drew out a small tube. Mendoza was around the desk in an instant, taking it from him, opening it. "All right—in a minute—just one," gasped Ingram. With some difficulty he swallowed the little tablet, and rested for a long moment with closed eyes. "Thanks." And after another moment, "Said I had a shaky ticker. Damn nuisance. Have to carry those—in case . . . Winthrop's a damn liar. That's a lie. He never heard anything like that—because I never said it."

Mendoza gave him a minute more and then said, "He also says that as your wife left a few minutes later, she said to you, 'When I get home we'll have this out,' and so on. Is that true?"

"She said—something like that. Not as—strong words, as I recall——"

"What was that about?"

Ingram was still breathing deep and quick. "Nothing much," he said. "Nothing at all, really. Silly. She was—poor Bella—such a damn suspicious woman. She didn't approve of organized charities, for instance—thought they wasted money. There'd been a young fellow at the door—while she was getting dressed, about eleven-thirty—collecting for this Refugee Children's Fund." He moved restlessly, made an unfinished gesture. "Hell of a thing, just kids, no clothes, no food. . . . Molly never had any, she'd have liked—we were sorry—only she was always at me, no regular home life—— Hell, the kids didn't make the world they got to live in." Since his little attack his grammar had slipped once or twice, his accent roughened; but he was pulling himself together. He rested a minute, eyes shut, and in a stronger voice said, "I saw his credentials, he was level. Gave him ten bucks—all I had on me. Well, Bella came in just about then, and—I told her it was a single, see. She didn't believe me. She went on about it, giving good money away. That's all the argument was about." His eyes were still closed.

"It was your money," said Mendoza, "wasn't it?"

"Sure it was my money. With her, it was the principle of the thing, you know? . . . It's no good just saying it to you, I know—told you the truth—why the hell would I want to . . . ?" He sat up painfully and looked at Mendoza, meeting his eyes frankly.

A nice guy, thought Mendoza helplessly.

"I tell you, Ingram," he said, "it's not a cinch hand for you, or me, or anybody in this thing. I'll tell you what it's like—a bunch of females playing draw by their own rules, every other card in the deck wild." Ingram laughed; but Mendoza was exasperated. "Will you for God's sake open up with me?"

Ingram sat up straighter. "I've told you the truth," he said. "I've told you the truth—that's all I can do, isn't it? Are they—are they going to hold an inquest? Just on —those things?"

"I don't know," said Mendoza between his teeth.

CHAPTER SIX

MENDOZA'S temper was not improved by the necessity of attending a scheduled discussion with a representative of the D.A.'s office. Holmes would be sitting in too. The Ingram case had flared into life again in all the newspapers; today, for the first time, the press had been given the facts about the teeth, the glasses, the rug, and the maid's statement about the car. None of the papers was playing it up as a mystery, only as a new sensational murder; on the known facts, it looked pretty open-and-shut. The *Times* had a rather scholarly column wondering whether it was judicious in law to hold an inquest without a body, and citing cases in which it had been done. In two of the cases quoted, the presumed deceased persons had turned up alive and well later on. The *Herald,* as if unwittingly determined to annoy Captain Holmes, had a couple of paragraphs lauding Lieutenant Mendoza and recalling a few of his more spectacular arrests.

Holmes was sarcastic about the article, before the D.A.'s boy arrived. Because he wouldn't have been indifferent himself, he couldn't quite believe Mendoza was. He had a few things to say about playing to the grandstand, and added significantly, "I suppose you noticed the by-line."

Mendoza had; but he knew that Holmes was well aware of little César Rodriguez' motives, which had nothing personally to do with Luis Mendoza, but solely with the question of racial prejudice in a town where a good many delinquents and pros mentioned in the papers happened to possess Spanish names. He did not call this to Holmes's attention.

The D.A.'s man, when he arrived, was vague and unhelpful. Neither he nor Holmes had any serious doubt that the woman was dead or that Ingram had killed her; but they all agreed that it would be nice to have a body.

"I don't think it's a foregone conclusion that Ingram's guilty," Mendoza told them. "Yes, yes, I know he's the obvious one. But I don't think this case is as obvious as it looks. I want to do a lot more poking around, and so I'd very much rather you decided against an inquest. You needn't tell me that if we held one now, on what we have, the odds are that Ingram would be found responsible for his wife's death. Particularly with Winthrop getting up and swearing he heard Ingram threaten her."

"You don't believe Winthrop did?" asked Holmes. He massaged his jaw thoughtfully. "Well, I will say——"

"I can't believe, if he really had overheard a thing like that, he'd have forgotten it until now. Not when he's been shoving Ingram down our throats as a murderer. It's not possible."

76

"That certainly seems—er—logical," agreed the man from the D.A.'s office in his soft, vague voice. "Well, shall we leave it a day or two, and—um—perhaps you'll come up with more evidence, Lieutenant. If we only had the body——"

"We're pressing an intensive hunt," said Holmes. "The Forest Rangers are covering every mile of their areas, and of course the press publicity may help."

"Er—yes. Well, we'll leave it then—just for a day or two."

Which was something. Mendoza went back to his own office and met Hackett just coming in. "Got a little for you," said Hackett.

"Give it to me over lunch," said Mendoza. "I need cheering up, God knows." They went downstairs for the Ferrari and drove up to Federico's on North Broadway. Hackett said they both needed a drink, Mendoza on account of the D.A.'s man and himself on account of all the dust over at the Hall of Records. "Dangerous," said Mendoza. "You know what it does to me, and I'm mad enough now at everybody mixed up in this damned business." But he let himself be persuaded.

"Bruce Lauderdale, Linda's boy friend," said Hackett, "has a little record. One arrest as a juvenile, grand theft auto, probation."

"Well, they say every dog's allowed one bite," said Mendoza.

"No, it doesn't say much. There's not much on Ingram, either. On the application for the marriage license he gave his original home town as Providence, Rhode Island. Both his parents were born in the British Isles—father in Edinburgh, mother in Liverpool. At that time he'd been a California resident for four years, when they were married, I mean. Gave his occupation as retired salesman. Born on February 3, 1901. I looked for him in our Records too, but he's not there. Not as Ingram anyway."

"I didn't think he would be," said Mendoza, and broke off to order. Hackett abandoned Ingram temporarily and looked mournfully at the menu. His Angel was a superlative cook, and fond of feeding him exotic things ("But you're a big man, Art, you *need* lots of good food"), and if he was to pass his next physical, he must somehow shed fifteen pounds. He told the waiter gloomily he'd have a small steak and coffee. "And I don't think," added Mendoza, "the F.B.I. will have anything on him either."

"Why should they? What *is* your little idea about Ingram, anyway?"

Mendoza finished his rye and looked at the empty glass thoughtfully. "There are tricks in all trades," he said, "and sometimes we give ourselves away by doing little things automatically in a certain way. That jacket fits you well enough." He eyed it critically. "I can't see any obvious bulge from the shoulder holster. But you give it away by that unconscious little reaching up to adjust the gun comfortably when you sit down."

"So what?"

"So, one of the trades I happen to know more about than most is pro gambling. Pro crooked gambling. I don't say the old man worked at it regularly, but he knew most of the tricks. And before I joined the force I worked at a couple of gambling houses. Then, though you may not remember, I put in eight years in Vice before I got switched to Homicide."

"And if you'd admit it," said Hackett, "you ought to have been a pro yourself."

"*¡Dios me libre!* It's too damned hard work," said Mendoza with a grin. "About the hardest way to make a living there is. It takes constant practice, a memory long as God's, and an eye like a hawk. No, thanks. . . . Well, when I first talked to Ingram, he started fiddling with a deck of cards. He wasn't thinking about what he was doing, you know—he was trying to size me up. His hands were just moving automatically. And he's an artist at handling the cards, obviously a man who's played a lot of cards all his life."

"But that doesn't say——"

"I was watching him," said Mendoza lazily, "because I'd noticed the way he picked up the deck. He handled it with that old mechanic's grip, whole deck across his palm, thumb on top diagonally. Look out for the fellow who picks up a deck like that.

"It's one of the earmarks of the crooked gambler, because it's the easiest position to start a crooked shuffle from. Several kinds of crooked shuffles. I watched Ingram's hands, and it was the damnedest thing to see. He wasn't sitting in any game, he wasn't starting to set up a crooked deal, he was just shuffling the cards to occupy his hands. But automatically he was keeping up his practice at the overhand stack. Very smooth work too—he's good."

"What's an overhand stack?" Hackett wasn't much of a card player.

"One of the commonest crooked shuffles. You put the cards you want on the bottom of the deck. Then, as you shuffle, you slip one card off the bottom and one off the top at the same time. Easier said than done, it takes practice. You're shuffling from your right hand to your left, and you riffle the cards through once for each card you want off the bottom. As you pass the bottom and top cards into your left hand, you shuffle out of your right hand two cards fewer than the number of players. Then, when you've got all the cards you want in your left hand, you just slap them down on top of the cards in your right, and the deck's set up for a crooked deal."

"Sleight of hand—it sounds impossible," said Hackett.

"I said it takes practice."

"But there'd be a cut——"

"No trouble. Any good sharper can set it up—by crimping a card, for instance—so the position of the cards is unchanged, or he can spot his little picked hand in the deck. More sleight of hand. And watching Ingram, I said to myself, *¿Vaya, qué mas?*—and when he was so careful to present himself as a man who didn't really know much about cards——!"

Hackett looked at his steak and picked up knife and fork. "Maybe that's what she'd found out about him?"

"That wasn't the first thing that leaped to my mind," said Mendoza, "no. Though it could be. Pro gamblers I know, Art. I know them *de arriba abajo,* from top to bottom. There's a popular superstition, fostered by the Westerns, I suppose, that they're big bad men with a gun always primed to hand. Well, they're not. They're sedentary men—they have to be—and every one I've ever known had the soul of a rabbit. All they want is to stay out of trouble. If trouble looks like it's heading their way, ninety-nine times out of a hundred they'll just run. Very few of them ever get into police records —unless they get mixed up in something else, and as a rule they don't. They tend to be pretty moral fellows, oddly enough. Generally they don't drink much—they can't, because they need all their wits to do a good job. Now and then you find a chaser among them, but usually their main interest centers on the cards. A lot of them are very nice fellows. They're a little like con men that way, you can't reform them, but——"

"Wouldn't you classify 'em *as* con men?"

"No," said Mendoza, "I wouldn't. Con men there's a point to catching and stashing away. Although in a lot of cases their victims wouldn't have been hurt unless they were crooked enough themselves to be lured into getting something for nothing, in other cases they're just poor, ignorant people. But your inveterate gambler, who can't keep away from the table, he's inviting the crooked gambler to come and take him. He's got larceny on his mind to start with. He's asking for it. As long as people want to gamble, there'll be crooks to oblige them. Now I don't mean to say that I like the idea of legalized gambling. You can't make human beings moral by writing laws and it's a human instinct to gamble. But legalized gambling's always an invitation to the syndicate to step in—which, I needn't tell you, is why Gardena's a thorn in the Chief's side. We've managed to keep the syndicate out, so far." Mendoza finished his steak and picked up his coffee cup. "But your crooked gambler, average specimen, is a nice quiet non-violent fellow strictly on his own. No hookup with any other pro crooks. Sure, he *is* a crook—but of all the varieties, he does the least harm to society, he's the most sympathetic, and certainly he's the least violent." He got out a cigarette. "That's off the record—don't quote me to the Chief."

Hackett laughed. "I can hear what he'd say!"

Mendoza emitted a long stream of blue smoke and leaned back in his chair. "Me, I like a friendly session of draw, with congenial companions," he said. "I come out ahead a little oftener than I come out behind, because I play a lot of cards—and practice is bound to give you an edge. But I never pick up a hand with my whole mind fixed on getting some of the other fellows' *money*. What I'm interested in is winning the hand. And I know the odds, which most people don't stop to figure. Your chances of collecting a royal flush are just one in six hundred and forty-nine thousand, seven hundred and forty."

"I'll remember that to console myself next time I miss one," said Hackett. "What's this got to do with Ingram?"

"Well, for one thing," said Mendoza, "I've been a cop for a little over twenty years, and I can think of just one pro gambler who committed a murder. And that was more or less by accident—his wife was cheating on him and he took a poke at lover boy and fractured his skull."

"Maybe something like that happened here?"

"It could be, yes, but I doubt it, Art. I really do. Bella seems to have had a sharp tongue—not a very pleasant woman—but he never, apparently, lost his temper with her. He couldn't afford to. . . . To tell you the truth, also off the record, I can feel for Ingram, you know. Here he is getting into his sixties, with a bad heart, and probably very little money. That's another thing about pro gamblers—when they've got it, they throw it away, and half the time on their girl friends and old pals and quite often on charity. I don't believe in Uncle Thomas Bailey for a minute, though we'll look. I think Ingram had a little nest egg he'd painfully tucked away, forcing himself to save. He has this bad heart, needs medicine, he's not getting any younger—and it *is* a hell of a hard way to earn a living. Not so bad when you're young and healthy—getting a kick out of taking the marks, and shop talk with your pals, and always a new town to move on to. You don't mind the cheap hotels and the greasy-spoon restaurants. Sometimes you have to hock the flashy diamond ring, but it's all in the game and you'll get it back, or a better one. Always tomorrow coming along, and you always know it'll bring the biggest take. But when you get old, you're not so sure any more, and the cheap hotels get to matter. You begin to want a settled place, with a good mattress, and decent meals to soothe your digestion. You don't always feel up to par any more, and maybe find your hands not quite so steady, and your memory for what cards are where not so quick as it was——"

"You're breaking my heart, boy," said Hackett.

"All right, all right. But I can see how it went. I think, if we could trace it back, Ingram had Bella pointed out to him somewhere—or maybe just saw her name in a society note—and made a dead set for her. If there was a little mention in the paper of her going on the Mexican tour, that was it. She's been prominent in volunteer charity work, she'd get into the papers now and then. He took some of his savings and bought a ticket on the tour himself—made up to her. And wouldn't she jump at him! Handsome, courtly, quite a catch for a plain widow. If it crossed her mind that he was more interested in her money, well, she wasn't a romantic young girl and he *was* something to flaunt before her lady friends. . . . It was a gamble that paid off, for Ingram. I think we'll find that it was tacitly agreed she'd take care of all the household expenses. He had what was left of the nest egg to keep himself in cigarettes and so on—and he could wander down to Gardena a couple of times a week. He would anyway. It's been a way of life to him, he couldn't keep his hands off the cards. . . . All he wanted, you see, was a safe berth. A home base, with creature comforts guaranteed —security. And maybe to Bella he was a symbol—that somebody was interested in her even to that extent. He'd have to keep it up all the time—pleasant to her, giving in to her. And one thing I'll swear, Art—he was telling me the naked truth when he said he wished to God she'd never left him anything. All Bella was to him was present security. I don't think he did expect to outlive her—we'll see what his doctor has to say. Well, you see what I'm driving at. He's a man of a type very unlikely to do a murder in the first place, and he hadn't any real motive to kill her. Not when you look beneath the surface. He had what he wanted from Bella. For a little courtesy, a little flattery, he had a comfortable living. I can't see him losing his temper and killing her by accident or otherwise when he's kept his temper with

84

her for two years. I certainly can't see him planning to kill her."

"There's a saying about the straw that broke the camel's back."

"So there is. It could be, of course. . . . I hope to God we can locate the body. And I still can't see why in God's name it should have been concealed. Damn the whole mess," said Mendoza. "Are you finished? Let's get back. I've got a program for this afternoon. I want you to go up and prod at that maid—you look so much more formidable than me. She knows something she's not telling, and I want to know what it is."

Mendoza sent off a wire to the Chief of Police of Providence, Rhode Island, requesting any available information on Francis James Ingram, reputedly born there—date and parents' names thus-and-such. He sent a wire to the F.B.I. asking whether they knew Ingram. Just on the off chance, he should get Ingram's prints.

He intended this afternoon to see all the women present at the bridge party that Tuesday; but before he left the office Sergeant Lake came in and announced a visitor. "Quite a dish," he added. "If I wasn't a moral married man—— Name's Kay Webster. Says she's got some information."

"That I could use," said Mendoza.

Kay Webster was eighteen, and both confident and shy at once. She had glossy chestnut hair, a delightful wide-mouthed smile, a luscious figure, and a pleasantly husky voice. Mendoza regarded her with approval and asked her to sit down.

"I thought I'd better come and tell you," she said. "I

mean, probably it doesn't mean anything, but I talked it over with Dad and he said I'd better, the police always want to know every little single thing. Just in case. After what it said in the papers today."

"Yes? About the Ingram case?"

"That sounds just like a detective novel," she said with satisfaction. "Well, of course I'm sorry for her, if she *was* murdered, but it's sort of exciting to be mixed up with——" Her nice brown eyes were eagerly taking in him and his office. Mendoza had the sudden irrelevant feeling that it might, after all, be rather interesting to have those twins and watch them grow up to be eighteen. "You see, I've just got my driver's license," she said, "and I'm saving up to buy a car when I start college in September. So I sort of notice cars, because it'll have to be a secondhand one, naturally."

"Yes? If you'd——"

"Oh dear, I'm telling it all wrong, I'm sorry. You see I remember the day because it was New Year's. I should've said we live at 306 Sycamore Terrace."

"Ah," said Mendoza.

"And Anne and I had a date to go to the movies that night. A French picture, at the Granada. We both take French and it's a good way to keep it up, you know. That's Anne Madison, I don't suppose you want her address because she didn't see anything. The car, I mean. Well, I asked if I could have the car that night— Anne doesn't drive, I mean she's just learning . . ."

"Won't you have a cigarette, Miss Webster?"

"I guess so, thank you." She beamed at him; she was being treated like a grownup. "I don't, much, but——" She bent to his lighter. "Well, anyway, I was going to pick up Anne at six-thirty and she lives way down toward Culver City so I left about six. It was just getting dark. And I ought to explain, we sort of knew Mrs. Ingram because she and Mother both worked for the same Red Cross unit as volunteers. And I did too, a couple of times in the summers, and I knew her from that. I didn't like her much, she was terribly bossy. Anyway, you see, I knew her house. Because I always think it looks so funny—that ranch-type house sort of sandwiched in between two awfully modernistic houses. Well, the whole point *is*, you see"—she gestured inexpertly with the cigarette—"when I came past her house, there was a car in front of it, and it wasn't a Cadillac like she had. I just happened to notice it because there weren't any lights on in the house—not in front anyway—and it was about the time people were turning them on. Still light enough to *see,* outside, but —— And I thought, just casually, you know, no company at her house—it must be somebody calling on a house across the street. Dad's always complaining about people parking in front of our house and going somewhere else."

"You're sure of the place and day?" This could be a little something.

"Oh yes. I've got a very good memory for dates and things," she said seriously. "I always get A's in history and math."

"Can you make any kind of guess as to what make and year the car was?"

"I've got what they call a visual memory. I *see* things in my mind. And I thought—well, it probably isn't important at all, it was just somebody going to another house—but it said you thought, the police, I mean, thought she was killed between six-thirty and nine-thirty, and—— So I tried to remember, and how it looked and so on. And I'm pretty sure it was light tan. It was a sort of medium car, like a Dodge or Buick, and not very old but not new either."

"I'd like you to make a formal statement on this," said Mendoza.

"Ooh, I'd love to! Do you really think it *is* important? But I don't see why, the paper said Mr. Ingram had a Cadillac too, and it was him——"

He smiled at her. "Well, it just could be important. We'll see. It was very good of you to come in." This might be very useful—though the D.A., or a jury, wouldn't think much of it at all as evidence. Would say the girl couldn't possibly remember such a trivial thing so far back, when she hadn't any real reason to remember it. Himself, he thought Kay Webster probably did have a very accurate memory, and that she wasn't the type to come in with a made-up story just to get a little publicity. He was interested in her statement; though he'd need better evidence to back it up.

"Well, Dad said I'd *better*," she said conscientiously. "Just in *case*."

CHAPTER SEVEN

HE TOLD Sergeant Lake to have somebody look up data on the cars used by everybody involved in the case, and set off belatedly to interview as many of Mrs. Ingram's friends as possible in one afternoon. As he waited for the elevator, he wondered how Hackett was doing with the maid.

Hackett wasn't doing so well, and that was due at least in part to his small but lusty son Mark, aged five months. Hackett hadn't got much sleep after three o'clock, and a morning spent poring over documents had made him sleepier than ever. Now he was trying to swallow yawns and to sound stern and official, and not meeting much success at either.

"Come now, Miss Glass," he said. "We know there is something you haven't told us." He wondered whether there was; Luis had a powerful imagination, and his besetting sin was that tortuous mind. He didn't *like* things to be simple. "It's very foolish of you, Miss Glass," said Hackett, sounding pompous even to himself, "not to be frank with us. You want to help Mr.

Ingram, don't you? Only the truth—and all the truth—can help him."

It wasn't the first time he'd said all that.

"I've told you all the truth I know!" she said. She was crying, she was scared, but stubborn as they came; she faced up to him defiantly. "You can't know nothing like that, because it's not so! It's not! And I—and I won't be bullied into saying nothing—— He never did such a thing, and I——"

She had said all that before too. She was saying it a good deal louder this time, and suddenly Ingram appeared at the door of the living room. "What's going on, Sylvia? Oh, more police." His tone was resigned as he looked at Hackett.

"He's bullying me to say bad things about you, sir! It's not true I didn't tell all I know——"

"Well, we think it is," said Hackett. Ingram looked older, and tired. He looked from the girl to Hackett.

"I don't suppose you'll get anywhere with the third degree——" He paused.

"Sergeant Hackett. And——"

"Sergeant. I thought that was a little old-fashioned."

"I've just been asking her questions," said Hackett mildly.

"Nothing but questions," said Ingram. "If it isn't you people, it's the press. All around like flies this morning. Getting damn tired of it." He passed a hand over his face.

"You ought to rest up, sir, what with all the worry and the awful things people——" She gave Hackett a spiteful glance.

He saw he wasn't going to get anywhere with her. He

thought it might be a good idea to scare her a little more by taking her downtown, let her think she might be arrested. She wasn't a bright girl, wouldn't know there wasn't a thing they could hold her on. If she did know something—— He'd suggest it to Luis.

He frowned at her, said they'd want to see her again. Coming away, he wondered if there'd be any little cautious talk between the man and the girl, Ingram probing to find out if she did know anything. Or whether there had been collusion already.

He went back to the office. Mendoza was still out. A little information had begun to drift in on the people in the case. Hackett looked at the reports. Mrs. Barron had an income, from invested capital, of about forty-five hundred a year. She had been a widow for ten years. Hugh Barron had once come to Juvenile's attention, about nine years ago, as one of a group of high school vandals caught breaking car windows. He'd been put on probation; nothing on him since. At present he was a salesman at a Chrysler agency in Hollywood, and apparently well enough thought of by his employers. But he'd drifted around in jobs a lot, never staying in one long. He lived well up to his income and maybe beyond it, paying for a newish car, buying stereo records—his hobby was jazz—living in a new apartment. Not much on his fiancée, Marcia Wills; nothing known against her. She lived with another girl in an apartment on Fountain Avenue.

As Hackett finished going over the reports, Sergeant Lake came in with more papers. "Some stuff he wants, on the cars."

"Why cars?" asked Hackett, and heard about Kay

91

Webster's statement. He didn't think much of it at all. "Luis just wants to make it complicated, damn it. What does this say? The girl couldn't possibly identify, one glance a month and more ago, and who'd believe her if she did?"

"Well, he's right a lot of times, Art."

"He's wrong sometimes too." Hackett glanced over the notes. Lawrence Winthrop drove a tan Dodge sedan, four-door; it was two years old. Hugh Barron had an off-white Buick two-door hardtop, a year old. Mrs. Barron didn't drive and had no car. Linda Barron had a six-year-old gray Ford two-door. Bruce Lauderdale had a light green Dodge two-door hardtop, three years old. Mr. Harley Stevens had a five-year-old off-white four-door Buick.

It didn't say much. Even if the girl were straight, not just out to get in on the act, the light had been uncertain; she could be wrong about the color. In her statement she said she wasn't sure whether the car was a two-door or four-door, a hardtop or a convertible with the top up, but she thought it wasn't the latter. And the chances were, of course, it had just been parked there by somebody visiting another house.

He put the reports on Mendoza's desk and called the Chief Ranger's office to ask how the search for the body was progressing.

Mendoza came in at five forty-five, looking tired but pleased, and looked over the reports. "Meet some nice gossipy females?" asked Hackett.

Mendoza grinned at him. "*Eso ya es llover sobre mojado*—adding insult to injury. I think they get worse as they get older. But I've got a couple of things. I saw all seven of the other women who were at that bridge party. Three of them—Mrs. Widdows, Mrs. Sprague, and Mrs. Kirsch—were about Bella's closest friends. They were all very eager to talk. All I had to do was listen. I'll spare you the irrelevancies, and there were a lot of them." He took out some folded notes. "Two of them—Mrs. Widdows and Mrs. Sprague—are coming in tomorrow to make statements. Now. To start with, they're all very surprised that Ingram should have done such a terrible thing. No question in their minds that it *was* him, but that will be the result of the slanted stories by the press. They'd never have thought, et cetera. He seemed such a nice gentlemanly fellow. Of course all the women—all but one—are thinking about *de mortuis* and very reluctant to say anything against dear Bella. The exception is a Mrs. Katz, who—I gathered from a couple of the others—had had a little run-in with Bella over some Red Cross business. Most of what she says we already know—that Bella was domineering and tactless and that a lot of people didn't much like her. But I did get one interesting thing." He shuffled the notes. "Here. Mrs. Willard Sprague, a close friend of Bella's. She says that Bella talked to her a good deal about her family, things she wouldn't say to anyone else. And since Bella had married Ingram, there'd been quite a few family quarrels on and off, for reasons we know about.

"And Mrs. Sprague said that on Saturday, the week before Bella vanished, they had lunch together, and Bella said something rather odd. She'd been talking about her family in general and she said, in a rather vindictive tone, that if *she* hadn't been taken in, she knew somebody who *had* been, and it would be gratifying to prove it. No names mentioned."

"Interesting," agreed Hackett, "but elusive." He yawned. "What's the second point?"

"Mrs. Widdows said, among a lot of other things, that she'd wondered if maybe dear Bella had begun to *doubt* her handsome husband. Because some time ago—she was vague, placed it as either two or three weeks before Bella disappeared—Bella had asked her if Mr. Widdows could recommend an honest private detective. Mr. Widdows is an attorney, and she thought perhaps he could advise her. He couldn't, incidentally, and we don't know whether Bella went to one on her own. If she did, whatever agency it was isn't speaking up, you notice. I want somebody to check with every one in town—yes, I know, a job, but it'll have to be done. Bella wouldn't tell Mrs. Widdows why she wanted a detective, just let it be understood it was to do with a maid she suspected of stealing. But Mrs. Widdows didn't believe that because Sylvia Glass, the only maid Bella had, used to work for the Widdows and seemed to be an honest girl."

"Well, all this adds up like two and two," said Hackett. "Something made her suspicious of Ingram——" Palliser and Dwyer came in together. They looked tired; it had been a warm day.

"Have a nice time, boys?" asked Mendoza. "Sit down. Find any possibles?"

"I got four who I'm pretty sure recognized the photo," said Palliser. "About twenty men said they'd seen his face, and a few of 'em knew his name. They said so after pushing, they didn't want to get involved. I only got one name—Antonio Morelli. The others, I just put down descriptions."

"All according to Hoyle. Bert?"

"I collected three. I think. Same thing—no names. I guess Higgy's still looking, unless he got lured into a game."

"He'll be in. More or less what I expected."

"Look," said Hackett patiently. "It's open-and-shut, Luis. So Ingram's a crooked gambler—a sure-thing man. We can't guess how Mrs. Ingram found out, but that's the most probable thing, isn't it? That's what she was talking about that day when she said that about getting the truth out of him. When she got home Tuesday she accused him again, told him to get out—maybe threatened to denounce him to the police. There was a fight, and he killed her. Probably didn't mean to, but there she is. And he knows the maid will be back pretty soon———"

"Why did he hide the body?"

"Panic," said Hackett. "He got one of his Gardena pals to help him———"

"I don't like that much," said Mendoza. "I'm not buying it yet. What'd you get out of the maid?"

"Damn all," said Hackett, and outlined his suggestion about bringing her downtown. Mendoza agreed, looked at his watch, and said he was going home. He added that he wouldn't be in in the morning, but would probably check in at lunchtime to see if anything had turned up. He tucked all the notes into his pocket and departed.

When he got home, he found the front of the house deserted, and wandered back to the kitchen looking for Alison. He found her standing on top of a five-foot ladder putting a new light bulb into the recessed ceiling fixture over the sink. All four cats were sitting at the foot of the ladder watching her with fascinated eyes.

"Damn!" said Alison. "Hello, *amado.* Oh, curse the thing—why on earth they had to use screws with practically no head to get hold of———"

"It was my understanding," said Mendoza, "that you were planning to go to the hospital about six months from now and, with the aid of Dr. Feininger, produce a bouncing pair of twins."

Alison looked down at him over her shoulder. "Somehow that 'with the aid of' sounds rather immoral—but that is more or less the general program, yes."

"Then, *por el amor de Dios,* what the hell are you trying to do, break your neck and the twins' too? *¡Baje —ven acá—*come down here at once, *inmediatemente!"*

"I will, as soon as I've got this maddening thing in." She was still struggling with the screw; the ladder rocked and Mendoza uttered a loud yelp, startling the cats.

"*¡Santa María y todos demonios——— Cuidado!* Come down! Come down from there at once!"

"There!" said Alison. "An invention of the devil, if you ask me. You'd think they could design something easier to——— All right, I'm coming." She began to back down the ladder. "I'm being careful, don't fuss, Luis."

"Listen," he said, turning her around in his arms as she gained the floor, "these antiquated notions about a houseful of children I may not agree with, *chica,* but after all I've got a vested fifty per cent interest in these twins—if it is twins, which I doubt. You have no right to go around risking my property. Will you for the love of God be sensible? Why couldn't you wait until I got home to change the damn light bulb?"

"Don't be silly," said Alison, kissing him again. "You know how you hate to be asked to do any little job around the house."

"I have been known to screw in a light bulb on occasions."

"Well, it's done now, so what's the odds? If you really want to make yourself useful, you can find my engagement ring. El Señor's stolen it. I took a bird away from him this morning, and that was his revenge. He waited until I took the ring off to wash the dishes, and walked away with it."

"*Señor Ladrón!* He used to steal my cuff links until I got a box with a lock. Have you looked under the bed?" That was a favorite hideaway.

"Yes, it's not there, I moved the bed out——"

"*¡Diez millón demonios desde infierno!* Have you no sense at all? Lifting that——"

"Oh, I just shoved it," said Alison. "You do fuss. You know something?"

"What, *querida?*"

"*I* think," said Alison, straightening his tie, "that all this cynical talk about antiquated notions is just a front. *I* think you'd be awfully pleased about twins, and probably spoil them horribly."

"Oh, you do?"

"And we'll have to decide on four names, you know. Because it could be one of each, or a pair of each. And John's all *right*, but rather ordinary, isn't it?"

"And I suppose these will be very extraordinary infants."

"Well, what else? They're ours. What do you think of Adam? It's almost the same in English or Spanish."

"And maybe call the other one Noah? *¡Bastante!* Let me go, I'll hunt for your ring."

"But we've got to decide on *something*," said Alison.

Mendoza spent half an hour shifting furniture, feeling along the tops of shelves, and turning up rugs—eagerly assisted by all the cats—before he found Alison's emerald ring lying innocently in a big glass ashtray on the coffee table. He told El Señor he was a bad cat; El Señor returned his stare remotely and disassociated himself from the whole affair by polishing one forepaw.

CHAPTER EIGHT

On Wednesday morning Hackett drove out to Syca-more Terrace to pick up the maid, and was frustrated. She wasn't due at the house until ten o'clock. He went back downtown and looked at a couple of overnight reports that had come in.

Giorgio Copas, the Filipino houseboy employed by Winthrop, had been questioned, and substantiated Winthrop's alibi. Winthrop had come home that night about seven-fifteen, dined alone—on, the report stated precisely, chicken à la king on toast, asparagus, custard, and coffee—and had spent the evening reading. Copas had been in and out of the room several times between eight and eleven, when Winthrop went to bed. It was possible that Copas had been bribed to back him up, but it was a remote possibility. Hackett didn't see why Mendoza was trying to make the case so complicated. The really annoying thing was the lack of solid evidence; there wasn't much mystery about it.

There was to be more annoyance. When Lieutenant Ames started redoing his homework, he had gone through the Ingram house again, and had the maid and Ingram look at Mrs. Ingram's wardrobe, to see whether she'd changed her clothes. At the party she'd been wearing a gray and mulberry printed nylon jersey dress; and that was there, tidily hung up in her closet. She had also, the maid thought, changed from medium-heeled black pumps to a pair of low-heeled tan walking shoes. The maid wasn't positive what dress Mrs. Ingram had changed into, but thought it was a blue and white cotton house dress, which was missing and not in the laundry hamper. On the dresser were the hat and the jewelry she'd worn with the gray dress—Mexican silver necklace, brooch and earrings, and an old-fashioned gold-mounted diamond ring she usually put on to "dress up." That didn't look so good for Ingram, because she wouldn't have gone off voluntarily in a house dress and old shoes. Even if she could have left without her glasses, which had been lying folded behind the hat.

When Hackett got back to Sycamore Terrace a few minutes before ten, Ingram opened the door; his face lit up and before Hackett could speak he said, "I was just going to call Headquarters, Sergeant. Come in, I've got something for you. Damn surprising thing, too—it staggered me! You see——"

"Yes?" Hackett went in. "Is Miss Glass here yet?"

"No, you want her? She will be. But this is the damnedest funny thing. I can't explain it, but maybe it'll suggest something to your lieutenant—or you," added Ingram tactfully. "I just found it out ten minutes ago—Bella's jewelry is gone! At least, the best pieces, the things that'd be worth anything. You see, I hadn't any reason to look through her things, and I've been so worried and so on, I'm afraid I haven't been keeping the room very neat. I'm not as tidy as Bella was anyway—I'd better explain, you see, Bella never liked a maid to tidy her personal things, she took care of them herself, so Sylvia hasn't touched the dressing table. Habit. I should have done it myself, after the police had searched, but I didn't until just now, this morning. There was her jewelry, where she'd put it when she took it off, and when I opened the jewel box to put it in—well, see for yourself." He had led Hackett back to the master bedroom as he talked, and now gestured.

Hackett looked at the dressing table, which was a feminine-looking affair in Salem maple. On its glass-covered top sat a couple of bottles of cologne, an empty silver vase, a little tray with an empty cut-glass atomizer, and a fairly large box covered in green leather. He lifted the lid with the tip of a finger; the box opened out into three tiers of velvet-covered trays. There were a few pieces of costume jewelry scattered in each tier.

"There should be more—quite a lot more," said Ingram. "I noticed at once. Her first husband—she said he thought jewelry was a good investment—he bought her a lot of good pieces. She didn't care much for it herself, she didn't wear much as a rule. It was insured, I think—yes, I think I recall her saying that—— But why should it be missing? Could it be that it was a burglar, after all, that she came back and surprised him?"

Hackett felt a little exasperated, which he didn't let Ingram see. He supposed the family could corroborate her possession of the jewelry; but where the hell did Ingram think it would get him, to lay this new false trail? He wondered what Ingram had done with the stuff; he'd have more sense than to pawn it, or hide it around the house. Probably it was in the custody of some pal.

He heard the maid come in the front door. "What exactly would there have been?" he asked.

"I couldn't say definitely, there might be a list somewhere. I think Sylvia could help, she always admired the jewelry, and I believe one day Bella did show it all to her because she was interested. There'd have been three or four diamond rings, and a diamond and sapphire bracelet, and some earrings."

"Yes, well," said Hackett with a mental sigh, "I think you and Miss Glass had both better come down to Headquarters and try to make up a list for us." There hadn't been a list of the jewelry in the house; that, Ames would have caught. Maybe the lawyer or the bank had one.

"Yes, of course, glad to. But—I've been thinking about it—it must have been taken that afternoon, when you reason it out," said Ingram. He sounded bewildered, earnest, and anxious to help. "Because if there had been a sneak thief some time since, when the house was empty, surely he'd have taken at least the other diamond ring that was lying there in plain sight. And you know, Bella probably didn't realize the jewelry was missing herself—she didn't open the box to put her jewelry away, probably intended to later. Though she usually did right away. I can't understand it——"

Hackett wanted to swear. They'd have to follow it up, of course—go through all the motions. And it would probably confirm Luis' wishful thinking about the case being a lot more complex than it looked. But what Ingram hoped to gain by such an obvious red herring—— Well, of course, exactly that: to make the police think the case wasn't as obvious as it looked.

Hackett sighed again and turned to call the maid in. He wondered irrelevantly what wild goose Mendoza was out chasing this morning.

There was a large gilt-framed mirror just inside the double glass doors of Benny's Poker Palace, and Mendoza stopped to straighten his tie. He was pleased with his appearance, though not for the usual reason. He had chosen a suit a good deal less discreet than any other he owned—he had seen the bolt by artificial light: a rather gay purplish tweed. He had stopped and bought a garish tie, not possessing any remotely to be so described. He had taken off his gold signet ring and his watch, and at a cheap jeweler's on Main had bought two flashy-looking zircon rings for nine dollars apiece, and a brass-cased wristwatch. Standing in front of the mirror, he'd just swept off his widest-brimmed black homburg.

He certainly didn't look at all like a cop—if there was any special way a cop ought to look. He stared at the slim dark man in the mirror, with the widow's peak of polished black hair, the cynical mouth under a precise line of mustache, and thought pleasedly that he looked rather like a screen villain.

Oddly enough, he also felt about twelve years younger. Twelve years ago he'd still been down in Vice, doing this kind of thing a good deal—though not down here in Gardena, and not for today's purpose.

He was armed with the descriptions of about a dozen men who might have been lying when they said they did not recognize Ingram's picture. He was looking for one of them.

And he wasn't at all sure why. He didn't know exactly why he felt that Ingram couldn't be guilty of murder. It didn't feel like one of his famous hunches. He told himself it was because he knew the breed, that was all, and knew it to be as nearly incapable of violence as human nature can be.

He hung up his hat on a modernistic brass rack, turned, and went through an archway to the first of several large rooms. It was a nice setup, clean, airy, high-ceilinged; everything very plush. The tables were not set too close together, the padded chairs looked comfortable. There were fifteen or twenty men in the room, even at ten in the morning; three tables of play, a couple of men sitting alone at one table. Mendoza lit a cigarette and waited where he was.

Benny, recognizable from Palliser's description, came up at once. His little shrewd dark eyes sized up Mendoza at a glance. "Don't believe we've seen you here before, have we? Can I do anything for you, sir?"

"I guess maybe you can," said Mendoza casually. "No, I just blew in from Dago. Haven't hit L.A. in the hell of a long time—thought I'd come up and see how she's changed. I used to have some friends here—Eddy Roehampton, Carlos Reyes—but I've kind of lost touch."

"I see," said Benny, and his eyes flickered at the names. That placed Benny on the wrong side of the fence; he knew the names of pro sharps, had linked

Mendoza with them, and was doing nothing about it. It didn't matter to these proprietors who played at their tables; they got a cut of every jackpot anyway; but the Gardena force tried to see that the only proprietors who got licenses were those who'd shoo away the pros. They didn't always succeed.

"Well, you know how it is," said Mendoza, jingling coins in his pocket. "I feel like a couple hands, but nobody to sit in with. You set up tables?"

"It's a bit early," said Benny, "but, sure. Tell you what, I'll introduce you to a couple guys right now, they're waiting to meet another guy here. What's the monicker?"

"Moreno—Rodolfo Moreno. That's nice of you, mister."

Benny led him across to the table where the two unoccupied men sat and was expansive and friendly, introducing Al Pressman and Fred Light. Pressman was dark and angular, about thirty; Light, middle-aged and bald. Neither corresponded to any of the descriptions. Mendoza sat down at the table on invitation. It was the standard special poker table, a high-class job, with green baize top and slots to hold glasses; these places couldn't buy a hard-liquor license, but served beer.

Benny stayed for a while to get the ball rolling, very talkative and all-pals-together. Mendoza suggested a friendly little hand, and Pressman said, "Aw, let's wait until Buck gets here, he's late now—no fun with only three."

Light began to tell a long, pointless story about a girl he'd met in Syracuse. Mendoza lit another cigarette and looked around the room.

He knew the breed, all right. After all, he'd grown up under one of them. The ones who couldn't leave the cards alone—and the sure-thing men always ready to take them.

At the nearest table ten feet away, six men were playing a hand. The man squarely facing Mendoza was a jolly-looking fat man in his fifties, with horn-rimmed glasses and a Cupid's-bow mouth. He was puffing a cigar and talking a good deal. As Mendoza's eyes turned on him, he laid his hand face down on the table, knocking cigar ash into the ashtray; his right hand was laid carelessly on the cards, index finger touching the margin of the design. He was discreetly telling some pal opposite him that he held a king.

Mendoza knew them, as he'd said to Hackett, *de arriba abajo*. And sure, they were crooks, technically speaking. But they didn't, like another breed of con men, victimize the innocent.

They were, the sure-thing men, otherwise very harmless—and seldom very happy. Nothing much ever happened to them if and when they were caught up with—police generally just moved them on out of town. They were necessarily wanderers; and because part of their stock in trade was a good front, they spent their money on that front and lived cheap, in third-rate hotels, and traveled cheap. A lot of people had the idea that a cardsharp could take every pot; that wasn't so. The tricks and devices gave them a big edge over honest players, but not a certain edge—chance being what it was. They won often, but they lost too. The hell of a hard way to earn a living. Skill at cheating depended on many things: abnormally keen eyesight—the marks on some decks of readers were almost microscopic; a long memory for where key cards were at any given moment; hands as practiced and skillful as a surgeon's: and long experience at play.

No, they weren't happy men. Some of them didn't know that. They drifted into it as a way of life because they couldn't take routine, liked the thrill of taking a mark, maybe because they were irresponsible men, or drifters by nature. But, as he'd also said to Hackett, that was about the only moral count against them—that they were weak men in some way. He'd known very few who were drinkers or chasers or homos or venial in any other way. He'd known more who, after cheating a big take out of the marks, couldn't keep away from the race tracks where they usually lost it all. A few of them had wives, and they were usually model husbands. Most of them didn't, because they were wanderers, and few women are. They died as they lived, vagrantly. They ended up on the state pension, in old people's homes, or in the General Hospital, or sometimes they killed themselves, but not often; they were optimists by nature.

It wasn't an easy life. They drifted into gambling when they were youngsters eager for adventure or excitement. It wasn't until they got old, and every tomorrow wasn't something to be looked forward to . . .

Ingram. Why the hell did he feel like this about Ingram? On the surface, it looked so obvious. . . .

He was down here hunting a pal of Ingram's, hoping to get such a pal to open up to him, believing Mendoza also to be on the wrong side of the fence. There was always the possibility that Ingram had told a pal more than he'd tell the cops and that a pal might know something pertinent about Ingram's movements the day his wife disappeared. It was even possible that Ingram might have an alibi of sorts, but be willing to gamble on not producing it to maintain his respectable surface. Or, more likely, if the alibi depended on somebody known to the police, the man was refusing to speak up, chary of being involved. This kind didn't like trouble.

Ingram.

The jolly fat man at the next table laughed, throwing his head back. And all of a sudden Mendoza knew why he felt the way he did about Ingram.

Ingram reminded him of little Niddy.

And it was a purely irrational thing, meaning nothing.

Little Niddy had always laughed like that, throwing his head back.

Ingram didn't really look much like Niddy—he was handsomer; but Niddy too had had that curly silver-white hair and very blue eyes. His name was Axel Nidstrom, but everybody called him Niddy. From around 1900, he'd been about the slickest pro cardsharp in the business; even the people who disapproved of him had been forced to admire his skill. He'd had small, rather pudgy hands—he was a short, stoutish little man, and he bounced when he walked—but he could riffle through a deck, spotting the cards he wanted and sliding them into the right places to get naturally dealt to him, as easy and smooth as cream. An artist.

He'd been a nice, genial, friendly little man, Niddy. Even the cops who'd picked him up, in every city in the country, had liked him. Niddy had been picked up, and warned, and moved along, oftener than any other pro, because he *was* so good; anybody will eventually suspect a ninety per cent consistent winner, and lay a complaint. But he'd never held a grudge or made trouble —he was like most in that: just accepted it cheerfully.

He'd been married once, and had a boy; his wife divorced him, and got the youngster. But he'd never missed sending money for the boy. He was quite frank about it. "It's no life, but it's my life," he'd said to Mendoza once, fifteen years ago, in a place very much like this. God, how time went! That had been to Sergeant Mendoza, fifteen years younger. "I guess I couldn't change now, but I want my boy to have good schooling and maybe be a professional man—he's plenty smart."

But the rest of the money, after he'd paid his bills and got a bigger diamond ring, half the time he threw away. On his friends, or kids in the street—Niddy liked kids—on anything. When the war was on, he'd once given the Red Cross a thousand bucks, on impulse.

Mendoza had picked him up, that hot August night, and introduced himself by his real name, and read out the charge and the evidence. Niddy had looked resigned, and then laughed. "O.K., Sergeant," he'd said. "O.K., I'll come along quiet. You sure took me in, boy —anybody less like a cop! You're good, boy, I'll say that. But you're better off your side o' the fence, you just stay there. Me, I'm too old to change now."

Niddy had liked kids. . . . That night there had been a row in the Blue Grotto—the drunk going berserk with a loaded .45—that had been before Niddy knew Mendoza was a cop. Niddy'd dived under a table and stayed there until the drunk was knocked out. "I'm a coward, boy," he'd said with his happy grin. "Got to admit it. A little fellow like me, he's got to be either one damn good fighter or one damn good runner. Long time ago I decided I was the runner kind."

And Niddy had run, that rainy night just before Christmas of 1949, when he came out of a bar on Third Avenue and waited to cross Main where he'd catch the bus back to his hotel. When that big truck swung around the corner just as the little boy started to run across on the green, Niddy had run—in the right direction. He'd shoved the boy back safe, but the truck had got him—little Niddy, seventy-two and still the slickest pro in the business, with his ostrich-skin billfold stuffed with money from the suckers.

Mendoza had often wondered whether that boy of his had turned out the way the old man had hoped. He remembered little Niddy vividly—*It's no life, but it's my life.*

And he also remembered that Kevin O'Shea, the ten-year-old boy whose life Niddy had saved that night, had died in the gas chamber at San Quentin last year for the rape-murder of an eight-year-old girl.

What was the answer? There never was any answer —any easy answer, he thought savagely.

And Francis Ingram wasn't little Niddy. It was just irrational, a fleeting chance resemblance. No logic.

On the surface, it looked so open-and-shut. . . .

CHAPTER NINE

THE expected pal turned up after a while, and they played a few hands. Mendoza watched the room start to fill up, looking for someone who matched one of the descriptions. Just as the inveterate gamblers would start playing first thing in the mornings, the pros were early birds too.

He won a few dollars, lost a few dollars; they were playing low stakes. About eleven o'clock the other men at the table decided to move on somewhere else. Mendoza declined an invitation to tag along; he'd hang on here a while longer. He didn't want to approach Benny, who probably didn't know Ingram well; what he wanted was one of the fraternity.

He sauntered out to the lobby to the cigarette machines, got into conversation with another customer there, and managed to attach himself to the fellow when he went back to his table. None of the other men there interested him; he hung around, aimlessly watching the play. Benny had the place running smooth and quiet, all right; there were plenty of house attendants.

The minute there was a showdown at any table, there was a house man there, smiling, to collect the house cut, and it was a high one—ten per cent of the pot.

He watched the door. The place was still filling up, but nobody came in to match the descriptions. It was nearly noon; he ought to call his office. And then maybe go on somewhere else, have better luck.

He was making for the door when a man came in alone, who added up to one of Palliser's possibles; a medium-sized man about forty-five, sandy and going a little bald, brown eyes, small scar through his left eyebrow, ear lobes joined to his cheeks, left shoulder carried low. He was even wearing what looked like the same suit Palliser had seen him in, a chalk-striped charcoal affair with padded shoulders.

Mendoza slowed to a saunter and changed his direction. Chalk-Stripe walked rapidly across the room to a table containing four men, was greeted loudly, and sat down. Mendoza drifted over that way, making a circuit of the room. Benny would have a lookout man, but not to spot sharps; just to spot developing trouble.

He stopped near Chalk-Stripe to light a cigarette. There was an empty table nearby, and Mendoza sat down in one of the chairs. The five at the other table were very genial together, getting ready to cut for deal. Timing it nicely, Mendoza leaned over and said in a hesitant voice, to the nearest man, "Say, excuse me, but is there any rule about how you get into a game in this place? I've just hit L.A. from San Diego, and I don't know anybody here—I thought——"

They were cordial; a couple of them had had a few

beers. Chalk-Stripe said nothing, but Mendoza knew he was being sized up.

"Well, sure, the more the merrier——"

"Glad to have you—what's the name, hey?"

The rest of them all looked like straight marks. And of course there was no guarantee that Chalk-Stripe was a pro; he might, for all Mendoza knew, have been one of Ingram's marks. But no harm taking a chance.

He dragged his chair over and sat down, beaming gratefully at them. They exchanged names; Chalk-Stripe was Neil Davenport. "How do you play?" asked Mendoza. "Straight rules? That's good enough for me. What's the limit?"

"We been freezing it at ten, O.K.?" said Davenport.

"O.K. with me. Chips?"

"Start with a half buck."

"O.K.," said Mendoza again. It looked as if these pals had played together before; and at those stakes Davenport must be making a nice thing of it, if he was a pro. Four bits a white chip—and a ten-buck ante. One of the attendants hurried up, at Davenport's lifted hand, with cards and a rack of chips.

"Who'll bank?" The man on Mendoza's right was a beefy farmery-looking young fellow.

"Doesn't matter much," said Davenport casually. "O.K. if I shuffle? You bank if you want." But Farmer-Boy declined, and in the end one of the others, a thin older man with glasses, took the chips. Mendoza sat and looked amiable, watching Davenport. He was sitting under the gun, to the left of the edge and two places away from his quarry. They cut for deal and

Davenport got it with the ace of hearts. He shuffled rapidly, passed the deck to the edge—the thin man—for cutting, and dealt around. Everybody bought chips.

Mendoza looked at his hand—a pair of fours—and waited until Davenport glanced up from his cards for a minute. Mendoza laid his right hand flat, palm down in front of him. His gaze roamed around the table and caught a flash of comprehension in Davenport's eyes.

"Well, off to a good start," said Davenport casually. He was holding his cards in his left hand; he laid his right flat on the table with thumb upraised.

Mendoza smiled at his cards. For what it was worth, he had found his man. His gesture had said to Davenport, "I'm a sharp, anybody want to team up?" and Davenport's had said, "Sure, rank me." As Mendoza maneuvered his cards, he let Davenport know what he held and received information about Davenport's hand.

Play started. (And damn it, he ought to have called his office.)

The four marks were insatiable; the six of them sat there until after three o'clock, and Mendoza lost track of the hour and the number of hands. It was a long time since he'd knowingly sat in a crooked game and been forced to keep tabs on a sharp. The necessity for absolute concentration started his head aching dully—that, and too many cigarettes. Naturally, as time went on, he and Davenport came out ahead oftener than behind.

"This guy has the damnedest luck," said Farmer-Boy. It wasn't funny the first time he said it, and the twentieth time Mendoza could have strangled him.

And he could have kissed Davenport when, at long last, he scattered the deck on the table after a show-down and said, "I guess I won't push my luck, boys. See you," and stood up. Mendoza rose with him.

"Same for me. Very nice to have sat in with all of you." He didn't hurry out after Davenport; he knew Davenport would be waiting.

He was, in the lobby, twirling a soft felt hat on one finger. Mendoza collected his homburg and they went out. "Buy you a drink?" he offered.

"Fair enough," said Davenport. They started up the street; he gave Mendoza a sideways glance. "New beat for you? Haven't seen you around before."

"I've been down in Dago, like I said. Had a kind of reason to come up, but now I'm here I don't know—— Well, it's a funny thing." Mendoza's tone was troubled. "Maybe you can tell me something about it. I was look-ing for somebody who might, see. Didn't see any famil-iar faces, and I wanted a local contact. . . . You're damn good, by the way. I thought I was pretty smooth at a two-handed shift, but you beat me, brother."

Davenport laughed. "Practice," he said lightly. "You satisfied with the take, Moreno?"

"Any time. I didn't hit L.A. on business exactly, like I say. I just made a kill down south."

They turned into the first bar they came to, and Men-doza led the way to a rear booth. A waiter came up and they ordered. "What's on your mind?" asked Daven-port. He leaned back, relaxing. "Brother, what a ses-sion! I met up with those four marks three weeks back, and I love every hair on their heads. The whole bunch

115

of 'em are assemblers or something at Lockheed, and Wednesday's their day off. They make a beeline for Gardena, see. And you saw what they're like."

Mendoza laughed. "Marks from Marksville, sure. I appreciate your letting me sit in. Like I say, I'm loaded right now, but who ever gets too much?"

"You said you wanted to ask me something."

"Wait for the drinks."

The waiter came back with Mendoza's rye and Davenport's highball. Mendoza took a sip, set the glass down, and took out his billfold, extracted a folded newspaper clipping. Then he hesitated, looking at Davenport. "I don't know," he said doubtfully. "It's a hell of a business. I wouldn't have come, except I owe him something. He's a nice guy, see. But I don't suppose—— Well, anyway, it was this dragged me up here. I saw it in yesterday's paper, and——" He handed over the clipping. It was a cut of Ingram, the caption running, *Francis Ingram, 62, under suspicion of murdering his wife Bella, whose body has not yet been found.*

Davenport looked at it and his expression smoothed out to utter blankness. "What about it?" He handed the clipping back.

"Well, look, I know him," said Mendoza. He didn't dare call Ingram by name, because it was possible that the fraternity knew him as Joe or Bill. "The last time I was up here. He's on the job too. Maybe you knew him?"

Davenport was silent over his drink, but his eyes were wary.

"If it's the same guy, and it must be," pursued Mendoza. "But I just can't see him mixed up in a thing like this—murder! I didn't even know he was married, but like I say I haven't hit L.A. in a while. I owe him a favor—he helped me out once, got me out of a jam, a bad jam."

"You looking for trouble?" asked Davenport, eyes on his drink. "That's poison."

"Am I crazy? But he's a good guy. Look, I made this kill. The hell of a kill, Davenport. If he needs an alibi, well, I guess, you know the ropes, you can still buy one. And I owe him a favor, God knows. But, sweet Jesus, *then* when I get here I think—how the hell to contact him? There'll be cops all over."

"If you want advice," said Davenport softly, "keep out of it. That's what I said to Killeen. Sure, I'm sorry for Ingram—not that I ever knew him much, except, you know, just seeing him around and knowing who he was. But who wants to get mixed up with cops?"

"Well, sure. But—listen, it *is* him? I mean, I can't connect it, even when the picture—he isn't the kind to do a thing like that——"

"Know him pretty well?" asked Davenport, signaling the waiter. "I'll buy you a refill."

"I guess I did, awhile," said Mendoza. "I guess you could say so. Thanks. My God, I can't believe it—he wouldn't do a murder. They're railroading him, way I figure it."

"That's his lookout, brother," said Davenport. "Sure, I guess that's how anybody'd feel about one of his sidekicks. But I don't want one damn thing to do with it."

"Neither do I," said Mendoza in heartfelt tones. "All I thought was, if the folding stuff'd be any use to him. I know what the papers said about that dame's will—my God, imagine him coming into the long green like that—but it takes the hell of a long time to really get your hands on it, with the lawyers and all, I know that. I just thought—but I didn't dare go in a mile of the house, and I guess the cops'd have a tail on him——"

" 'S what Killeen said," said Davenport. "Real shook he was. Well, I guess natural. Man, he was ready to cry. I was talking to him in at Carlson's last night. He kept saying he doesn't know what to do. Well, like I told him, the way the setup looks, it wouldn't do Frankie Ingram any good if Killeen or anybody else stood up and alibied him. You couldn't, see? What the papers say, he could've killed the dame any time inside twenty-four hours. And not even Killeen wants to stick his neck out for nothing, who would? If you get me."

"Sure. It's a funny setup," said Mendoza. Who in hell was Killeen? "I guess, reading between the lines, what the papers said, this dame was strictly on the level and didn't know about Ingram being in the business. Papers call him a retired businessman—that's a good one. I can see it'd be another count against him if the cops——"

"Say it again," said Davenport. "And leave it alone. Me, I'm all for repaying favors to pals, but not if they're playing footsies with the cops. No, thanks. But then, he never was a pal of mine."

"Sure," said Mendoza. "But you see how I feel. My God, I don't want to show to the cops, but if there was some way I could—— Know where I'd find this Killeen? And who he is?"

118

At once he knew he'd made a mistake. Davenport glanced at him sharply, and his eyes narrowed. "Don't you know—— Who the hell are you, anyway? You're buddies with Ingram, but don't know—— What the hell?" He stood up; he'd finished his second drink. "Not that I'm pals with either one, but—— Well, I'm doing no more talking. Trouble I don't want. Of any kind, get me? Thanks for the backup and the drink, and *adiós.*" He slid from the booth and walked out fast.

Mendoza swore at his untouched rye. What had he said wrong? But he'd got something—and there was something more here to be got. Who was Killeen?

A little something he had. Frankie Ingram—his own name, then. And Killeen. He hadn't been wrong about Ingram; and, as he'd suspected, Ingram hadn't quit the business when he married a rich wife. Gamblers so seldom did quit, for any reason. Ingram was known down here—to most, as a steady customer; to a few, as what he really was. And there might be a mine of nice solid evidence to be had, from somebody down here (Killeen?) —but it wasn't going to be easy to find.

Damn it, what had he said to raise Davenport's suspicions?

Mendoza looked at the rye, swallowed it in one swift gulp, laid two singles on the table, and went out. He found a phone booth on the corner and called his office. It was three fifty-five.

"Anything going *on?*" said Sergeant Lake. "I've been trying to get you all over town, Lieutenant! There's a new witness just come in who blew Ingram's story all to hell, and now Ingram's claiming all his wife's jewelry's been stolen—— Art's been——"

119

"¡*Una limosna, por el amor de Dios!*" said Mendoza. "All right, I'm coming in, see you in twenty minutes!"

Ingram said steadily, "I'm sorry, gentlemen, I can't change the truth just to please you. The boy's mistaken, that's all. It wasn't me he saw."

Mendoza stared at him in exasperation. The boy, Mike Skene, just looked miserable and sullen. He was about nineteen, good-looking, tall and broad-shouldered, with a crest of dark auburn hair like an Irish setter and honest brown eyes. He was a good kid, nothing on him, but he was still young enough to be wary of any authority. Right now he was obviously wishing to God he'd never said anything about recognizing the newspaper picture. Mendoza swung around to him. "Well?"

"I already said it's him," muttered Skene. "Sure I'm sure."

"I'm afraid it wasn't," said Ingram pleasantly. "It can't have been. I'm not all that unique, you know." He had kept his temper and his head; he wasn't enjoying this, but he was facing it out well.

Sergeant Lake brought in the boy's statement neatly typed, and Mendoza took it to read it over. Baldly, what it said was that Mike Skene had seen Ingram that New Year's Day. He hadn't happened to notice the picture of Ingram when the papers first carried it, but since the case had got into the news the second time, during the last week, he had; and he'd said so, and his father had got all excited and said if he was sure, he ought to tell the police. Mike worked for his father, who had a

Richfield station way out on Western, just this side of
Gardena. The boy remembered the day for a pretty
good reason; it had been a holiday and he'd wanted the
afternoon off to see the Rose Bowl game with a couple
of pals who had tickets, but his dad had made him stay
on the job because it would be a heavy day, a lot more
customers than usual. But he'd said Mike could go off at
six-thirty, to meet the same bunch for the evening, and
the man Mike remembered, and now identified as Ingram, had been his last customer. It had been about six
twenty-eight when the light blue 1961 Caddy drove
into the station. There'd been another man next to
the driver.

"No," Ingram kept repeating, shaking his head. "No,
the boy's honestly mistaken, that's all."

Mike hadn't got a good look at the second man, but
the driver was right under the lights. He'd had Mike
fill it up with ethyl, and handed him a five-spot. While
the tank was filling, Mike had polished the windshield;
and when he came back with the change, the driver had
said, "You did a good job on that, boy, thanks," and
handed him a dollar bill. Which was another reason
Mike had remembered him, because getting a tip was a
thing that practically never happened.

Mendoza gave Skene the statement to read and
turned to Ingram, who'd been brought downtown (for
the second time that day) to let the boy look at him.
"So, you weren't just stepping into Chino's at about six-
fifteen for a lonely dinner. You said you were home at
five-thirty when your wife arrived, and you said you left
the house at six or a little past. Well, you could have

121

been there at five-thirty, but you wouldn't have been there at six—not if you were that far out on Western at six twenty-eight, through home-coming traffic."

"The boy's mistaken, that's all," said Ingram. "I can't help it if you believe him instead of me. It wasn't me he saw, but somebody who looks like me."

"Driving a 1961 light blue Cadillac just like yours?" said Mendoza. "Quite a coincidence, Mr. Ingram!" He turned back to Skene. "Are you satisfied with that, ready to sign it as it is?"

"I guess so, sir."

"All right. Did you notice which direction the car took when it left?"

"It headed up Western toward Inglewood."

"And points north, such as Hollywood. . . . Thanks very much for coming in, Mr. Skene—we appreciate it." When the boy had been ushered out, Mendoza eyed Ingram grimly. "You were on your way back from Gardena," he said. "I think you'd had a profitable day, anyway you were feeling expansive—in spite of your incipient cold—hence that dollar tip. Very unwise, Mr. Ingram. You might have known he'd remember you! Who was with you? Did you go straight home after dropping him, or did he come with you?"

"I can't make up any lies for you, you know," said Ingram. "I'm very sorry, but you'll just have to take this as a coincidence."

Hackett, on the other side of the desk, sighed and shifted.

"You weren't home at all," said Mendoza suddenly, "were you? Or———" Ingram very possibly felt (rightly or wrongly) that police suspicion would increase if he changed his story. It wouldn't look very good, at that; depending on what he changed it to. But why had he told a lie in the first place? Why did he have to, unless he knew she was dead? It wouldn't necessarily have incriminated him to say he'd been down at one of the poker palaces. Quite honest citizens sometimes had the urge; it wouldn't have given him away on that line. So possibly he'd been up to something else that would incriminate him. Or, of course, he did know she was dead and was covering himself. And now this second man had showed up—a friend of Ingram's?—and he might have been right there to help start planning the cover-up. Killeen?

Why the hell hide the body?

He stared at Ingram and said suddenly. "Look, *amigo*. I don't think you did it, you know. I'll level with you—everybody else around here does, but not me." Hackett uttered a little sound of disapproval at this man-to-man approach; Mendoza ignored him. "Call it a hunch. Say it's because you remind me of a fellow I liked once. Say I'm a fool. But for my money, you're not guilty. Will you use some common sense and help me prove it?"

For a half second, he could swear, Ingram wavered. Then the very blue eyes dropped from his, and the long hands lifted in a little gesture. "Thanks, Lieutenant," said Ingram in his pleasant deep voice. "I appreciate your saying that. But I really can't invent a lie just to please you. I've told you the truth."

Mendoza looked at him for another moment and then turned to the door and held it open. "Until the next time."

Ingram got up, hat in hand. "It's too bad all these extraneous things keep coming up. Like the jewelry. I can't understand that—and I can't understand why her body hasn't——"

"We're working on it," said Mendoza, and shut the door on him.

CHAPTER TEN

"So WHAT about this jewelry?" he asked Hackett abruptly, sitting down at his desk.

"You've got to admire his nerve, I will say," said Hackett. "Never say die. The hell of it is, you know, we'll have to look. Make all the gestures."

"Does it occur to you that he might for once be telling the truth?"

"Frankly, no," said Hackett. "We got a list from her lawyer. Here it is. The jewelry was evaluated at approximately ten thousand dollars."

"Mmh." Mendoza ran his eye over the list. Diamond solitaire ring with twelve side stones; twin-diamond ring, round brilliants, with six side stones; diamond-set wristwatch; diamond and sapphire bracelet, forty diamonds adding to six carats . . . "Yes. Ingram's quite right in saying that it must have been stolen that afternoon, of course. If he's not lying. And this and that, now, shows me a few pretty pictures I hadn't seen before."

"You're in the wrong line," said Hackett. "I've always said so. You should be writing T.V. scripts, with your wild imagination. Or telling fortunes."

"Indulge me five minutes, Arturo, and let's assume Ingram is innocent of the murder at least. Where does he tell us he was that afternoon?" He hunted among the papers on the case. "Here. He says he had lunch after his wife left, watched the rebroadcast of the Rose Parade on T.V., and later on went out for about twenty minutes, drove down to the boulevard for cigarettes, and came home again. How fortunate for him that he gave himself that out, now this robbery has turned up. Though I suppose, if he hadn't casually said that, he could have claimed to have been reading in his den and just didn't hear the sneak thief. Well, that doesn't matter, because we know now he wasn't home at all. The problem is, where was he? Apparently coming from the direction of Gardena, but if he'd been whiling away the afternoon taking a profit off some marks, surely a couple of them would have showed up to say so by now? Leave that a minute. Now, here's one picture I'm seeing. Bella probably came straight home from her bridge party, and got to Sycamore Terrace about five-thirty. Practically every woman, young or old, pretty or plain, goes through a little automatic routine when she gets home from somewhere. Alison snatches off her earrings first, and dangly bracelets if she's wearing them——"

"It's shoes with Angel," agreed Hackett, "and then earrings."

"Yes, well, the point is that a lot of women, especially if they're going to be getting a meal, change their clothes when they come in. Especially if they've been

126

rather dressed up. We know Bella did. She took off her dress, after unpinning the brooch and putting it on the dressing table. Then she hung up the dress, and being in the closet for that purpose she put on the cotton house dress and also changed her shoes. And then she came back to the dressing table to finish taking off her jewelry and put it away. It's a pity," said Mendoza, "that there doesn't seem to be a happy medium between the fanatically neat people and the hopelessly disorderly ones. I know I annoy people by going around straightening pictures and so on, but you're built one way or the other. And Bella seems to have been one of those too. Ingram himself says she always put her jewelry away at once, just as she hung up her clothes on taking them off. But on New Year's Day she didn't—put her jewelry away, that is. I think very possibly she was interrupted just as she was about to. By, say, the doorbell ringing."

"Enter X," said Hackett.

"Just admit to me it could be."

"Oh, it *could* be. But as I've said to you before on these little hunches, the obvious answer is usually the right answer. Just because you're a complex piece of goods yourself doesn't say that everybody has such a labyrinthian mind."

"Four-syllable words yet," said Mendoza. *"¡Vaya, qué hombre!"*

"You're trying to make it complicated. Not just because, for God's sake, you like the guy——" It was half question, and half incredulous exclamation.

Mendoza smiled. "I haven't slipped that far, Arturo. There are very few likable murderers in the world, and if I ever ran into one, I've been a cop too long to let personalities influence my judgment. No. It comes down to pure feeling—the nuances I get from him—and the type he is, which I know up and down." He got up, sorted out the papers he wanted, and added, "I'll brief Goldberg."

Downstairs in Burglary, he told the tale to Lieutenant Saul Goldberg, who listened in silence except for sneezes. When Mendoza handed over the list of jewelry, Goldberg looked at it, looked at him, and sneezed again.

"I see," he said, getting out fresh Kleenex. "You want me to send out half a dozen men looking in all the usual places for this collection of ice which you're not sure's even been stolen."

"It's got to be done," said Mendoza reasonably.

"Oh, sure!" said Goldberg. "We're always happy to oblige you, Luis, you know that. All I will ask you— damn it to hell," as he sneezed again and groped for Kleenex, "is, have you had a little hunt for it yourselves? For all you know, he's buried it in the back yard. After all, we're kept fairly busy on honest-to-God break-ins."

"I know, I know! We'll look around too. But you'll run a check on pawnshops and so on? And remember, if this is on the level, we're more than a month late on it."

"And you don't even know that," said Goldberg, "not for sure. Hell and damnation!" He began to sneeze again.

"Having a bad attack?" asked Mendoza with guileful sympathy.

Goldberg emerged from the Kleenex to say with quiet venom, "You know the latest thing they tell me I'm allergic to? Paper. Just ordinary paper. That I got to handle all day long. They say to me, keep away from it. Just like, keep away from the glue on postage stamps, and the cat, and my wife's face powder, and grass. I think they're all nuts—just plain nuts." Goldberg gave the Kleenex box a petulant shove, and it fell off his desk. Mendoza picked it up and lined it tidily with the desk blotter. "Look, I say to them—these specialists!—I say, What do you expect me to do? I'm only forty-four, I got a family to support, I got to work, and in my job I've got paper work. Have I got paper work! Am I supposed to quit and go on relief? Do I have to kick the cat every time she comes near me, or make the kids hate me if I take her to the pound? Do I have to pay somebody to lick all my stamps for me? Every time I want to kiss my wife, does she have to wash her face first? And who the hell can afford a gardener?"

"It's a problem," said Mendoza.

"They're nuts, that's all," said Goldberg. "Ivory-tower nuts, like some guys I could mention in Washington. Just no common horse sense. You know what I said to Dr. Lowenthal? I said, 'Doctor, I tell you—what it comes down to,' I said, 'if I want to get rid of all my allergy troubles I'll have to live alone in a hermetically sealed room the rest of my life, with meals shoved through the ventilator. Isn't that what you're telling me?' And d'you know what he said?" Goldberg sneezed violently.

"What?"

"He said, 'Well, Lieutenant Goldberg, all we can do

is analyze and explain your problem. The rest of it's up to you.' I ask you! And of course," added Goldberg bitterly, "he went on to say something about it being psychosomatic. The hell with the whole bunch of them."

"You're absolutely right," said Mendoza. "But you'll run this little check for us, and see what turns up? Thanks very much."

"Oh, I suppose so," said Goldberg gloomily.

Mendoza told him to cheer up and went back to his office. It was getting on for five-thirty. But his hopes of getting away by six were sabotaged by the message Sergeant Lake had for him. He was expected immediately in Captain Holmes's office for another consultation with the D.A.'s representative.

"Hell!" said Mendoza. "Talk about a waste of time——" But he'd have to be there.

It was, as a matter of fact, less a consultation than an ultimatum. The D.A.'s office had decided on an inquest.

"In view of the—ah—sensational press coverage the case is getting, you understand, we feel——"

And certainly, if ever a case had been tried in the papers, this one was being so tried. "Slanting" wasn't exactly the word for it, thought Mendoza; no paper had any interest in railroading Ingram. A couple of them had more sensational reporting than others; but the facts set out in journalese curiously distorted the characters and events.

In the press coverage, Mrs. Ingram appeared as a distinguished high-society member of several volunteer charity organizations, a diligent worker for the Red Cross, the California Committee for Underpriviliged

Children, the Beautify Our City drive, and so on, all worthy groups. The late Simon's philanthropies were also recalled. Somehow it was implied that the Ingrams had lived much more lavishly than was the case—the high-society element improved the sensational value of the Ingram murder as news. Although all the facts were reported faithfully, the dinner party given on the night before she vanished had taken on all the attributes of a formal reception at the governor's mansion. As the press hadn't been handed much of anything new since Headquarters had taken over, and space had to be filled somehow, they'd relied a good deal on interviews with the family. Winthrop, his fussiness and old-maidishness played down, appeared righteously as "retired from local political activities and the directorship of a well-known brokerage," and his late wife's fortune was mentioned. The Barrons couldn't be sensationalized easily, and the high-society factor was sadly lacking there; but Linda was played up, inevitably, as the Beautiful Model. Though there was no question of libel, the facts themselves damned Ingram, and an unspoken tacit acceptance of his guilt underlay all the reporting. The press hadn't got hold of anything about Ingram's past; unless they got it from the police, they probably never would. But what they did know—or what they'd been told—a retired ex-businessman with far less money than his new wife, naturally led to the inference that he had married this upright, worthy widow for her money. The story of the will had come out too, from Winthrop, who said forthrightly that Ingram had deliberately worked on her with flattery and charm until she left him the greater part of her fortune.

Nuances, thought Mendoza, nuances. He looked at the D.A.'s man and at Holmes. They knew the facts; but they hadn't met the people. And the people . . .

That was something else. He hadn't said anything to Holmes about his own knowledge of Ingram's past, which he should have. Time enough, he said to himself. If he had time, and luck, he might turn up the truth and show Ingram innocent. Meanwhile, if Ingram's gambling connections came out it would only damn him further; there were always so many people ready to confuse moral values, to believe that obviously, if a man was a cardsharp, he was all the likelier to turn to murder. If in the end it came to a charge on Ingram, the whole business would have to be made public. But right now, Mendoza knew that that revelation would make both Holmes and the D.A. all the more certain of Ingram's guilt. They would bring up the matter at the inquest, to make the coroner all the more certain too. People . . .

So they were going ahead with the inquest, damn it. It could still be an open verdict. A hundred-to-one chance.

"I'm sorry," he said, "about this decision, Mr. DeVries. I'm afraid that an inquest now might end in an official charge on Ingram, and I don't think he's guilty."

DeVries looked politely surprised and Holmes said, "Oh, for God's sake, Mendoza! You got a message from your crystal ball, maybe? If I ever saw an open-and-shut case! The only question there ever was about it was, did we have enough to charge him on? I didn't think so, but if the D.A. does—— And with what's just turned

132

up, this gas-station kid blowing Ingram's story to pieces——"

"We thought Friday," murmured DeVries, rising.

"The point is," said Mendoza, knowing he wasn't getting through, "once there's a charge, we won't have a chance to do any more looking around. And I think——"

"That's O.K. with us," said Holmes loudly. "Anything you want, DeVries, just ask. . . . I want to talk to you, Mendoza." The D.A.'s man left and the captain sat back in his chair, a big solid gray man—hair, face, eyes, suit all gray—his face like granite.

In the last year Holmes had been increasingly difficult to get on with; not only Mendoza had experienced that. The captain was due for retirement in six months; it was the general consensus that he wasn't well, maybe had an ulcer or something that sharpened his temper. Now he was eying Mendoza contemptuously.

"Listen," he said, "you think I don't know what's in your mind? Always playing to the grandstand, our glamour boy Mendoza! You know damn well Ingram's guilty. After the first day, it'd have been just an ordinary murder case reported on the back pages, if it hadn't been for the missing body and all the money. But if you can spin it out and make it look mysterious, you'll get a lot of publicity, and how you love that! I know——"

Mendoza stood up. "You know that's a damn lie, Holmes," he said coldly. "That couldn't matter less to me. I'll tell you what does matter to me, Holmes. This force has a little reputation as being about the tops anywhere, and I wouldn't like to see it railroad an honest man. And I wouldn't enjoy the feeling that I'd had a hand in it."

Holmes let out an expletive. "The honor of the school! Don't give me that, I know what you're after!"

"Then you know more than I do," said Mendoza, and stalked out. In his own office, he called Hackett and Palliser in and told them about the inquest. "It's the time element, damn it, you can see that. Only a day left to look around, and *terminar*. Because I'll lay long odds that what's going to the coroner on this so far will result in a verdict holding Ingram guilty, and he'll be charged and we're out of it. And I tell you frankly, I'd feel uneasy about it the rest of my life."

"Well," said Hackett slowly, "I've laughed at a lot of your ideas that turned out right, Luis. I don't deny it, you feel things. Honest to God, you think he's innocent?"

"Of the murder, yes. I think he's being used as a scapegoat. Yet, you know, the funny thing is that I still have the feeling this was a spur-of-the-moment business, which doesn't square with the complicated affair it seems to have turned into. At any rate, I know damn well there's a lot more to find out. We're all going to be putting in a lot of overtime until the inquest, in the hope that we can turn up something that will show the coroner it isn't as open-and-shut as it looks. John———"

"Yes?" Palliser looked resigned.

"Have a date with Miss Silverman?" asked Mendoza sympathetically. "Sorry, but that's how it goes. Give her my apologies. I want you to go and question that servant of Winthrop's again. Pin him down about times.

Art, you chase up that Wills girl. We haven't seen her yet. She looks very much out of the picture, but you never know. I want to see the maid again."

Hackett also looked resigned and said O.K.

"Tomorrow, we'll dig as deep as we can into the backgrounds of all these people. And I want that hunt for the private detective pressed—if Bella did hire one I'd like to know why."

"What about a tail on Ingram?" asked Hackett. "He just might lead us to that very hypothetical alibi you dreamed up."

"No. He'll be very careful not to do anything suspicious. And we haven't got the men to spare. I didn't like this case to start with and I'm liking it less and less, but while I'm on it I'll work it. Good luck, *hasta más ver*," and he reached for his hat.

Alison met him at the door of the house, having heard the car. . . . "Among several things I *don't* like about these twins," she said presently, "is that I can't seem to get quite so close to you any more, they get in the way. I'm looking worse every day."

"No, you're not, *querida*. Just slightly more fecund." But his tone was absent. Alison cocked her head at him.

"You're worried about something," she said seriously. "Want me to be a good listener?"

"Later."

He told her about it over dinner, with the usual interruptions from the cats, who demanded a sample of everything that was going. Alison listened in silence and then said, "You know, Luis, there's something in what Art says—you have got a tortuous mind. How sure are you he isn't guilty?"

"I can't be a hundred per cent sure, naturally," said Mendoza irritably. "I'm not psychic. There're just a dozen little irrelevant things I don't like about the case against Ingram—and there's the man himself."

"There might be an open verdict at the inquest."

"About one chance in a hundred."

"Yes. And then it'd be out of your hands."

Mendoza laid down his fork. He said, "Legally speaking, it would be. But I tell you, if it comes to that I'll throw away the rule book. I'm not going to stop work on this thing until I get at the truth."

CHAPTER ELEVEN

S Y L V I A G L A S S stepped back, looking frightened and stubborn at once, when she recognized him on the porch. "You!" she said. "I don't know why you got to go *on* at me all the time! I already told——"

"This is something different," said Mendoza. "We're sorry to annoy you, Miss Glass, but in a case like this—— May I come in?"

"I s'pose," she said, and gave way reluctantly. "Mother's out, gone to the movies with Mrs. Kraut. I guess we can talk in here."

It was the usual California bungalow, one long front room combining living and dining areas, a much-worn dark red carpet covering its whole length. The furniture was shabby old-fashioned velours and there was an old golden-oak upright piano in one corner. The inevitable garish seascape hung over the mantel. "Sit down," she said, not wanting to say it.

Mendoza sat down and offered her a cigarette. She told him she didn't smoke, but brought him a dime-store glass ashtray. "What is it now, anyways?"

137

"I'm not going to ask you to say anything against Mr. Ingram." He gave her a persuasive smile. "But, as I expect you noticed yourself when you read over the statement you made, sometimes the written word doesn't sound quite the same as what you've really said, and everything you've said doesn't always get into the formal statement. When you told Lieutenant Ames what you knew about the case he put what he thought was important into the statement. Well, I'd like you to tell me, just in your own words, some of what you said then."

"Oh. What part?"

"I'd like to hear about the dinner party that Monday night, when Mrs. Ingram told her family she'd made a new will."

"Oh, *that!*" said Sylvia. She looked relieved. "Sure, I'll tell you about that, and it'll show you what they're like and what *he's* like! I——"

"I want every little thing you remember, please."

"Sure. See, it was kind of a dinner party to celebrate that Hugh's getting engaged. And what any girl saw in him—well, he's not so bad-looking maybe, but smart-alecky and like that. I mean, anybody could tell, the way he'd make up to Mrs. Ingram, he was blarneying her for money, and I know a dozen times she'd give him some, him saying he had overdue bills—she'd call him extravagant and so on, but she'd give it to him. He's got what they call kind of a way with him. And then he's a *man*—they always get things easier. She was real pleased he'd got engaged. She said a good wife'd make him steadier, see?" Sylvia was garrulous, on this safe subject; Mendoza sat back and let her talk. "She didn't like Miss Wills, though—the dinner party was the first time she'd met her, see. Miss Wills got off on the wrong foot right away, because she tripped on the step coming in and said damn. Mrs. Ingram was real old-fashioned about ladies swearing, and she always spoke up and said what she thought. She did then, and I don't guess Miss Wills liked it much. But Hugh said something to her and she didn't say nothing. Well, I didn't hear what any of them said in the living room before dinner. I was naturally in the kitchen getting things ready, see. It was a good dinner———"

"I'm sure it was," said Mendoza. "I'd bet you're a good cook, Miss Glass."

She giggled self-consciously. "Well, if I do say so——— There was chilled tomato juice to start, because it was a kind of warm night, see, like January is a lot out here. And a nice tossed green salad with two kinds of dressing, and French beans with little bits of bacon in them and roast beef and browned potatoes and hot rolls and a dish of olives and celery. And for dessert there was Bavarian cream and little cookies, only hardly anybody ate that because by then they were all rowing. All except Mr. Ingram, of course, and he was trying to make them stop and smooth things down. Well, you can see I was in and out a lot of times, serving things, and when I wasn't there, well, the dining room's right next to the kitchen and there's just one of those louver doors—I couldn't help hearing every word."

"Yes, I can see that."

"Well!" said Sylvia. She was enjoying herself. "I could see Mrs. Ingram didn't think much of this Marcia Wills. I didn't neither. Bleached hair and red nails

139

an inch long and a silly sort of laugh and she had on a bright red dress and too much jewelry. You know what I mean? But she—Mrs. Ingram—couldn't come right out and say so. I mean she didn't have much of what you call tact but she wouldn't do that. Only I bet she'd have said so to Hugh later on, if she hadn't—— Well, Mr. Ingram was awful polite, of course, like he always is. And Linda just sat sizing Marcia up" (one of the things Sylvia was enjoying was calling them all by their first names) "but Linda don't care much about anything but herself, same as her mother. And of course Mr. Winthrop was taking up most of her time——"

"Whose time?"

Interrupted, Sylvia stared at him. "Why, Linda's, naturally. See, he's just crazy about her, Mr. Winthrop is—thinks she's the most beautiful, wonderful girl God ever put on earth. I guess it's because he never had any kids of his own, he kind of takes it all out on her, you know how some men are about their daughters. I don't know an awful lot about her—she's a model, isn't she? She didn't come to the house much except, I figure, when her mother made her—being nice to her auntie, know what I mean, on account of all the money. But anybody can see she's, you know, pretty snobby and thinks an awful lot of herself. But Mr. Winthrop just can't see any wrong in her at all. He wanted to pay for her to go to college, I heard Mrs. Barron say that, only Linda didn't want to. The funny thing is, she isn't all over him, the way Hugh was over Mrs. Ingram. I guess he'd give her anything she asked for, and he's got money too. But the way she acts, it's like she was kind of —uninterested, or wants to laugh at him when he keeps patting her hand and calling her darling and so on. But you wanted to hear what they *said*. Well, it all started when Mrs. Ingram said wasn't that a new bracelet Mrs. Barron had on and Mrs. Barron said yes and wasn't it pretty and it'd been on sale, only nine ninety-five, and Mrs. Ingram said—sort of sarcastic, you know—that she didn't think, in *her* financial position, Mrs. Barron ought to be so extravagant on unnecessary luxuries. And Mrs. Barron said, well, it was her money and she was used to nice things. And then Mr. Ingram, like always, tried to smooth things over in a nice way, you know, and change the subject, and he asked Linda how her modeling job was going and she said all right, and she'd had the most marvelous time at Lake Arrowhead last weekend. She'd gone there from Friday till Sunday with Bruce—that's the fella she's going steady with, I guess—and another couple. Well, Mrs. Ingram had kept going on at Mrs. Barron about the bracelet, but she heard *that,* and she looked right up—see, I was there then, I'd just come in with the coffee because Mr. Ingram always likes his with his dinner—only I was behind her and she didn't know I was there—and she said, sort of cold and nasty, 'I must say I'm surprised to hear you confess your gross immorality in public.' And Mrs. Barron spoke up and said she, Mrs. Ingram, was just a prudish, suspicious old woman, nobody thought anything of nice young people going around together like that now. But mind you, Mrs. Ingram had the right of it, because that's not so. A real nice girl wouldn't dream of doing such a thing. And Linda just laughed but Mr. Winthrop got awful mad and excited, so he could hardly talk, and he said Mrs. Ingram hadn't any right to say such a terrible thing about her own niece, and she was to take it back right away. And before Mrs. Ingram could say anything, Mrs. Barron spoke up kind of fretful like she does and said she supposed if Mrs. Ingram had *her* way they'd never have any little fun at all —and all this while poor Mr. Ingram was trying to smooth things down. Well, I mean, it wasn't the way people that was any real class go on, you know, was it? Fighting right out like that. And that was where Mrs. Ingram got real mad. She did sometimes, you know—I guess it was her high blood pressure. She'd go awful red in the face and say whatever came into her head. It used to embarrass poor Mr. Ingram something terrible, especially when it was in front of people—when they were alone and she went on like that, he'd say, 'please don't make a scene, I don't like scenes.' Well, anyways, she did then—she said, only not saying but kind of shrieking, 'Well, at least I've got better sense than to leave my money to fools and prostitutes!' " Sylvia blushed. "I mean, she said *that* right out, it was awful! Then she said, 'I made a new will, when I began to suspect all of you for what you are, but I'm going to make another now and leave Francis *everything* so none of you will get a penny. He gets most of it now but I want him to get it all! I won't have my money go to——' And then all of a sudden, see, she stops—she kind of holds herself in, because that Marcia Wills gave a kind of silly little laugh, and it reminded Mrs. Ingram she was there. She's a stranger really, and Mrs. Ingram didn't like her anyways and I guess all of a sudden she was sort of ashamed of going on like that in front of somebody she'd just met, you know? But gee, none o' the rest of 'em minded! You shoulda heard the row!"

"I can imagine it," said Mendoza. There was no mention in Sylvia's original statement that Mrs. Ingram had informed her family that they were mentioned in the present will but would get nothing under the new one she meant to make; or that Ingram knew that, if he sat tight for a while, he'd get it all. Very interesting. And what had Bella begun to suspect about her family? Anything specific, or just that they were all after her money?

"He—Mr. Ingram—was awful embarrassed. He just hated every second of it, you could see, and I sure didn't blame him. The names they called him! And right out before that girl they'd never seen before—I hope they're sorry now, the way she's blabbed all about it to the newspapers!" Yes, Marcia Wills had been very forthcoming about that little scene, even if she hadn't reported the exact details of dialogue; the press had covered it fully. Funny nobody *had* mentioned the terms of the new will before; but in a way, it was natural. In a confused uproar of voices, exact words wouldn't be remembered—what had registered was "a new will."

"The *things* they said!" Sylvia was still wrapped up in her story. "Like Mrs. Ingram wasn't right in the head, and he was a confidence man after her money from the start—— He's *not!* You never saw anybody nicer and kinder, and she talked real sharp to him sometimes too. And, listen"—Sylvia leaned forward earnestly—"I got to thinking about it. I mean, it's just awful the way everybody seems to think just naturally he's the one that murdered her, it isn't *right*—listen,

143

he's got a weak heart. He goes to the doctor twice a month regular to get checked up, and he has to take medicine—listen, I don't guess he *could* do anything, well, like—like hitting somebody or—— You know what I mean?"

Mendoza regarded her somewhat as Balaam must have looked at his ass. Out of the mouths of babes . . . See the doctor, yes, and get an opinion. It wouldn't be worth much, because they didn't (minus the body) know exactly how the woman had died. But . . .

"That's all very interesting, Miss Glass," he said. "You've given me a couple of ideas."

"He never did such an awful thing," she said earnestly. "I know him, and he *never*. I don't want you to think"—her hands twisted together—"there's anything—anything bad about my saying I—you know—like him. Listen, I'm going steady with Jack Reinfeld, see? It's just—Mr. Ingram's not the *kind* to do anything like that——"

"I agree with you," said Mendoza, standing up.

She stared at him, her agate eyes widening. "You *do?* Oh—but I thought——"

"Unfortunately I'm not the ultimate authority. But we'll do what we can. I want a new statement from you, with all these details in it."

"Anything I could do to help him, sure."

Hackett had found Hugh Barron with Marcia Wills in her apartment. Her roommate, she said, was out on a date. She said it coyly, and fiddled with her charm bracelet while she glanced sideways at Hackett under improbably long lashes. Hackett, whose resemblance to

144

a big dumb cop had nothing to do with the way his mind worked, instantly found himself wondering about a couple of things.

One of them was Hugh Barron's alibi (which had checked out). He'd said with a wink that his fiancée was "kind of prudish about what they call premarital behavior." Hackett could think of several adjectives for Miss Wills, but "prudish" wasn't among them.

He also wondered what her permanent attraction was for Hugh Barron. That one got answered almost at once. Barron said only half lightly, "Don't flirt with the nice big sergeant, pet," and she turned her eyes to him; they were sitting side by side on the couch.

"Ooh, Hughie, you know I'd *never!*" she said. Her expression was blindly adoring. So, thought Hackett. He was the Big White Chief as far as she was concerned —do anything for him, believe anything he said—as per Milton, he for God only, she for God in him. And Hugh Barron was just the boy, maybe, to like it that way.

"You fellows are certainly thorough," he said now, with a faint echo of his sister's mocking tone. "What in heaven's name do you think Marcia could know about this?" Hugh Barron had obvious and superficial good looks. He was middle-sized and wiry, with his sister's regular cameo features. His dark hair was curly, but unfortunately there were already signs that he would lose it early. He had ugly, short-fingered hands, and a too light tenor voice.

"Routine, that's all," said Hackett. He hadn't actually any questions to ask Marcia; they had her statement. As Mendoza said, she seemed well out of it.

Hackett had just wanted an impression of her, and that he had now.

"Ra-ather hard on old Ingram," drawled Barron, "prolonging the agony like this. I should have thought he'd have been arrested long before now."

"I thought, Mr. Barron," said Hackett, "that you'd expressed the opinion that Mr. Ingram isn't guilty."

"So I did," said Barron. "He hasn't got the guts to commit a murder. I'm surprised he hasn't been arrested because there's so damn much against him, and because"—his eyes traveled up and down Hackett's bulk—"well, there aren't usually any big brains in the police force, are there?"

"I'm afraid you've got some old-fashioned ideas there, Mr. Barron," said Hackett.

"Oh, d'you think so? I should've thought the deduction was obvious. Like the people in civil service, you know"—Barron flicked his lighter with a self-conscious gesture, like an amateur actor—"the ones without much ambition or individuality, just after security." He was trying to annoy Hackett, and succeeding. Hackett wondered if any victim of Barron's would-be sophisticated needling had ever given him the indicated treatment, a good swift kick.

"Don't you ever read the newspapers?" he asked politely. "I wouldn't call it a very safe job, you know. Every now and then there's a little item about a police officer getting killed——"

"My dear man, consult your dictionary for the difference between 'security' and 'safety,'" said Barron insolently.

Marcia giggled. "I do think you're mad at him because you thought I was flirting with him, Hughie!"

"Well, one thing about it," said Hackett, hoping that in the course of the case Barron would run up against Mendoza, who would take him down several pegs, "we do meet—all different kinds of people," and he looked from one to the other of them.

"Oh, if you have any questions to ask, ask away, Sherlock, and get it over! You're spoiling what started off to be quite a nice date."

Hackett made up a few random questions and left. . . . When he got home he told Angel he sometimes wondered why he'd ever joined the force. "Some of the people you run into——" He also commented bitterly on the peaceful silence emanating from the bedroom. *"Now* he sleeps. Like a cherub. If you'd deliberately keep him awake all evening maybe he——"

Angel said, "Don't be ridiculous, Art. I see this is one of the times you really need a drink. Sit down, take off your tie and relax, I'll get you one."

Palliser finished his assignment a little before nine, and though it was too late to take in the show they'd planned, he called Roberta Silverman to ask if he could come up for a drink. She laughed.

"You do sound wistful. If you don't mind the drive——" She lived in South Pasadena.

"Oh, I don't mind the *drive,*" said Palliser.

Unusually for him, Mendoza couldn't sleep. He lay awake going over every detail of the case; he couldn't switch off his mind. Round and round it went like a squirrel in a cage, evaluating the people, the few facts they had; and remorselessly the whirr of the electric clock on the bedside table seemed to get louder. Time, time! There was only one day more—and not if he had a hundred men to send out in all directions could he collect all the information he wanted in one day. If he knew exactly where to look, maybe one simple question and answer would tell him the truth—or send him in the right direction. But he didn't know where.

Killeen. Who was Killeen and who was he to Ingram, or Ingram to him? What was it the maid hadn't told? It was something concerned with the time after she came back to the house from the garage that night. Or was that just imagination?

Ingram . . .

Alison was sleeping soundly. There was nothing but aspirin in the house. Mendoza got up, waking the cats, who were surprised and annoyed and said so. He went out to the front room and reread the statements.

Finally he began to feel sleepy—it was past three—and went back to bed.

The telephone woke them all out of sound sleep at ten past six. "*¡Porvida, qué demonio——!*" muttered Mendoza drowsily, turning over and reaching for the extension phone. Alison sat up sleepily. "Mendoza."

"Sorry if I woke you up, Lieutenant," said the voice of Sergeant Thoms, who was on night tour this month. "I figured you'd want to know right away. The Ranger office called in ten minutes ago. They've just found the body and the car."

Mendoza sat up. A great thankfulness filled him.

Now the inquest would be postponed, probably over the weekend, for the results of an autopsy. And a whole list of new facts might show up. . . . "Where and how?" he asked eagerly.

CHAPTER TWELVE

RATHER obviously, the intentions of X had been to fake an accident. That explained the disappearance; X hadn't intended Bella to disappear. His bad luck had been in choosing the place he did to stage the accident.

He had picked a sharp curve of the Angeles Crest Highway, on the way up to Arrowhead and Big Bear. The cliff fell away just below the road, at an angle, and at the end of a sheer drop of nearly five hundred feet was a heavy growth of twenty-year-old Douglas pine. The Cadillac, so the Rangers said, and they were nearly as expert on accidents as the Highway Patrol, had plunged straight down to the trees, knocking two of them down and damaging others. The fallen trees had lain partly over the car, which had rolled under the bulge of the cliff, out of sight of the road above. The Rangers added philosophically that it was going to be the hell of a job to get her out of there. Even more unfortunately for X, the curve had been guarded by a separate section of white-painted guardrail. Ordinarily, somebody would have spotted a broken section of rail and reported it; there'd have been an investigation. But this section the Caddy had carried away clean, no broken parts left, so nobody had noticed.

And, uncomfortably, Mendoza remembered the honest bewilderment in Francis Ingram's voice when he said, "I can't understand why her body hasn't been found." X must indeed have been puzzled about that; he'd have expected it to be found almost at once. The Angeles Crest was a well-traveled highway. Of course X had chosen the place in the dark; and he—and his pal—must have been in a hurry to get away. And after all, in a big metropolis like this, anyone might be surprised she hadn't been found sooner.

The car had finally been spotted by a Ranger, up early and riding under the cliff on a routine inspection to see how the young trees were doing. He had recognized the plate number.

By the time the Chief Ranger's office called Headquarters, an emergency crew had been dispatched to the place and it was too late for Sergeant Thoms's urgent warning not to touch the body until a Headquarters team had seen it. When Mendoza and Hackett reached the scene, about a quarter to ten, the body had been removed from the car and was on a stretcher, awaiting the ambulance. The Rangers said sure, it had been in the driver's seat.

"I'll tell you one thing," said Mendoza grimly. "The lab's going to justify its existence on this. I want everything examined—every last little thing!"

They looked at the body, which wasn't a pleasant sight—but not as bad as it might have been. Fortunately the car windows had been closed, and by some odd chance the driver's window had remained unbroken; the car had come to rest on its right side, and the body had been protected from scavenging animals. It was in fair condition; the weather had been dry, of course. And there didn't seem to be as much blood as there should have been if it had been a real accident. The car was just broken metal; Mendoza didn't want it touched until the lab experts had been over it.

The ambulance came and took the body away; the lab experts arrived. Mendoza and Hackett left them to it and headed back for L.A.; Mendoza paced the distance on the speedometer. It was just eighty-nine miles back to Sycamore Terrace. And that might be another small point against Ingram, since he'd have had less time to deal with the body than any outside killer who could have taken it farther away; on the other hand, of course, X's object had not been distance but plausibility.

Mendoza saw Holmes, called the D.A.'s office; the inquest was postponed until Monday. It would be awhile before there was any word from the coroner's office or the lab; those boys were always so precise, and got annoyed when you said for God's sake hurry it up. Mendoza, telling himself to preserve patience, had a hurried lunch and went to see Ingram's doctor. He had to wait, but finally was ushered into the office.

"All I want is an opinion," he said.

Dr. Withers leaned back in his desk chair and smiled delightedly at him. "I read a lot of detective novels, you know," he said pleasantly. "First time I've been mixed up with the real thing. Damned interesting. Of course I've been following the case. Ingram missed his appointment with me last week—maybe he feels conspicuous, going out. I gather the press has been hounding him, the way the case is staying on the front page. Mind you, I like him—he's a nice chap. Offhand, I'd have said he'd be the last man—— But everything seems to point to him, doesn't it?" He looked at Mendoza eagerly.

"Sometimes things aren't the way they look, Doctor. All I want to know is, what physical activity is he capable of? Could he have knocked her down—with his fist or a weapon—without overstraining his heart? She wasn't a small woman, you know—weighed one eighty-five."

"Yes, I know, I've met her, of course." Withers hesitated. "Well, the heart's a peculiar thing, Lieutenant. By Ingram's history, he's been a very healthy man all his life, until this hit him. He was a fairly heavy smoker, but that's about his only vice. He tells me he used to play a lot of golf, it was a little blow to him when he was told to quit it. It's the type of physical action involved, you see—and he has this sound constitution to, er, help him along. He can drive, and do all the ordinary things, and while he's had difficulty cutting down his smoking, the ten or twelve cigarettes he has a day don't seem to have hastened the progress of the trouble. He can still take a drink or two. If you're asking me whether sudden violent physical effort would make him drop dead, well, I'm bound to say that if he ran up a flight of stairs at top speed, it probably would. But he'd be quite capable of knocking her down, without too great a reaction. It'd be over in a second, you see— that's the point—it's sustained exertion he can't take.

With ordinary care, he should last another ten or fifteen years quite comfortably." The doctor looked shaken suddenly, and laughed mirthlessly. "Unless, of course——"

"Yes," said Mendoza. The D.A.'s office, which thought of everything, would subpoena Dr. Withers to give this opinion at the inquest. But there it was. "What about lifting or dragging her?"

"He shouldn't lift anything heavy, of course. He could have dragged her, if he took it easy and rested now and then. I've *thought* about all this, naturally, knew you'd be asking. And it struck me, Lieutenant—I know you must have thought of it too," said Withers apologetically, "not trying to tell you your job—but it struck me that he must have had help. Because wherever he took the body he'd have had to get *back*—and if he left her car——"

"Yes, of course," said Mendoza absently.

"So his accomplice could have—— I'll tell you one thing, Lieutenant. I know—he told me—that Mrs. Ingram's occasional fits of temper, and her tactlessness, disturbed him a lot. He'd had one or two mild attacks, had to take a nitroglycerine tablet, on that account. He hated—he hates scenes. Like many of us. I only met her once or twice, but from what he said—well, he's a quiet, easygoing fellow. I was sorry for him. Tell me, Lieutenant—is there any evidence that he *didn't*—that he——"

Mendoza apologized for the necessity to be secretive, thanked him, and left. When he got back to his office, a little something had come in—information from Providence. It suggested nothing at all. Francis James

Ingram had indeed been born there; Providence had his birth certificate on record. Both parents had been naturalized citizens; his father had been an accountant, in civil service. Ingram had attended public schools in Providence and graduated from high school in 1919. From what the Chief of Police could discover, he had left town immediately after that and returned briefly only at the death of both his parents, during a 'flu epidemic in 1924. He had been an only child, and his father's modest savings and the family house had passed to him by will. He had sold the house.

Nothing there. Hell. Well, what had he expected?

About then Palliser came in and, after asking questions about the morning's discovery, said, "That Filipino of Winthrop's, Copas, acts all right to me. He's very clear about his story—it's lucky it was a holiday, you know, people remember the day. Winthrop came in about seven-fifteen and stayed in all evening. I will say the Filipino's got a thick accent, but he understands English O.K. He said Winthrop had 'a big, big book' he was reading. It turned out to be, of all things you'd think of, a cookbook. Seems Winthrop fancies himself as a gourmet."

"¡Maravilloso!"

"Isn't that something," agreed Palliser. "Winthrop told us he'd been at the house of this Godwin, an old friend, actually for the purpose of showing him this book, which he'd just got from the library the day before. Godwin's also a gourmet. Godwin backs him up and says Winthrop left about five-fifteen. Well, of course it wouldn't have taken him more than half an hour to drive home—so where was he in the interval?

He says he stopped to buy a few things at a drugstore—aspirin and toothpaste. Well, what's to say he didn't? The Filipino doesn't remember any packages, but small parcels like that would have gone in a pocket. Anyway, if Copas isn't lying, Winthrop never stirred out of the apartment, so he couldn't have been up to anything with the body that night. Copas has only worked for him a year, no reason to feel loyal enough—old family servant—to lie for him. I think the Filipino's honest. . . . Of course, he *could* have been bribed, I suppose, but it doesn't seem likely."

Mendoza was silent; and then he said, "Yes, but I think we'll ask the gentleman's bank, all very polite, whether he's hard up for money. Or has made any large withdrawals. Just in case. We want to cover everything."

"They'll dig in their heels," said Palliser. "Banks always do."

"So they do." Mendoza looked at his watch. "I wonder if I dare call the coroner's office—if they have any little thing for us yet. Take a chance." He called, and after delay reached the doctor scheduled to do the autopsy, one of the coroner's bright young men, Lippman.

"Give us a chance, will you, Lieutenant?" said Lippman. "Rome wasn't built, et cetera . . . Of course you realize there'll be nothing like a definite time limit? She's been dead anywhere from twenty-eight to thirty-four days, take your choice. Well, I can give you a little. She died at least four hours before she went over the cliff. She sustained a lot of miscellaneous injuries when she landed—broken bones and so on—but there was no

bleeding. The wound that killed her was a head wound
—left temple. Something hit her a good hard wallop
and fractured the skull, drove the bone right in on the
cerebellum. She might have lived ten minutes or so.
The weapon was something long and straight, not very
sharp—something like, oh, say the edge of a golf putter."

Mendoza stared at the table lighter sitting just to the
left of the pen tray on his desk. An affectation, it was:
like a lot of other things Luis Mendoza owned; he acknowledged it. Something else to negate the years when
Luis Mendoza had been just another Mex kid running
the slum streets (and the old man sitting on all that
money, miser-wise). It was a fourteen-karat gold globe,
the lighter, and he'd paid a hundred and forty bucks
for it. At the moment it needed filling. "Like a golf
putter," he repeated. "I see."

Dr. Withers had said, *He tells me he used to play a
lot of golf. . . .* Well, if it was an unusual hobby for a
pro sharp, people had a right to pick their own hobbies.

"We'll hope to get more for you with—ha-ha!—digging," said Lippman. "I'll call you. Say late tomorrow."

"Yes, thanks very much," said Mendoza. He put the
phone down. He stared at the lighter for another long
minute, and then, abstractedly, he opened the bottom
left drawer of his desk, took out a screwdriver and a can
of lighter fluid, wrested the lighter mechanism out of
the fourteen-karat globe, unscrewed the tank cap, filled
the lighter, replaced the screw, and jammed the thing
together again.

He took out a cigarette and flicked the lighter. The

157

wick was wet and refused to catch. He lit the cigarette with a match. Palliser was watching him curiously, hesitant to ask questions.

Hackett wandered in with a newspaper under his arm. "Maybe *I'm* going psychic," he said. "I've got this and that to say about little Hughie Barron and his girl friend, but first of all, have you noticed this?" He folded the newspaper over, laid it on Mendoza's desk, and pointed a blunt forefinger at a one-paragraph story on the back page.

Matthew Carnahy, owner-operator of the Ace Service Private Detective Agency, was found early today severely beaten, in his Hollywood apartment. Taken to General Hospital, he could offer no clue to his assailants.

"Once in a while," said Hackett, "I let my imagination off the leash. I mean, we do know she asked about private eyes. And it just occurred to me——"

"*¡Camarada, hermano!*" said Mendoza. "You do cheer me up, Arturo! I do see what you mean indeed. *¡Adelante* for the General Hospital!"

Somebody had certainly given Mr. Carnahy a going over. He had lost a number of front teeth, and had two black eyes, three broken ribs, and a broken arm.

He had told the Wilcox Avenue officers who questioned him that two men had forced the door of his apartment and immediately started to beat him up. No, they hadn't offered any reason, but probably, said Mr. Carnahy, they'd been some tough guys hired by somebody he'd scored against on the job—some guy cheating on his wife that Mr. Carnahy'd found evidence against. It had all happened so fast he couldn't give any kind of a description of them, sorry. What case was he working on at the moment? Well, he kept his business confidential. And so on. He was no more forthcoming, from his bed of pain, to Mendoza. Mr. Carnahy was a small, rather scruffy-looking man about fifty, chronically suspicious.

"Did you ever have a Mrs. Bella Ingram as a client?"

"No."

"You're sure? Here's a photograph. Did she ever come to you giving another name?"

Carnahy barely glanced at the photograph. "No. Never heard of—oh, this is the dame that got knocked off. No."

He didn't ask why they thought she might have hired him. He was reluctant to speculate on what might be behind his beating up. A guy in his line of business ran that risk, he said philosophically. He checked up on a lot of husbands and wives, that sort of thing, and sometimes the cheating ones got real sore. Well, half a dozen cases he'd worked just lately might have left somebody mad enough to——

"You'd think they'd realize after a while," said Mendoza in the corridor, "that we're reasonably smart these days. And also keep an eye on them. Or try to."

What was fishy about Mr. Carnahy's story was that in this state, which recognized a number of reasons for divorce, private eyes didn't get much husband-wife business: more creditors, suspicious employers, that sort of thing. And it just wasn't creditable that whoever had gone to the trouble of hiring a couple of thugs to beat up Mr. Carnahy had told them to make the beating anonymous; almost without doubt words would have passed. "This is from So-and-So," one of the thugs would have growled before starting operations. Credit where credit was due.

The state board tried to screen applicants for private-detective licenses, but venial individuals slipped through. It looked very much (as Wilcox Avenue agreed) as if Mr. Carnahy, stumbling on a secret of some kind, had tried blackmail and got his just reward.

Nothing, of course, said that the blackmail was tied up to the Ingram case. But he'd been very quick to deny that Mrs. Ingram had come to him as a client. Which didn't say anything either.

Overnight they got a search warrant and on Friday morning invaded Mr. Carnahy's office, in an old building on Fourth Street. There were just two small, dusty rooms; the first held two chairs, a small table with a few tattered magazines on it, and a lamp; the second, a scarred pine desk, a telephone, two chairs, and a portable typewriter. Mr. Carnahy employed no clerk; he subscribed to a phone-answering service. There was nothing in the desk drawers but some cheap paper, a few racing forms, a half-empty fifth of Scotch, and a very old and tired deck of cards. Mr. Carnahy, all there was of the Ace Service Private Detective Agency, kept his business really confidential.

"Hell," said Mendoza, looking around the inner room. "Not even one little file case." He picked up the cards and riffled through them. "Well, well. Very funny how cards and crook gamblers keep haunting us. Though I can't say I'm surprised, after meeting Carnahy, to find a deck of readers in his desk."

"Marked cards?" asked Palliser interestedly. "I've never seen any."

"This isn't the kind of crooked deck a really good pro uses. Not very subtle." Mendoza handed it over. "It's a deck of concave strippers. Look at the high cards—court cards, aces, and tens. The vertical sides are just slightly bellied out in the middle, you see? You can spot them in the deck by feel. A deck like that would cost you about one seventy-five plus tax, from any of several Eastern firms that specialize in such items. They sell them cheaper by the dozen."

"I'll be damned," said Palliser. "You mean, a regular business firm?"

"They even put out catalogues," said Mendoza absently. "Of course their mailing lists are—mmh—restricted. You might even say screened. Oh yes. Catalogues with nice clear pictures of all sorts of interesting devices. There's the holdout—little mechanical thing you wear under your shirt, standard model about fifty bucks. And special dice boxes and so on. And really artistic readers. Go down to Vice sometime, John, and look at some they've picked up—improve your education. One reason I say it's the hardest way there is to earn a living. Take a deck of trim-work—the high cards have about a sixteenth inch of the margin shaved off, the margin of the pattern on the back. Would you like to try to spot that, during play, from across the table? And the most artistic of all use the back design itself. There'll be a tiny piece of the geometric design filled in, in one corner, or vice versa—two little circles from the margin for a deuce, and so on. You need eyes like a hawk, as I say. But of course the real artists don't rely on readers—just, as the magicians say, the quickness of the hand deceiving the eye. I think, however, we'll deprive Mr. Carnahy of his obviously well-used deck. I wonder where he got it—probably from some unsavory client, and a long time ago by the look of it. Well, there's nothing here, let's go."

CHAPTER THIRTEEN

On Friday afternoon the reports began to come in, and Mendoza seized on each one eagerly. There wasn't as much meat in them as he had hoped.

The lab boys had found Mrs. Barron's prints (and *how* the family had howled at being asked for sample prints—except Ingram) on the back-seat ashtray in the car, but that didn't prove anything as Mrs. Barron would have ridden in the car fairly often. One of Ingram's prints was on the front-seat ashtray, but the same thing was true there. There was no blood in the car, nothing that looked unusual or suggestive. The standard paraphernalia—a cleaning rag and whisk broom in the glove compartment, a few maps.

Mrs. Ingram's prints were on the steering wheel. X hadn't forgotten that. The trouble was, there weren't any other prints on the wheel at all, which wasn't natural. Ordinarily, there'd have been dozens, superimposed on each other. That said that somebody had carefully wiped the wheel and then carefully pressed the dead woman's hands on it, before sending the car over the cliff. They knew, by the teeth and the glasses, that she hadn't driven up there herself. And something else was just a little odd. There were no prints at all on the light switch. X had slipped up there; he should have put the corpse's prints on the switch as well as on the wheel.

Mrs. Ingram's supply of insulin, and her hypodermic needle in its case, were in the glove compartment. The maid had slipped up a little, too, on the clothes; and so had the police, in not realizing that, if the intention had been to make it look as if she'd gone off for the weekend, she'd naturally have taken a bag with her. Ingram had said so, hadn't he? The bag was in the car, an alligator overnight case, containing a few cosmetics, a change of underwear, the blue and white cotton house dress. She was wearing the tan shoes and a beige cotton dress. X had thought of almost everything. He hadn't noticed the absence of teeth; well, probably he hadn't cared to study the corpse's face. And he had overlooked the glasses—probably meant to take them along and forgot. . . . Which was another little something against Ingram, because the glasses had been in the bedroom and the strong implication was that the woman had fallen dead in the living room. What outsider would take the glasses into the bedroom as he prepared to deal with the body? He'd be in a hurry, afraid that the maid or Ingram would be coming in any minute. But Ingram—concealing the body somewhere so the maid wouldn't see it, wandering around building his plot, waiting for Sylvia to come in and go to bed so he could get on with it . . . And the throw rug—what about that? If the rug had (as it probably had) anything to do with it, how very unlikely that an outsider, a non-resident of Sycamore Terrace, would take it away and dispose of it in Mr. Underwood's—— Or was it unlikely? If the intention was to make Ingram the scapegoat? The so obvious scapegoat. And any of the family could easily have known what night was refuse collection night along Sycamore Terrace.

Another mildly interesting point was that a single print (and not a very good one) of Bruce Lauderdale's left thumb showed up at the edge of the Cadillac's trunk. Lauderdale was asked about that right away, but there was nothing to disprove his explanation. It sounded all right; it could be all right. He was a little nervous, which was only natural; he blustered, and that was in character too. He said finally that a couple of times he'd been with Linda, either in her car or his, when she stopped at her aunt's house, and he guessed once anyway the Caddy must've been parked there ahead, and that he might have touched it without noticing. It was the kind of thing that happened. Since everybody told them readily that Mrs. Ingram had often left her car in the street, if she was going out again, there was nothing to say the print meant anything.

The wound was, the autopsy report said, four and three-quarters inches long, and ruler-straight. The offered suggestions were a heavy steel ruler, a length of cut wood, possibly the edge of a table or a raised hearth. (There hadn't been a table within ten feet of where she fell, if that was on the rug, and the hearth was flat). Something fairly blunt. There had been no traces of any extraneous material in the wound, conveniently pointing at metal, or wood, or telling them that the weapon had recently been in the vicinity of a mill or a bakery. The report said a lot more about the body, but nothing at all useful to Mendoza, and he swore at it. What the hell good was it to him to be told that the woman's last meal had consisted of chicken salad, white bread, and chocolate cake? They couldn't add how long before she died.

But wait a minute. Wasn't it of use? That must have been her luncheon party. Yes. So she hadn't had dinner. That said a little something. Since normally she'd have had dinner about seven o'clock, she must have died before. Or had she? It had been a holiday—routines got changed on holidays. It had been a late lunch. Also there was Ingram and the maid. It was the maid's day off, and Ingram had been some distance from home at six-thirty. It could be that his wife had known he'd be out for dinner, and had intended to have a pickup meal alone. In which case she *might* have changed to the dress she was found in, but more likely to a house dress.

The doctors and the lab boys had done their best on the autopsy, but there just wasn't any really helpful evidence. Mendoza knew very little more than he had before. Somebody had hit Bella Ingram hard, with something heavy, on the left temple and killed her. He —or she, of course—had then got the body into the Cadillac and, trailed by an accomplice in a second car, had driven up the Angeles Crest Highway and staged the fake accident. Several mistakes had been made—for one thing, X hadn't known or had forgotten that corpses don't bleed and the police would find out that the woman had been dead when she went over the cliff. Or was that a double bluff? But as it was, Mendoza was about as far from even guessing who X was as he had been the first ten minutes he was on the case.

Which he didn't like at all.

He went home in an irritable mood, and Alison looked at him and wisely forbore to start a discussion on her latest idea, which was the Hispanization of various British names. There were distinct possibilities in several; Andrew-Andrés, for instance, and you could say Andy for either one. And there was also Luisa, and Martha-Marta, and Alexander-Alejandro (you could call either Alex) .

But all she said was, "It's being sticky, *amado?*"

"It's being," he said, "damned annoying." He went down the hall to the bedroom to take off his jacket and tie, absent-mindedly left the closet door open, and later on swore to find that El Señor had pulled all his ties off the rack and made a nest of them on the floor.

Instinctively Mendoza always felt people to be more important than facts. This conviction had got him into trouble before; and had solved some difficult cases. On Saturday he went and took a good look at everybody concerned in the case. He manufactured questions to ask as an excuse, but what he wanted was an impression of their emotional temperatures, the kind of people they were.

In so far as he was sure of anything about this business, he was convinced that the murder had not been planned; it had been done on impulse. The planning had come later.

Linda Barron, he thought after seeing her, probably had a quick temper. She would flare up often, over little things. She was self-centered, but covered it up better than her mother did. She was greedy, and probably quite cold sexually. Was she capable of physical violence? Under certain circumstances she might be. She was also very shrewd, materially speaking.

He agreed with Hackett's reading of the boy friend, Bruce Lauderdale. Very much the Neanderthal type—hulking, loutish, affecting a beatnik vocabulary. Lauderdale, he judged, would be entirely amoral: the genial hail-fellow-well-met on the surface, the salesman type, but he'd do anything for money. Also very self-centered, and shrewd only up to a point; not nearly as shrewd as Linda. Definitely capable of violence, and probably had a hot temper. He was, Mendoza also noticed thoughtfully, wearing a custom-tailored Italian silk which had set him back at least a hundred and fifty bucks. Well, maybe he liked clothes and saved his pennies; his salary wouldn't run to that. Then again maybe he had another source of income.

Janet Barron hadn't much brain, but she was smarter than she liked to pretend. That sort of woman usually was. She was (like all such women) a kind of animate euphemism; she'd never look at facts squarely—it would be, "So nice for two lonely people to come together" instead of "I've got to annex a man with some money." She was, in that sense, also amoral. But surface appearance would always be all-important to her; she'd be cautious because of What People Might Say. A temper? No. Again up to a point, she was calculating—though it was halfway unconscious, or unadmitted.

Hugh Barron was a puppy with bad manners—a puppy being naughty to attract attention. "Well, well, another sleuth!" he had greeted Mendoza. "And *such* a suave-looking one this time. A definite improvement over that lout of a sergeant, I must say." And when Mendoza introduced himself, "Ah, I should have guessed. The pride of the force, according to the *Herald*. But I looked at the by-line and took that with a grain of salt. How you minorities will stick together. Race *and* religion in this case, I suppose——" He laughed.

Mendoza, who happened to be an avowed agnostic, looked at him coldly, unwitting that Hackett's wish was coming true. He said very gently, patient nurse to willful child, "When you've quite finished your adolescent showing off, little man——" And Hugh Barron had gone brick red and looked sullen.

Hughie boy. What about him? Spoiled child. Must be the center of attention all the time. Hugh, thwarted in some desire, might throw a temper tantrum; just possibly he might hit out in violence. But also he'd be a coward, and more apt to stop short of real trouble. That charge of vandalism—yes, in a sense he was still the delinquent, the vandal: hitting out spitefully at a world which hadn't given him what he'd been led to expect and thought he deserved.

Marcia Wills. A lot less brain than Mrs. Barron. Shallow, silly, cheap. All that. But according to what Hackett said, she'd do anything her Hughie told her to, blindly. As per Milton, yes. But would she, could she, have been the accomplice? Faced with a corpse, even with Hughie in charge of the situation, could she have kept her head and her nerve enough to have trailed him up there in his car? She had had a driver's license, had let it lapse a year ago. . . . She would, of course, be attracted by money. And there was Hugh's fifty thousand, even if that hadn't been the immediate motive. But, come to think of it, had Hugh known about the legacy?

Mr. Harley Stevens was a respectable, somewhat slow-witted fellow with a Texas accent, a voluminous knowledge of and interest in the history of American railroads, and gentle manners. He told Mendoza that Janet Barron was "a real womanly little woman, you know, sir—I do feel for her in all this family trouble." Mendoza really didn't see him as her accomplice in trying to cover up a murder. But you never knew.

And—on second thought—yes, had X made any mistakes at all? Details, details. The whole thing *could* be a double bluff. For, if the intention was to make Ingram the scapegoat, then why had X taken away the body to stage the fake accident? Quite possibly the whole thing had been carefully thought out, the teeth and glasses deliberately planted, and the throw rug, to tell the police that the murder had happened in the house. Yes.

Winthrop—well, he had a fussy sort of temperament. The kind of thing Winthrop would lose his temper over was a necessary deviation from routine, or a breakfast egg too hard or too soft, or a train being late. . . . Of course, he had talked murder before there was any evidence, and Mendoza was convinced that he was lying about the overheard threat from Ingram, but where was the proof one way or the other?

Sylvia Glass. She was the one person who was demonstrably innocent, really out of it. She could prove she had been with her boy friend, Jack Reinfeld, all that afternoon and evening, until he had dropped her at the house at nine-thirty. All the same, she was lying —retracting statements and concealing evidence. And how to get it out of her? How the hell?

"You," said Alison at seven o'clock on Sunday night, "are brooding. It doesn't do any good, Luis. Just have faith that *something* will turn up, and it will. . . . *Not* my earrings, Sheba! *Oh,* how provoking! Oh, damnation! Darling, would you mind? I do want to wear these shoes, and what with this tight skirt I can't possibly reach to buckle the——"

Mendoza came into the bedroom obediently and found her in her newest, smartest maternity suit, clipping on her emerald earrings. "And where are you going?"

"I did mention it three days ago, but you've been so involved in this case—Angel's having a shower for me. The shoes, *amado.*" The shoes, elegant green kid and high-heeled, had a slim strap across the insteps. "Six more months! I'm getting bigger every day."

"Well, it was your idea," said Mendoza, buckling the straps. "And I don't like your being out alone at night. That's quite a drive, way over to Highland Park. I don't like it at all. And these heels are too high."

"I refuse," said Alison, "to look dowdy just because I've temporarily lost my figure. Don't fuss. I wish you'd go out somewhere too and stop brooding. It's bad for you."

"You be home by eleven, *¿comprende?* And take a flashlight, that street's damn dark, and those heels——

Lock the doors of the car, and *not* over thirty-five. And——"

"And don't forget to say Thank-you-Mrs.-Hackett-I had-a-very-good-time. Yes, Papa. I'll be careful. . . . You *will* think about what I said? Andrew-Andrés and so on?"

"If I have a spare moment. And stick to the freeway, or well-lighted streets. I don't like——"

"*¡No seas tonto, querido!*" said Alison impatiently, rescuing her bag from El Señor, who was practicing on that sort of catch. She took up her jacket.

Mendoza went out with her to the garage and supervised the locking of the doors on the Facel-Vega. "That reminds me," he said, leaning in the window to kiss her, "what you just said. If you ever, now or forty years from now, have the effrontery to start calling me Papa, or Daddy, or Father, implying that that's my single role, I will divorce you *inmediatamente*."

"*¡Caro mío, qué atrocidad!*" said Alison. "As if I'd ever dream of it . . . Yes, yes, I'll be careful."

He watched her back out to the fork of the drive, and went back to the house. He stood in the middle of the living room staring at nothing for five minutes. Bast and Nefertite were tangled together in sound sleep on the sectional; Sheba was playing with an ancient catnip mouse, and El Señor was brooding to himself, crouched on the credenza. Brooding . . .

Mendoza went down to the bedroom, stripped off his clothes, ring and watch, redressed rapidly in the loud tweed suit and garish tie, zircon rings and cheap brass watch, and left the house.

By eight o'clock he was down in Gardena, entering

the Little Reno. It was a question, of course, whether the pro, Neil Davenport, had passed on any little word of warning. . . . Mendoza said to the house man in a confidential undertone, "Say, I'm looking for Killeen, is he here? Well, you got an idea where I might locate him? It's kind of important——"

CHAPTER FOURTEEN

THE inquest was called for ten o'clock. When Mendoza and Hackett came into the big room at five to ten, everybody was there, in various states of emotion. Ingram was sitting alone, handsome and well dressed in a discreet dark suit. Sylvia Glass sat a couple of chairs away; she was obviously wearing her best clothes, and looked nervous. The three Barrons were whispering together. Janet Barron looked pleased with herself, Linda haughtier than usual. Hugh wore a self-satisfied smirk. Marcia Wills, rather conspicuously dressed, sat with them. Winthrop was alone, as were Mike Skene and Underwood.

Mendoza slid in next to Ingram and sat down. "Last chance, Mr. Ingram. Take my advice and bare your soul. Open up and tell all. Who knows, the coroner might be sympathetic."

Ingram met his eyes. "I've told the truth." He looked pale and tense, as well he might. "You said you didn't think I was guilty. I'm not guilty. I couldn't have done a thing like that. What—do you think they'll bring it in?"

"Mr. Ingram," said Mendoza, "right now I wouldn't lay a dime on the chances of an open verdict."

"It's not fair," muttered Ingram as if to himself. "It's not fair! Hell, I never did anything——"

"If you want my private opinion," said Mendoza softly, "somebody made a damn good try at framing you. . . . Is that how it was?" Ingram shot him a side glance but said nothing. "Look, friend. I've been working overtime hunting for something—anything—in your favor, or against somebody else. Something to show the coroner this isn't as nice and obvious as it looks. I haven't got anything, not one damn thing. I have a hunch that if you'd open up with me and tell me all you know it might hand me a few clues. But you know how the law reads. If the verdict today is what I think it will be, I'm out of the whole case. The next time you'd see me would be giving evidence at your trial. For God's sake——"

"I can't," said Ingram under his breath, involuntarily. "I—I've told you all I——"

"Ingram, who is Killeen and where is he?"

Ingram went dead white, and shut his eyes for a moment. Then he turned and looked steadily at Mendoza, with tight-compressed lips. "I'm sorry," he said politely, "I don't know who you mean."

Mendoza sighed. He hadn't had much luck last night. A couple of men had known the name: house men and proprietors. But they'd been cagey, very cagey. That said that Killeen wasn't the average honest citizen. Two of them had said openly, "Sorry, no idea where he's living and he hasn't been in lately," or words to that effect. The rest had denied any knowledge of him at all. Mendoza thought he had a fairly clear idea of what part the mysterious Killeen had played in all this, and he saw how awkward it might be for Ingram to come out with the whole truth, but——

"Ingram," he said urgently, "think about it, man! It's all very well to be loyal to a pal, but it doesn't make sense to risk the dance hall just to keep a pal out of trouble with you." Because he'd figured out that angle by now.

Ingram glanced away. He had recognized the cant term for the death house, and he looked grim. Then he gave Mendoza his sudden shy smile. "They wouldn't need as much cyanide for me, would they, with this shaky heart?"

The coroner came in and called order. Mendoza went back to Hackett. He'd never worked a case he'd enjoyed less.

While the jury was sworn, he watched the other principals. Janet Barron went over to her brother and whispered, evidently asking him to join their party, present a solid front. Winthrop shook his head at first, shooting some odd uneasy looks at his niece and nephew; Mendoza's interest was aroused. But eventually Winthrop shuffled over and sat next to Hugh.

The first witness was called: Ames. The police evidence was got through quickly, for all its details. And how damning it sounded, against Ingram. Hackett took the stand to testify to Headquarters' part in the case. Then Ingram was called. He made a good impression; he looked like a senator, and his quiet, pleasant voice sounded sincere. He told exactly the same story he'd been telling all along, and it sounded plausible, until

176

you remembered the things that didn't fit—the teeth, the glasses, the autopsy report. The coroner—this coroner was a tough old boy—never took his eyes off the stand. And quite possibly the coroner, and some of the jury, were thinking that Ingram sounded just a little too glib and polished. You never could tell what a jury was thinking.

When the coroner let him go, he went quickly, passed the row of seats where Mendoza was sitting, and sat down at the rear of the room.

Sylvia Glass approached the stand reluctantly, which wasn't surprising. Mendoza had wondered if she'd get cold feet at the last minute; although she wasn't an intellectual, she'd know that perjury was a punishable offense. But her sympathy for Ingram, or obstinacy, held firm: she testified in a small but steady voice that she had been mistaken about Mrs. Ingram's car being in the garage that night. It hadn't been. And she also remembered Mrs. Ingram saying she meant to get rid of that throw rug, and Sylvia really couldn't say now but what it *had* been gone a couple of days before New Year's.

The coroner peered at her over the tops of his spectacles and asked, "Miss Glass, do you know the meaning of 'perjury'?"

"Yes, sir."

"In the first statement you made to the police you were quite positive that the car was there. You said you noticed it particularly."

"Well, when I came to think it over I knew I was wrong, I made a mistake, that's all. It was Mr. Ingram's car, it's a light color too and just for a minute I thought it was white and then I saw it was blue, so it was his," she said defiantly.

He looked at her for a long moment. "You also said you specifically asked Mr. Ingram about the rug, because you were surprised to see it gone."

"Yes, well," said Sylvia breathlessly, "once he told me that she'd thrown it out, *then* I remembered her saying she was going to."

"Why did you not say that in your first statement?"

"I don't know, but I was confused, I guess—all the upset and people asking questions—I remember *now*, that's all."

He couldn't shake her, and of course there was no proof she was lying. Just as there was no proof that Winthrop was. You could say one thing: the coroner was fair. Winthrop was also reminded that his original statement hadn't included any overheard threat, and with his old-maidish fussiness Winthrop didn't make a good impression. But when he was followed by Mike Skene, who showed Ingram's story to be at least partly a lie and by inference wholly a lie, the jury was probably ready to believe that Winthrop had heard Ingram threaten his wife. It built up. They didn't like Hugh Barron either but that was neither for nor against Ingram.

When the jury was sent out, Mendoza didn't move. He said resignedly, "They won't be long."

They weren't. They took just ten minutes—time enough for a smoke—to bring in a verdict of willful homicide by Francis Ingram. And they made it first degree—malice aforethought.

The coroner read the verdict, paused to adjust his

glasses, and added, "The—er—officer in charge of the investigation——" and then he stopped dead. He had been looking around the room from his raised desk, and he was now looking surprised and disapproving. "May I ask where Mr. Ingram——"

Mendoza and Hackett sprang up and turned. "Bailiff!" said the coroner testily. "Did you allow Mr. Ingram to leave the room? Come here!"

Ingram was certainly gone. A buzz of voices raised excitedly. Winthrop exclaimed loudly, "So he has run away—that proves his guilt once for all!"

"Bailiff!"

The uniformed bailiff came forward slowly. "I—I beg your pardon, sir. I didn't think——"

"Speak up, speak up! You let him go out—why and when?"

"It was about fifteen minutes ago, sir. I didn't see any reason not to—he said——"

"Don't mumble! *What* did he say?"

"—wanted to—er—visit the washroom, sir, and said he'd be right back——"

Mendoza said violently, "*¡Válgame Dios, que pedazo de alcorno! ¡No faltaba más que eso!* This is all we needed! My God, the fool, the goddamned fool!"

It was easy to trace Ingram—up to a point. He had left the Hall of Justice at once, by a side door to avoid the crowd of reporters waiting in the foyer, claimed his car from the lot attendant, and driven off. They weren't half an hour behind him then, but it had been enough. At the house, they found most of his clothes gone; since he couldn't have risked taking time to pack, with so narrow a lead, he'd probably packed the night before, in readiness. If the inquest turned out the wrong way, he'd be all set to run.

Captain Holmes said, "For the love of God why didn't you put a tail on him?"

"Because I didn't think he was such a damned fool, and I was keeping all my men busy on other people in the case, damn it! Oh, the damned idiot——"

"Does this convince you, at least, that he's guilty?"

"It does not. Just the other way," said Mendoza coldly. Which might not sound very sensible, but on the other hand . . . Police officers got to know criminal types. There were many different kinds of murderers, and many different motives for murder; but those who murdered in hot blood, or strictly for gain, as in this case, shared one trait—they were usually cocky. They kept on hoping and believing they'd get away with it until the last minute, until the judge read the verdict. They were very cocksure and cool. And Ingram hadn't been; he had been quiet and worried. He had weighed his chances, and when he saw how long the odds were, he'd decided to cut his losses. Or try to.

"The *damned* fool," said Mendoza helplessly. "Of course this convinces everybody that he is guilty. But don't I know how it went! He hung on, hoping that evidence would turn up against X, that somehow it would come out all right and he could sit back and wait for the jackpot, all that nice money she'd left him. But everything that turned up was against him. It must have seemed like a nightmare. And when everything had been going so well, too! He must have decided to take the gamble last night—had his bags packed ready. He knew how black all that evidence would sound to a jury."

"You're bucking a lot of evidence this time, on a hunch," said Hackett.

"Are you telling me anything? Ingram's as good as convicted now. We'll pick him up eventually, of course, and what trial jury will even admit he might be innocent, when he cut and ran like this? My God, the fool! I should have told him," said Mendoza suddenly. "I should have told him I wouldn't stop work on it, the hell with the inquest verdict. Maybe if he'd thought I'd eventually—— And of course it's a tough one. Very tough."

"He was a fool," said Hackett, "other ways too. He might have known that Skene kid would remember him and probably come in to say so."

"Oh, he didn't know that could be dangerous, then," said Mendoza absently. "He didn't know he was going to be making up any lies for the cops."

Hackett stared at him. "And how d'you know that?"

"I know, or I think I know, quite a lot about half of this case," said Mendoza. "The half I don't know about is the important part—who is X? There's Killeen —I've got to find Killeen, damn it—and that maid knows something—and there's the golf clubs——"

"*Golf* clubs?" said Hackett. "Where?"

Mendoza stabbed out his cigarette violently. "At the house. I don't know much about golf, but I'd say it was a nice expensive set of clubs. I was looking for it, you know. Of course it didn't mean anything to Ames, or to us, when we went through the place, just a set of golf clubs, in a bag, at the back of the hall closet. But then I heard from the doctor that Ingram's hobby had been golf, until he had to quit on account of his heart. So I looked. And there were a lot of clubs in that bag—I don't know all their names, but I do know a putter when I see one—but there wasn't one putter."

"Well, and so what?"

"The autopsy report, *chico*. Something with a straight, blunt edge, at least five inches long."

"What *is* this? You trying to say he's guilty after all, killed her with the putter? I don't get——"

"I think there must have been a putter, you know. And if I had to make a guess, I think I know where it is now. Tossed off a cliff somewhere and now at the bottom of the Pacific."

"You mean you think——"

"I think a lot of things," said Mendoza, "and most of all I think Ingram's the biggest fool walking on two legs. I'm wondering now—considering that putter— whether there were two frames set up on him. . . . But, by God, I'll have the truth out of this if it takes me the next ten years!"

He was not easy to get on with, the next ten days; Hackett had seldom known him so irritable. At home, Alison eyed him warily, fed him all his favorite meals, and asked no questions. Even Bertha, that irrepressible domestic, after one barked-out sarcastic answer to some question, kept out of his way.

They knew now, or were pretty sure, that Ingram had left L.A. A clerk at International Airport had tentatively identified his photograph as that of a man who had collected a ticket on a flight to Portland, which had taken off at one-forty that day, an hour and forty minutes after he'd left the Hall of Justice. The ticket had been reserved the night before, in the name of Thompson. Portland, of course, was looking, and thought he might have gone on to Vancouver. Vancouver was also looking.

The case had exploded nationally now, on account of Ingram's disappearance. His picture was splashed over a lot of front pages, and a lot of people from Los Angeles to New York were on the lookout for him.

Inevitably, a lot of people excitedly told their local police that they'd seen Ingram, and a lot of innocent men were hauled in, to be released on identifying themselves. Ingram was seen in Dallas, Kansas City, Indianapolis, Terre Haute, and Detroit; he had snatched a woman's bag in New London, Connecticut, and on the same day tried to pick up a blonde in Helena, Montana.

His Caddy was located the day after he ran. It had been parked along Main Street, not far from Headquarters, and a traffic officer, tagging it for overparking, had noticed the plate number. There were no useful new prints in it.

"And that," pointed out Hackett, "tells us somebody helped him. Somebody drove the car back from International. Who the hell is this Killeen you keep talking about?"

"Somebody," said Mendoza. "And, damn it to hell and back, is he still here? Has he run in another direction? Maybe with a later rendezvous fixed? No, I don't think so. There's money, first of all. Ingram would need as much as he could get together, to carry him as far as he could go and hide out on, so he may have had all Killeen's available cash too." They knew now that

Ingram had cleared his bank account on the Friday before he ran; he'd have had something over seven hundred dollars, which wasn't any too much for that kind of thing. "And then, you know, that fraternity—surprisingly moral fellows, there aren't many split cases among them——"

"Informers? And what——"

"He could lie low here as well as anywhere else. Waiting for a message."

"I'm a little way behind you, slow down. This is a pal of Ingram's, maybe another sharp?"

"I have an idea," said Mendoza, "that he's a very, very good pal indeed. Maybe more than a pal. Because most of the reason why Ingram's not talking, I think, is that he doesn't want to involve Killeen. Damn it, *damn* it, if I could find him! He might talk where Ingram wouldn't. Oh, God, the pair of fools! Ingram's bound to be picked up eventually—why he ever thought he could get away with it——"

Even with a million-odd people hunting him all over the continent, Ingram got away with it for nearly two weeks. And, considering the efficiency of most modern police forces, that was quite a record. A man couldn't hole up alone forever; he had to buy shelter and food, he had to let himself be seen by numbers of people; and without unlimited cash, he had to acquire money to live. Ingram was clever and canny, but if he had known more about the methods by which police forces co-operate to trace people, he wouldn't have tried to run in the first place.

A police artist had made a number of sketches, from

photographs, of Ingram as he might look in various disguises; these were wired all over the country. His prints were wired to all big-city forces, along with his official description, and such of his habits as were known. Mendoza had been annoyed at the necessity of keeping his knowledge of Ingram's profession a secret (could you call it a profession? as good a word as any) but he wasn't running the risk of letting the papers get hold of the information that Ingram was a pro sharp, to scare off Killeen permanently.

Ingram was no fool, and he gave them a good run. But it is almost impossible to disappear permanently from police vigilance, and twelve days after he'd so casually walked out of the L.A. Hall of Justice he was dropped on.

And at that, he wasn't found through any modern-miracle detective work. He was picked up in an ordinary police raid on a gambling house in St. Louis; a brighter-than-average desk sergeant looked at him twice and took his prints.

Then, of course, it was officially out of Mendoza's hands; the warrant served, the arrest made, and Ingram on his way back to L.A. under escort to await trial. The calendars were always full; he might wait for a couple of months. A breathing space; but where the hell to look further?

Mendoza sat over his coffee the morning Ingram's arrest was reported, and stared at the big cut on the front page of the *Times*. It showed Ingram, handcuffed to a plain-clothes man, at the St. Louis airport, ready to take off for L.A. and retribution.

The plain-clothes detective looked a little like Art Hackett.

Ingram had dyed his hair black, and it made him look much older. He was wearing a light suit, and there was no particular expression on his face—he looked vague and resigned. Studying it, Mendoza realized suddenly that it was a gentle face, almost a peaceful face. If Ingram no longer looked like a senator—the beautiful silver hair had aided that impression—he looked like a rather scholarly clerk. Perhaps one of those dull, precise accountants who expected you to understand figures (Mendoza had got consistent D's in math in his school days) and said things like, "That is not really a legitimate deduction, sir, I'm afraid you'll have to include it."

"Hell!" he said, and flung the paper down on the table. Alison jumped, and the cats fled, startled, except for El Señor, who was ensconced in his favorite Thinking Place on top of the refrigerator. "And if Holmes catches me going on poking into it—— The hell with Holmes. I'll get to the bottom of this if I have to resign over it!"

CHAPTER FIFTEEN

HOMICIDE had been kept busy; it usually was. At the moment, what with the unidentified corpse in the storm drain, another along the S.P. tracks in the freight yards, and all the paper work on a number of other less obscure cases, Mendoza hadn't any men to spare.

He went down to the County Jail to see Ingram. "Have you got a lawyer yet?" he asked abruptly.

Ingram looked surprised to see him. He was looking the same as he had in that cut, older and very tired. "I suppose you'll tell me I was a fool, thinking I could get away with it," he said despondently. "But—the way everything happened, it was like—like fate or something had it in for me. Nothing on my side at all. I began to see there never would be, never could be. It wasn't *fair*—and I was damned if I was going to get gassed for something I didn't do! I gave you a run, anyway." He smiled mirthlessly.

"You did. Do you also realize that you've convinced everybody you're guilty as hell? Obviously, innocent men don't run away. They stand their ground in pious consciousness of virtue, their strength being as the strength of ten because their hearts——"

Ingram said a rude word and then laughed unhappily. "What were the odds, Lieutenant? I'd have been convicted anyway."

"Yes, well, we'll see. This case is supposed to be closed as far as I'm concerned, but I'm going on working it when I can. Maybe I'll turn something up."

"Why?" asked Ingram. "That's real devotion to your job, Lieutenant." It was half a question; his expression was curious and wary.

"I might strike a noble pose and say it's a passion for justice," said Mendoza dryly, "but the truth is, I've got a strong sense of order. I don't like things left all in an untidy mess. Which, God knows, this is. What about the lawyer? And how are you fixed for money?"

Ingram shrugged. "I don't know any lawyers, except Bella's and that other fellow she knew, Widdows. I don't think they take criminal cases. He—her fellow—came and explained about the money. Very upstage he was, too—wouldn't touch me with a ten-foot pole. There's some kind of law about not profiting by a crime, so the whole deal's frozen, until after the trial. I cleaned out my bank account, I guess you know that. I've got about a hundred bucks." Probably spent a lot of the original roll on travel, and made a little kill in St. Louis or somewhere along the way, thought Mendoza.

"I see. Well, I'll fix you up with a lawyer. You've got to have one, and if I don't turn lucky and this does come to trial, you don't want to be relying on one of those nice inexperienced boys from the Public Defender's office."

"Listen, what I've got wouldn't go far paying a real good——"

"Don't worry about that. I'll guarantee him," said Mendoza abruptly.

Ingram stared at him. "Why the hell?" he asked incredulously. "Cops don't rake it in in six figures, I know that. Why the *hell*?"

Mendoza paused with his hand on the cell door. "I don't know that there's an exact term for it," he said thoughtfully. "Maybe a kind of vicarious atoning for sins? Or simple poetic justice?" He laughed. "You see, Ingram, my late villainous old grandfather made quite a little nest egg in your own—mmh—profession. Not that he'd ever have admitted it. And unlike most of you feckless fellows he saved it, and invested it very cannily, and in due course he left me a sizable piece of capital. You know something? I'll lay you ten to one he's chuckling away to himself in his coffin, pleased as hell that a little of it's going to aid and abet a member of the fraternity." He shouted for the jailer. "I'll find Killeen, you know. It might help if you gave me a little note for him, saying I'm to be trusted."

Ingram just stared at him blindly, still incredulous. The jailer came slowly up the corridor, keys jangling.

"Be damned," said Ingram at last. But his eyes were still wary, and as the jailer swung the door open he started to say stiffly, "I'm afraid I don't know what you——" He was still keeping up the front.

Mendoza gave him a careless salute and went out.

He took what time he could snatch from other legitimate jobs and went to see all the other people in the case. To each of them he made a little speech, to the effect that the police felt that the case had been tried in the papers and were not satisfied that the D.A.'s office had been justified in charging Ingram; that investigation was still going on into Bella Ingram's death. None of them, or so he hoped, would know enough about police work, or the law, to see through that.

He got one rather interesting reaction from most of them. Janet Barron said vaguely, "Well, I must say I think that's rather silly, because of course he's guilty, but the way you went about investigating before, it seems to me the police *are* stupid." And Hugh Barron said, "Oh, is that so? From what I've seen of your methods I don't suppose you'll get anything much, if there's anything to get." And Bruce Lauderdale said, "Hah? Well, what's it to me what a bunch of dumb cops are up to, anyways?" And Linda Barron . . .

What it added up to was collective derision and dislike of the police. And that was a very odd reaction to get from people in their class and circumstances. Generally speaking, people in settled middle-class lives, honest and respectable citizens, respected the police and trusted them. And especially they did so here, because (as Mendoza had reminded Holmes) the L.A.P.D. had a hot reputation as a very crack force; it was known for its high standards.

With the exception of Bruce Lauderdale, these people were not the type you got over in east L.A. or the other side of Main Street, where you expected to meet the automatic equating of Cops with the Bad Guys. But even prim Winthrop said testily, "Really, all I can say is that this fumbling about clearly illustrates what

I have always suspected, that the police are extremely inefficient and stupid! After all the trouble I had to persuade you to listen at *all*—and when the man is so obviously guilty——"

Linda Barron, thought Mendoza pensively. Something just a little funny there? She was, he thought, very young for her age—or permanently immature, shallow. She wore the sophisticated, mocking mask because it was smart, the thing to do; he suspected that she was aping the heroines of stories in the slick magazines. And yet she had brains of the cold calculating kind, he suspected.

He found her at home, just ready to leave the apartment; she didn't give him much time. "How thrilling," she said in a bored voice. "Just like a suspense story. Am I supposed to cheer?" At the same time, as if automatically, she was eying him—he could only think suggestively. Very aware of sex—his and hers. It was almost blatant. And yet Mendoza, who knew a good deal more about females than perhaps any honest husband should, felt from her, curiously, an emanation that was entirely sexless, utterly cold.

"Sorry, you'll have to excuse me, I've got a date," she said, and laid her hand on the door. There was a ring on her fourth finger, a large center stone with a number of side stones around it, set in either white gold or platinum; the stones flashed in the light.

"That's a very handsome ring you're wearing, Miss Barron," said Mendoza. She put her other hand over it, rather quickly.

"That! Just costume stuff, I only paid a few dollars for it. I really must go——"

Well, well. He knew a little about stones, and he knew diamonds when he saw them. . . . Lauderdale was a salesclerk at a sporting-goods shop, at a salary of three eighty-five a month. Linda's modeling jobs brought good money when she worked, but she didn't get many calls. So maybe she was the kind who saved up for some heart's desire? (And then didn't want to show it off?) And maybe also Lauderdale was mixed up in some lucrative off-the-record racket?

That private detective Bella had talked about hiring. Carnahy? And——

When they'd tied up this latest corpse and he had a few men free, he would check up on Lauderdale. . . .

Ingram had been committed to the County Jail on a Thursday. On the following Monday, Mendoza had just arrived at the office and was looking at the overnight reports when Lieutenant Goldberg wandered in and said, "I've got something funny for you. It looks as if Ingram was telling the truth—about one thing anyway."

"*¡No me diga!* The jewelry? Is the tide turning at last? Sit down and give!"

Goldberg sat down, sneezed, blew his nose, and gave. "We got a tip on a new fence yesterday, so we went out there last night, secondhand store on Second Street, and looked it over. Guy named Honeywell, Theodore Honeywell, he's got a little pedigree, petty theft. It seems he got smart and decided it's safer and more profitable to let other people do the dirty work for him. Well, he wasn't being very careful—new at the business like I say—and we came across quite a lot of hot stuff. Including a couple of pieces that rang a bell with me. Your old experienced fence breaks the stuff up right off, you know, but of course you don't get as much for it if you discard the mountings, which is the smart thing to do because usually the mountings are the only identifiable parts. But some greedy fellows hang onto it intact, hoping for a time when the heat's off. Or, of course, sometimes they got to hang onto it, waiting for their price. Anyway, there along with the other stuff was that diamond bracelet of Mrs. Ingram's, and one of her rings. I checked the description. I mean, the inventory said they were custom pieces, so there wouldn't be two."

"I'll be damned. Get anything out of Honeywell about it?"

"Uh-uh, and I probably won't. Well, look at it logically. Nobody wants to get the reputation that as soon as he gets picked up he starts co-operating and handing out names right and left." Goldberg blew his nose again. "What'd happen when he gets out and sets up at the same old stand? Everybody leery of doing business with him."

"*Se comprende.* But, damn it, if we knew where he'd got it—— Well, we ought to get somebody in the family to identify it."

"Sure, here it is." Goldberg put an envelope on his desk. "I knew you'd want it, but let me have it back—it's evidence."

Mendoza scribbled a receipt and upended the envelope. The ring and bracelet glittered exotically on his desk blotter. "Nice pieces. Worth about thirty-five hundred retail. Whoever sold them to Mr. Honeywell got about what?—say a third of that. Altogether, for the whole lot, somewhere around four thousand . . . I'd very much like another, closer look at that ring of Linda's. Not that it'd turn out to be one of Mrs. Ingram's —or would it? Yes, would it? She'd be very careful not to wear it in her mother's presence, or any of the family —but her mother wasn't there, and she was on her way out. . . . How very damned funny. You know, Ingram was quite right. We can pin down the time of the robbery. It had to be before Mrs. Ingram came home that Tuesday afternoon because when she got in she laid the jewelry she'd been wearing on the dressing table. If the thief had come after that, he'd have also taken the diamond ring she left there, and he didn't. And the robbery couldn't have been before about eleven-thirty that morning, or Mrs. Ingram would have noticed the stuff was missing when she opened the jewel box. I wonder——"

"Well, for what it's worth, there it is," said Goldberg. "Of course you can also read it that Ingram took it, any time between the evening his wife was killed and the day he said he discovered it was gone. We don't know how long Honeywell's had it. All I ask is, don't lose it, and let me have it back." He sneezed, cursed, and went out.

Mendoza took the jewelry to Mrs. Barron, who promptly identified it and was outraged to be told that she couldn't have it, and that the lawyer (executor of the will) couldn't have it either. Legal technicalities she brushed aside, and accused Mendoza of dishonesty, prejudice against "people like us," and stupidity. "It was my own *sister's* jewelry, after all, I don't know what right the *police*——"

"The estate will get it back eventually," Mendoza told her, and drove back downtown to hand it back to Goldberg, thinking hard and cursing the silence of the honorable fence.

Could it have been the thief? Just possibly? Or say thieves, because—— Had it, after all, been that way? He had thought he knew about the second half of the case, but he might be off the track there. Any of the family—— The double bluff. Which of them was cunning enough to plan that out?

One of them thinking, after that row on Monday night, "Well, maybe she can keep that money from us, but I'll have *something!*" They all knew she'd be out that afternoon. She'd been a self-centered woman, and had talked of her plans for the next day. But how could anyone know Ingram would be out? All that was necessary was to ring the bell; if he answered the door, say you'd come to leave a message for Bella. Or dear Auntie. If he didn't——

He came back to the anteroom of his office and dropped a list of phone numbers on Sergeant Lake's desk. "Here is one hell of a job for you, Jimmy. Console yourself that it was one hell of a job to make up." It was a list of all the quiet, cheap, third-rate hotels within a ten-mile radius of Gardena, composed with the aid of a map and Mendoza's nearly encyclopedic knowledge of the city, plus all five phone books. "In your spare moments, I want you to check all these numbers and ask if there's a Mr. Killeen registered."

Sergeant Lake looked at the list, groaned, and said, "O.K."

But as a matter of fact it was Mendoza who got the first faint trace of Killeen.

He had been deserting Alison nearly every evening during the last week, to don what she called his disguise and sally forth to Gardena. He'd won a little money, spotted a few other pro sharps, and got to know the insides of all the gambling houses down there, but he hadn't made any progress in finding Killeen.

That evening, Alison looked at him resignedly as he came in from the bedroom to kiss her good-by. "I thought detectives never wore disguises any more, except in implausible thrillers."

"Not exactly a disguise," said Mendoza. "I've got to look the part."

"Well, you most certainly do," said Alison. "You look perfectly horrible. Exactly like the city slicker in a third-rate Western—all you need are the sideburns. Anybody with eyes in his head can see you're up to no good. Do you really get honest people to play cards with you? I should think the minute they laid eyes on you they'd expect you to pull out a greasy deck of cards and say in a nasty, sinister tone, 'What about a li'l game, boys, heh-heh, just to pass the time?' I think it's mainly the mustache," she added thoughtfully.

"What's wrong with it?"

"There's nothing wrong with it," said Alison. "But villains, especially gambling villains, always have mustaches, you know. Same as all the rakes who go around

196

seducing innocent heroines. I wonder how you'd look without it." She studied him.

"¡Ay de mi! Has it come to that? You leave my mustache alone! I refuse——"

"I just wondered. Have a nice time, *amante*."

He was concentrating on the honest citizens now. Killeen would need money to live on, after all (if, of course, he was still here). And honest citizens, if they'd run across him, wouldn't mind saying so. In the last week Mendoza had sat in games with perhaps forty different men, and at some time, with each group, he'd said casually, "I've been expecting to run into a pal of mine down here, wonder if any of you've met up with him? Guy named Killeen." It was a little awkward; he hadn't an idea what the man looked like or what his first name was.

He'd got various replies. "I knew a guy named Killeen once, but he's dead." "That's an Irish name, isn't it?" "What's he look like?" But nobody had said, "I sat in with a fellow named Killeen the other day, I wonder if it was the one you know."

Tonight somebody did. Mendoza was back at the Little Reno tonight. He'd picked up a motley crowd of fairly hot players; he'd been holding bad cards all night, and had dropped about ten dollars. But his luck was in, another way.

When he asked his casual question, the off-duty Southern Pacific engineer looked up. "Killeen? I sat in with a guy named Killeen just last week. And, brother, did he take me! He was red hot that night. One of those days for me, anyway—I should of stood in bed."

The engineer was one O'Donnelly, a handsome young-ish man with a grin to charm a commissar.

"That so? Jack Killeen," improvised Mendoza, shuf-fling the deck. "He's from Dago too, I knew him from a house down there. He got transferred up here about the same time I did, but we don't work for the same outfits, see. I wondered if he was here yet—knew he'd make a beeline for some place like this, soon's he got settled." He laughed. "Tall thin guy about forty."

"Then this one wasn't him. . . . Give me some *cards* this time, will ya?" as Mendoza began to deal. "God, the luck I had lately. . . . Nah, this one was older than that, about sixty, short and kind of fat. Nice guy, seemed like, he was in real estate. What the hell was his first name, now? He said it." And it didn't mat-ter a damn, so far as the engineer knew, but in the way of meaningless, on-the-surface talk he groped for it in his memory. Mendoza concentrated on the deal. "Buh-rother!" said the engineer, picking up his hand as it came to him. "You're doin' better this time, man! . . . Irish name, isn't it? . . . Oh, man! Keep it up, keep it up . . . Danny!" he said triumphantly. "That was it, Danny Killeen. Same as my middle name, see. Nice fellow."

Considering what he'd said about the fictional Jack Killeen, Mendoza could hardly go on to ask eager ques-tions about the genial Danny who'd had such phe-nomenal luck playing with O'Donnelly. But he had a description now, and maybe other honest citizens could tell him more. *Paso a paso*—step by step . . .

198

CHAPTER SIXTEEN

HE PUT a man on Lauderdale—he had only one free. "Just pick up anything you can." Again he looked over the odds and ends that had come in before the inquest. They didn't suggest much; dead wood.

Winthrop hadn't bribed anyone with money from his bank account; he'd made no large withdrawals lately. By the figures on his latest statement, it was a bank account in a very healthy condition—he wasn't in any need of money.

Diligent research had failed to discover any record of Thomas Bailey, the archaeologist uncle who had died in Persia. That didn't surprise Mendoza; he thought Ingram had probably brought in Persia from a vague conviction that it would make it hard to trace the non-existent uncle, or show that he was non-existent. That didn't matter; also dead wood.

He was wondering now about two very nebulous little things. In regard to Linda Barron (and how he'd like a closer look at that ring!), it was odd that in spite of her dearth of modeling jobs she didn't seem to be hard up for money. Sylvia had said she didn't take the trouble to make up to her doting (and wealthy) uncle —as Hugh had to his aunt. Maybe Winthrop handed her money anyway, thankful for any crumbs of her affection? It was a small thing, but he'd like to know. Sometimes very small things gave you a hint.

The other point he was thinking about was the rather curious behavior of Winthrop just before the inquest. For some reason, Winthrop hadn't wanted to sit with the Barrons. Or was that just imagination?

He called Goldberg's office and asked if they'd found out any more about the fence. "Well, this and that," said Goldberg. "The way I said, he was hardly taking any precautions at all, and we did pick up three or four stray prints in his store. I mean, we picked up hundreds, but there were four of them in Records, so they were probably using him as a fence. Item, John Stead, two convictions on burglary. Peter Arnaud, one conviction breaking and entering. Vicente Martello, ditto. And a guy we hauled in once as a hot suspect on a holdup, but the evidence was pretty slim and he got off. Matthew Reilly, his name is. The trouble is, as you can see, it's no proof. They all say blandly, 'Sure, I'd dropped in there, I been looking for a secondhand table'—or bed —or stove—any damned thing." Goldberg sneezed. "So I say, 'How come you were in Honeywell's back office, by his desk? That's where we found all the prints except Martello's, which were on the front door. And they say, 'Why, he took me back there to figure up the sales tax on what I'd bought, or to show me something just came in.' What the hell? Sure it's suspicion, but nothing for me to haul them in on."

"Yes, I see. Well, thanks anyway." Mendoza knew he ought to be out seeing a new witness about the storm-drain corpse, which had now been identified. He sent Dwyer instead, and drove out to Mariposa Street to see Sylvia Glass or to discover where and when he could see her.

She opened the door to him, and her expression tightened. "What do you want now?"

"Just to talk to you, if you don't mind. Don't look so nervous, Miss Glass. I'm on your side, you remember? I don't think he's guilty either."

"So you said," she said dully. "Well, come in." He followed her into the shabby long room and sat down where he had sat before; she brought him the same glass ashtray.

"Haven't you found another job?" he asked.

"Oh, sure. Two jobs. But I quit both of 'em because it was all so—— See, I went to that Mrs. Widdows first, she was a friend of Mrs. Ingram's." He nodded. "She phoned and said did I want a job. That was before—before Mr. Ingram was arrested, see. But all the time she kept asking questions about, you know, what he was really like at home and what did they say to each other and all like that—real personal questions, and didn't I know why! I could just hear her saying to all the other ladies over their card tables, '*I* know all about it, because her maid's working for me now and *she* told me.' Well, I didn't," said Sylvia. "I never told her anything. And I'll tell you something else—before, when she came to dinner one night, she was all over Mr. Ingram, really flirting at him, it sort of embarrassed him, it was awful. But as soon as she thinks

201

he—— Just a ghoul, that's what she is. I quit after a week."

"Well, some people are like that," said Mendoza.

"If you ask me," she said miserably, "an awful lot of people are. I got another job last week, answered an ad in the paper, a Mrs. White up in Hollywood. And gee, soon's she heard my name, she'd have paid me a hundred a week just so's *she* could ask me things—all the same as Mrs. Widdows. Not if I thought Mr. Ingram *did* it—oh no!—but did I ever suspect he was dangerous, and so on. It's just wicked, the way everybody takes it for granted. Why, he wouldn't kill a mosquito! I quit that job too. I couldn't stand it, and I told her so, and why. I been thinking maybe I'll try to get a job in the dime store or something."

"Miss Glass," said Mendoza, leaning forward, "just listen to me a minute. It's supposed to be all over but the trial, now. He's arrested, and in jail, and I'm not supposed to be working on the case any longer. But I'm like you, I don't think he did it. I think somebody framed him for it. And I'm still looking, trying to get some new evidence. If I can find out who really did it, and prove it, then Mr. Ingram won't be tried at all."

"Oh!" she said, flushing excitedly. "Oh, if you only could! Is—is there any way I can help, sir?"

"I think so. Look, Miss Glass. A detective wants to know every single little fact about a case. Now, you know something you haven't told—no, don't interrupt me—you haven't told because you think it'd be something else against Mr. Ingram. But you're not a detective. It could be that what you have to tell might help, in the end, to show he's not guilty. You see, it's a little like putting a jigsaw puzzle together." He smiled persuasively at her. "You know how sometimes when you're doing a puzzle—there'll be a funny-shaped blue piece that you think will be part of the sky? But in the end it turns out to be part of a lake, or part of a woman's dress?" She was following him eagerly; she nodded. "Now, nobody's going to do anything to you for not telling us about it before—whatever it is. But I'd like to know, just in case it might be important."

She wavered for a long moment; and then she leaned back and said, "H-how'd you know I was? But it's not important! I guess—well, anyways, you must be a pretty good detective when you guessed I was. But, see, it isn't anything really! He—he just ran out of cigarettes or something." She looked defiant.

"You heard him leave," said Mendoza softly, "after you came back from the garage? Heard him go out and drive away?"

"Yes, I—— How'd you know that? I hadn't said yet. And why shouldn't he, anyways?"

"No reason. Did you hear him come back?"

"I—no, but he did pretty soon because I heard him moving around in the living room, and—— It doesn't really mean anything, you can see! I went on into my room and like I said I never heard nothing more all night. I went right to sleep. It doesn't mean any-thing——"

"But of course that might sound like damaging evidence. You committed perjury by——"

"I didn't!" she said breathlessly. "I didn't! I just—it wasn't important, I kind of forgot to say anything about it, and then later on I thought if I said anything you'd think I was dumb, not saying about it before, and wouldn't believe anything I——"

"Well. Thanks very much," said Mendoza, and stood up.

"If you just *could* help him, sir! Find out the truth."

"We'll try our best."

Behind the wheel of the Ferrari, he lit a new cigarette and smoked for a while thoughtfully. He'd hoped for something else—something she'd noticed about the house, some extraneous object, say. This wasn't very helpful to him, or to Ingram. And he thought that Sylvia knew quite well that Ingram hadn't returned very soon. Where had he gone? *And which car had he taken?* Not the body—he wouldn't have dared try to lift that. But . . . And she'd heard somebody "moving around"—but had it been Ingram?

He drove out to the County Jail. "Like the lawyer all right?" he asked Ingram. He'd sent young Shaughnessy, having seen his courtroom tactics.

"Nice young fellow. He's a live wire, isn't he?" said Ingram. He eyed Mendoza warily. "I haven't thanked you——"

Mendoza brushed that aside. "Forget it." The black rinse had started to wear off Ingram's hair, and he looked oddly healthier, plumper; but prisoners usually did pick up weight on prison food. "I want some answers. I'll tell you what I've dug up. There's good evidence that your wife was thinking about hiring a private detective. Did she ever mention such a thing to you?"

Ingram looked startled. "She did not. What for? You

mean checking up on me? She never susp— I can't imagine why——"

"I don't think she was checking on you. Mrs. Sprague tells us that the week before New Year's, when she had lunch with her, your wife made a rather odd comment. She said, 'If *I* haven't been taken in, I know somebody who *has,* and it'll be gratifying to prove it!' No names mentioned. The—mmh—first part of that, you gather, referred to the family's opinion of you." Ingram smiled faintly. "Did she ever say anything to you along these lines? Evidently she suspected one of the family of— well, what? Your guess is as good as mine. There's a hint that she may have hired a private eye—if so, she picked a wrong one. One by the name of Carnahy got himself beaten up recently, probably over one of his cases. We think he found out something and tried blackmail. There might be a link."

Ingram shook his head. "That sounds pretty wild," he said dubiously. "I can't see any of 'em mixed up with anything really—— No, she never mentioned anything like that to me. She never said much to me about the family anyway, except what she'd say to their faces. Janet was extravagant and man-crazy, and Linda was what she called fast and too modern about her morals, and Hugh was young and wild but she hoped he'd settle down. That kind of thing. I tell you, it was funny in a way—you know how some people are ostriches? She knew what they all thought about me, that I'd married her for the money." Again he smiled. "They didn't mind saying so in front of me. But she never—how shall I put it?—she never admitted it. She'd never fight back at them about it, just pretend not to hear, and between us she never mentioned it. . . . I don't know, I don't think she *would* have told me if she'd found out something really bad about the family. You mean, maybe she'd found out Linda was sleeping with her current boy friend, or Hugh had a finger in the employer's cash register? Which I wouldn't put past him. Something really bad against somebody, not just something she was old-fashioned about——"

Mendoza laughed and after a moment Ingram smiled with him. "Sorry," said Mendoza, "nothing to laugh about really. Moral values aren't so cut and dried as we like to think, are they? I had a hunch you're a very moral fellow, Ingram."

"Well, what I was going to say, you know how families are. Fight like cat and dog among themselves, but if any outsider sticks an oar in, they put up a solid front. I wouldn't know much about it, always seems damn funny fighting with people you're really fond of. But I never had any brothers or sisters, of course. . . . I mean, either you l-love people or not"—he stumbled a little over the word, slightly embarrassed—"and if you do, you make allowances, you give and take, you know. Why, I don't think Molly and I ever had any serious disagreement all the twenty-one years we were married."

"People come different shapes and sizes," said Mendoza.

"That's true. Anyway, I'd think Bella wouldn't have told me anything like that. In a way, I was an outsider. She was what they call a literal-minded woman, you know. Things were black or white to her. She hadn't much imagination. No, she wouldn't have told me, she'd have thought it was strictly family business."

Mendoza offered him a cigarette. "Do you think—suppose she'd found out that one of them had committed a real crime, police business—would she have given it away? Turned them in?"

Ingram didn't ruminate on that one. He said flatly, "Oh yes, I think so. She had that puritanical kind of conscience, you know? Well, of course I wasn't raised in any church, maybe I haven't any right to judge, but it seems to me a lot of these faithful churchgoers don't really know very much about real Christianity." He looked down at his cigarette. "I guess none of us ever get to be my age without having done some wrong things, but—well, in my book the real sins, if you want to call them that, are things like being mean and unkind and backbiting—and acting too damned righteous to walk the same ground with ordinary people. If you know what I mean. . . . There were times," he added to himself, "I was sorry I'd ever married her."

"I believe you."

"I mean, Bella was the kind—say Sylvia Glass had got into trouble, Bella'd have packed her off as a bad girl without finding out if she had anywhere to go or enough money. Not that Sylvia would, she's a nice girl. But you see what I mean. Bella was one of those seemed to figure anything that's a little fun's got something wrong about it. And like I say, literal. Letter-of-the-law sort of thing. If she had found out that one of her family was mixed up in a real crime she'd have thought whoever it was just had to take his medicine. She wouldn't have liked the scandal but she'd have done what she'd call the right thing."

"From what I've heard about her, I think you're right," said Mendoza, and got up.

"But what in hell could it have been? I can't say I like any of 'em, but I wouldn't have thought——"

"If you had to make a stab in the dark," asked Mendoza, "and guess who is likeliest to have killed her, what name would you say? After all, you know them."

Ingram shook his head helplessly. "How in God's name can I answer that? I don't—— Hugh," he said suddenly. "I think I'd say Hugh Barron. He's like a spoiled kid, never been disciplined, never had to pay for anything he's done wrong."

"Well, it could be. Thanks for the co-operation, anyway."

"Have you got anything really hot?"

"Odds and ends," said Mendoza. "Just odds and ends. But sometimes, if you get enough of them, they add up. I'll keep poking around."

A sporting-goods store. Lauderdale . . . Another very small notion had occurred to him; and on his way back downtown he stopped at a sports-equipment shop on Broadway and asked to see some golf putters. He looked at them speculatively, weighed one in his hand.

It was, he thought, the hell of an unhandy weapon. The balance was all wrong. Try to use it as a bludgeon, and the weight of the head made it swing around. To the glassy-eyed astonishment of the clerk, he tried swinging it like a club at an imaginary victim, and

every time the thing twisted in mid-air so that the victim would have been hit by the right-angle curve, the
back edge of the club, instead of the blunt bottom edge.

"Sir," protested the clerk faintly, "you don't use it—
I mean, if you're taking up golf——"

"Thanks, no," said Mendoza absently. "Just testing
out murder weapons." He handed back the putter and
went out, leaving the clerk with a story to tell.

That was on Tuesday. On Thursday Landers, who
had been taking a look at Lauderdale, handed Mendoza something. It was annoying that he had only
Landers to send out. A full-time tail would dredge up
more but he had lessened the odds a trifle by putting
Landers on night duty when Lauderdale would be
moving more freely.

"I don't know much about him," said Landers, "but
for my money we, or some department, are going to
know more eventually. He seems to be running with
a wrong bunch."

"Oh?"

"Not," said Landers, "that I've got built-in radar
like you, Lieutenant, but I didn't much like the look
of the two fellows he saw Tuesday night. They met at
a bar on Third Street, had a few, and then went to an
apartment up on Occidental Boulevard. Name in the
mail slot was Carlo Forelli. Well, I mean, I wouldn't
have been surprised to see any of 'em in a line-up. You
get to know the types."

"Isn't it the truth. And?"

"Lauderdale came out about ten and went to another apartment house on Beverly. Name there was

E. Smith. I think he had a key. Well, that doesn't say much. He didn't stay long—came out with a girl, but she drove off alone. Then last night he went to another bar and met a guy I recognized."

"¡Qué gratificación!" said Mendoza. "How?"

"Because about six years back, when I was still on traffic detail riding a squad car, I'd picked him up. He and another guy were spotted coming out of an alley right next to a supermarket where the burglar alarm'd been set off about ten minutes before. You remember, there'd been a kind of wave of market break-ins and we were all on our toes after the gang because the press had been after us. That's how I came to remember. We went over these two, but there wasn't anything to hold them on. But, like you know, I've got a good memory for names and faces, and I hunted around in my mind when I saw this guy last night, until I made the connection. His name's Reilly, Matthew Reilly, and I looked in Records and——"

"¡Ya estamos—uno quedo aturdido!" Mendoza sat up. "Don't tell me! I'll be damned!"

"Mean something to you, sir?"

"I think it might mean quite a lot," said Mendoza.

And that night he met Killeen.

The night had started out badly. He'd got down to Gardena by eight, and tried the Silver Dollar for the second time. It was a very classy setup, nothing but the best. He joined a game with some fellows he hadn't met before, but during the second hand, when he was just warming up to bring in Killeen's name, he looked up and spotted Eddy Roehampton not thirty feet away at another table.

He had thought he recognized Eddy from Palliser's description, before. Eddy must have changed his routine; he usually spent the winter down in Palm Springs or Coronado. And it was very damned awkward, but there he was, all three hundred asthmatic pounds of him, jollier than ever, upholstered in a greenish-gray Italian silk suit, booming out his friendly laugh. And it was very damned awkward because Eddy Roehampton, a run-of-the-mill pro, had once been dropped on by Sergeant Mendoza and knew him for what he was; if he spotted him here now, he'd pass the word around.

Mendoza made an excuse to drop out of the game after the showdown, slid out of the room unobtrusively, and collecting his hat strolled up Redondo Boulevard past several houses, undecided where to try next. He looked at the neon signs blinking on and off with cynical, if irritated, resignation. You sure as hell couldn't legislate morality.

Finally he went into the Lucky Horseshoe. He hadn't hit that one before. It was very much like all the others, and at the moment it was full. Air conditioning to carry out the smoke, a steady background hum of voices, with an occasional loud exultant cry or doleful exclamation, smiling house men scurrying about from table to table, and as more subtle background, the incessant soft insidious whirr of the shuffled cards. The tables were full.

And there was Killeen. Pausing on the threshold of the big room, Mendoza saw him almost at once; he was sitting at a table about ten feet away, playing a hand. He thought it was Killeen. A shortish, stoutish man— as he'd been described—about sixty or a little more, almost bald, a few dark strands of hair plastered carefully across the top of his head. He had a round, pleasant face, glasses, and wore a quiet dark suit.

A lot of men might conform to the rather general description he had of Killeen. But this was the first one he'd run into who did.

How the hell to separate him, get him alone and find out? Mendoza hesitated; he didn't dare get into a game here, run the risk of being immobilized.

Then, at that moment, as if a fairy godmother had waved a magic wand, the hand came to an end at that table; Killeen, if it was Killeen, said something smilingly, rose, and came out to the lobby. He turned past Mendoza, heading for the door discreetly gold-labeled *Men.*

"Mr. Killeen!" said Mendoza quietly.

The short stout man turned. "Yes?" He looked very much as you might expect a successful real-estate broker to look; he looked respectable, honest, and friendly.

"I want to talk to you, Mr. Killeen," said Mendoza, starting toward him. "Please believe me, I'm——"

An expression of pure terror froze on Killeen's round face. He said under his breath, "You must be the one—Davenport said—and Frankie——" and he ran. He made a blind lunge past Mendoza for the big double front doors, burst through, and was gone.

Mendoza ran after him; but when he reached the street Killeen had vanished. Probably turned down an alley between buildings.

"*¡Mil rayos!*" he said to himself. But he might have expected it. And how to proceed from here?

CHAPTER SEVENTEEN

PALLISER had been dealing with one of those nasty cases that come Homicide's way, and hadn't much enjoyed it: the wholesale slaying of his entire family, including three children, by a former mental patient. Palliser had nearly all the paper work cleaned up, and after his testimony at the inquest on Monday his part in the case would be over. Meanwhile, at the end of Saturday's working hours, he was chatting with Hackett in the sergeants' room. When Mendoza came in, looking purposeful, Palliser eyed him suspiciously.

"Good, you're here," said Mendoza. "I've got an interesting little job for you."

"Not *now?*" said Palliser plaintively. "Look, Lieutenant, it's Saturday night——"

"Another date? Too bad, but there it is."

"You're ruining my social life," complained Palliser.

"Well, if your intentions are honorable," said Mendoza, "she'll have to learn to put up with a cop's irregular hours. The sooner the better. Anyway, I don't think you'll be bored tonight." He laughed.

"You're up to something," said Hackett, regarding him shrewdly.

"I'd have picked you, but you wouldn't get to first base. You look exactly like what you are—in the vernacular, a ton of law. But John here might be anything." Approvingly, he surveyed Palliser's long, dark face with its heavy eyebrows and serious brown eyes, his lean height and noncommittal clothes. "You'll do very nicely as a decoy."

"Listen," said Hackett. "Am I right this is still the Ingram thing? I know you've been using your spare time on it. You know what Holmes'll say if he finds out you're still working it. Do you want to get hauled up to Internal Affairs for an official chewing out?"

"I'm hoping it won't come to his attention until I've got something to justify myself. And I have the feeling —there comes a time in every case when things begin to join up and come clear—I have the feeling we're approaching that point now. Damn it, if I only had the men to put full-time tails on the whole bunch of them! But as it is, little by little I think I'm getting a firmer hold on—mmh—the thread that'll unravel the mystery. John——"

"Yes?" said Palliser resignedly.

"Call Miss Silverman and apologize, get yourself some dinner, and meet me at this address at six-thirty. Are you anything of a poker player?"

"Not much," said Palliser, surprised.

"You *do* know how to play?"

"Well, sure, but I never was much of a one for cards——"

"That's all right, all the better," said Mendoza. "I'll see you."

Palliser obeyed instructions (relieved when Roberta was sympathetic and understanding) and at six-thirty found a parking place half a block up from the Peacock Hotel on 135th Street in Hawthorne. Walking toward the hotel, he spotted Mendoza's big black Ferrari in a public lot; and Mendoza was leaning against the building smoking a cigarette.

He said, "Jimmy spent three days locating this place for me—— Now, John." He looked around; there were no pedestrians near. This wasn't a very classy section, and the hotel was a cheap one. Mendoza dived into his pocket and brought out a roll of bills. "Here you are—gambling money—two hundred bucks. We are going to take a room in this hotel. You will register, and I'll go upstairs and stay there. Your job is to loiter down below and wait until a gentleman named Killeen comes out. As soon as we found him, and got the desk clerk to say he was in, I chased Landers down here to keep an eye on him—I took over from Landers five minutes ago. Killeen's had dinner, and he'll be going out again, I think, so let's make it snappy." He gave Palliser a graphic description of Killeen as they started in. Palliser went up to the desk and was assigned a room on the second floor for three-fifty. He registered; at a hotel like this no comment was made on his lack of luggage. He came back to Mendoza and handed over the key.

"O.K. Now, tag along after Killeen and get yourself in a game with him. You'll lose some money, but don't object to whatever stakes he wants to play. He's going to like you, and it shouldn't be hard to bring him back here with you. Mention where you're staying and he'll probably tell you he's here too. Stick to him until he heads home, and then insist on his coming to your room for a drink. It shouldn't—— Here he is." Mendoza turned abruptly away and unfolded the newspaper he'd been carrying under his arm. Palliser stepped back against the wall.

Killeen came down the narrow stair and made directly for the door. Palliser counted ten and followed him.

Mendoza went up to the second-floor bedroom, unlocked the door, and left it unlocked behind him. The room was reasonably clean; it had an old rag rug on the floor and contained a single iron bed, a cheap painted chest of drawers bearing a telephone, and two rickety straight chairs. There was a single overhead light. The bath would be down the hall. It wasn't a very inviting place to spend an idle three or four hours, but Mendoza eyed it philosophically and stretched out on the bed to do some intensive thinking.

A couple of rather curious new facts had come to light. . . .

Palliser trailed Killeen down to the next corner, where there was a bus-stop sign; Killeen stopped and waited. It was dark, of course, but while several other people were waiting too, Palliser wished fervently he had a newspaper to hide behind. But Killeen didn't seem to be doing much looking around; he stood waiting stolidly, wearing a serious expression. When the bus came, Palliser was the last one in, and strode quickly to the very rear; Killeen was looking out the window.

It was nearly half an hour later that Killeen reached up and pulled the bell cord. They were in Gardena now; the next stop would be Gardena Boulevard. This was an awkward moment; no one else seemed to be getting off here. Palliser managed it by waiting until the last moment to jump out, when the automatic doors were just closing. Killeen was ten feet ahead, walking quickly up the street.

He went into a poker palace called the Lucky Horseshoe a block down. Palliser went in after him; Killeen was just depositing his hat on a rack. Palliser walked around behind him and approached as if from the other end of the foyer. "Excuse me—oh, you're not one of the attendants, I'm sorry." He looked as callow and embarrassed as possible for a cop with seven years' service. "I was just wondering how you get into a game in these places. I'm alone and I don't know anyone——"

Killeen smiled genially at him, but it seemed to be with a little effort. "Well now, young man, I think I can oblige you. There should be a few fellows I know here, let's see."

"That's real nice of you, sir."

There were a few fellows Killeen knew; names were exchanged and they sat down to play. As Palliser had said, he'd never been a card player, and the effort of concentration was tiring. Moreover, he was not by nature a gambler, and it horrified him to see good money, never mind whose, passing out of his hands so recklessly. The stakes were fairly high; he got bad cards and played them ineptly compared to the other four men. But he went on grimly acting the part foisted on him, and by eleven o'clock he had lost nearly a hundred and fifty bucks, most of it to Killeen. At that point two of the others decided to call it a day, and Killeen, stifling a yawn, said he would too. Long before, Palliser had managed to bring into the conversation a mention of his hotel, and Killeen had remarked on the coincidence.

He said now, "I'm afraid we'll have to call a cab, the buses don't run this late. Do let me pay, Palliser. I feel guilty, the way the luck was running my way tonight."

"All right, sir," said Palliser (he'd been acting deferential, youth to age), "but you must stop by my room and let me give you a nightcap."

Killeen agreed to that expansively; he'd had no more than three beers through the evening, but it had loosened him up a little. When they reached the hotel he claimed his key at the desk; Palliser said quickly, "I never bother to turn it in, too much trouble." They climbed up to the second floor. It was almost dark—a low-wattage bulb at the head of the staircase—and very quiet. Palliser pretended to fish for a key, bent over the door, stood back to let Killeen precede him, and shoved the door wide.

"At last we meet, Mr. Killeen," said Mendoza. "Come in."

Killeen turned blindly and came up against Palliser, who shoved him all the way in and shut the door behind them. Mendoza tossed him the key and he locked it.

"You——" said Killeen. He was breathing hard; he

turned and looked at Palliser. "You, a fuzz! I wouldn't have guessed. Well," and he shrugged, "it's what the Aussies call a fair cop. All right, you've got me."

"Sit down," said Mendoza, "and have that drink John promised you. I filched some paper cups from the bathroom." He nodded at the pint of rye on the chest. "I think you need one, Mr. Killeen. All I want to do is talk with you, but I had to make you stand still first."

Killeen sat down heavily in one of the chairs and stared at him. "I don't mind, you know," he said suddenly. "I don't know how you dropped on me, but I don't mind. Shouldn't have run away the other night. I was going to see Frankie's lawyer tomorrow. Frankie said not to be a damn fool—last time I saw him, that Monday when he took off—but habit's a funny thing. I miss him like hell, you know. We might as well stick together now, we been doing it forty years. You'll have me up with him, but I don't seem to care. I know who you are—that head cop. Frankie told me about you." The dark eyes behind the heavy-rimmed glasses looked almost blank. "It's no good Frankie sticking to that story now, I can see that. I told him so then, but he said he'd be damned if he dragged me in, he said for God's sake don't mix myself in. I been kind of used to doing like Frankie says—but I'd made up my mind, see his lawyer. And anyway the truth was——"

Mendoza took the paper cup from Palliser and handed it to Killeen; Palliser had poured a very stiff one. "Go on, take it. You're jumping to conclusions, Mr. Killeen. I don't have a warrant in my pocket for you. I just want to talk to you, and I hope you'll talk to me. So far as I know, or have usable evidence on, you're a perfectly respectable citizen, and so is Mr. Ingram. Listen to me! I know you haven't been in touch with him lately, so you aren't up to date, shall we say? But I don't think he's guilty. I'm so convinced of it that I'm guaranteeing his legal defense. . . . John, you might forget you heard that. Internal Affairs wouldn't like it at all."

Palliser grinned and nodded.

"Listen, Mr. Killeen. If I can get at the truth and prove it—prove somebody else is guilty—Ingram won't come to trial at all. There'll be no bar to his getting what she left him in that will, and he'll be free as air. And so will you. I'll have no evidence that either of you ever did anything wrong at all." He held Killeen's eyes. And that was true: always so hard to get concrete evidence on the sure-thing men, anyway.

Killeen stared back at him dumbly. "Look," said Mendoza. "If you don't believe me, I can show you the canceled check to the lawyer. And this is off the record." He looked at Palliser. "If Mr. Killeen decides to level with me, John, you're going to hear some things that may burden your conscience. You'll just have to trust me. I'm playing the hand the way I see it. Or would you like to take a walk?"

Palliser smiled. "It's been a damned warm day, Lieutenant, and I'm tired. In fact, I'll probably go to sleep and never hear a word."

Killeen looked from one to the other of them. "L-level?" he asked hoarsely. "Frankie said you were— he couldn't make you out. But I don't care. Not any more. He made me swear I wouldn't, but—damn it to hell"—he took another gulp of rye—"it sounds like one of those damn silly kids' stories, all about honor and loyalty—but I don't care if it puts me up there with him. . . . The old Pavilion in Atlantic City, it was, where we first met up. It's torn down now. Forty-one years ago next month." He finished the rye and sat holding the cup in a lax hand. "He was just a kid like me, drifting around, only he'd been working regular jobs. Me, I was raised to the business, my dad was one of the best. Hell, I was practicing overhand stacks when I was still in grade school. We sort of took to each other, and I—well, cut a long story short, I showed him a few tricks, and he was a natural. He got to be better than I am even. Forty-one years next month. I mean, you get to think alike. Like telepathy. I don't suppose there's been a day we been apart in those forty-one years—except when he went off with Molly on a wedding trip —until he had to run. And he wouldn't let me go— get involved. He made me swear—— But you picked him up." He stopped abruptly, like a run-down clock, and Mendoza got up and poured him another four fingers of rye. He took a swallow of it.

"He said—last time I talked to him—don't be a damn fool, better one than two. But nothing's like it ought to be, him there and me alone. It wouldn't make that much difference to me, I guess. . . . I dreamed about Molly last night. God, it's been no fun, going on alone——" Killeen shut his eyes. "I never felt old before, but I feel old now. A thousand years old."

"Molly," said Mendoza very quietly.

"Molly, she was my kid sister. It wasn't fair, her dying like that, only forty. He's had some rough breaks, Frankie has. It was bad enough for me, but I had an awful time making him pull himself together, after she died. They'd been pretty close—you know—the three of us had been. . . . She didn't like moving around so much, women don't, but of course she was brought up to it same as me. Dad . . . There was a girl in Newport News I was struck on once but she didn't—— And I never had the urge for a permanent one, after that. The three of us always got on fine. Frankie and I both liked to play golf and—— Only Frankie'd throw away a whole take on some fool thing Molly wanted—but it didn't matter." He stared at the second half of his drink. "Frankie's like that. Easy come, easy go. I guess I am too. So it didn't matter. Forty-one years is the hell of a long time."

"So it is," said Mendoza softly. "And sometimes it's not so easy any more, when you get to be——"

"Oh, *Christ!*" said Killeen with something like a sob. "It was me put it in his head, God forgive me!" The liquor had loosened his tongue; he wouldn't be used to drinking this much, and he was coming out with all this tale in a torrent, anxious to be rid of it. "I saw it in the paper, this society woman going on a vacation in Mexico. It said about her late husband giving away money to charity, so I knew she'd be loaded, and I said to Frankie—he's got the kind of looks women like, you know—it was just a joke really—we'd just missed a big kill in San Diego, one of the house dicks spotted——" He stopped, discovered the cup in his hand, and drank. After a long moment of silence he said, "I never been so scared in my life as when he had that heart attack. The year before, that was. The doctor explained about it, how Frankie had to take care of himself. Good for

222

another fifteen years if he was careful, but he had to watch his diet and all that. It was lucky we'd just taken a nice piece of change. Eight hundred bucks the hospital bill was, and I had to hock my diamond ring at that. . . . It was a *joke*, damn it, when I said about this rich widow, but he got it in his head, said it'd be like a life preserver. I couldn't stop him. And of course, it was O.K.—in a sort of way—until all this happened."

"I can see that it was," said Mendoza as he stopped again. "Finish your drink, Mr. Killeen."

"Molly was a pretty girl," said Killeen. "She took after Ma. The prettiest little thing—dark curly hair she had and big brown eyes and she sang a lot. Ma, she used to sing a lot too, I remember." He finished the rye. He was feeling the two very stiff drinks now. "Ma was from County Clare in Ireland, like Dad's folks. There was one song Molly liked and she was always singing it. Funny, she used to say the only times you can sing a sad song is when you're really happy. I don't know—maybe just because of remembering old times, it keeps kind of going through my head. It went—I can't sing, but——

> "Oh, all the money I ever had,
> I spent it in good company—
> And all the harm that I've ever done,
> Alas, it was to none but me.
> And all I've done for want of wit
> To memory now I can't recall—
> So fill to me the parting glass,
> Good night, and joy be with you all. . . .

I don't know . . . Frankie's had some rough breaks. It's twenty years since Molly died. I miss him, you see.

You get *used* to each other. Having the same room, having breakfast and lunch and dinner together, talking—well, you get into habits. Sure, it was all *right*. He'd be down here most days, after he'd married Bella —we carried on the same way except he was living up there. It turned out an easy deal. He told her after a while he'd lost most of his money in lousy investments, but it was O.K. She always paid for everything anyway, for the house and so on. We took enough for him to get cigarette money and run that car she gave him. He made me keep the rest, because he was fixed up with a living, see. Oh, *damn* it to hell, why did he ever *do* it? We'd have been all right—he knew I'd always see to him. He didn't have to go and marry——"

Mendoza said, "Mr. Killeen. I want to know about that day. New Year's Day. You were together. What did you do?"

Killeen blinked, and his eyes focused on Mendoza. "New Year's——" he said. "I don't mind telling you. If you'll believe me—Frankie said nobody would, it'd be no good. I was going to see his lawyer to tell him. Break it open. I don't know if there'd be a chance, but we got to take the gamble. . . . Damn it, you get *used* to being together. Not that I suppose they'd put us in the same cell. . . . New Year's Day's my birthday. January 1, 1901, I was born. I'm just a month older than he is, see. That was kind of a joke too, we always take birthdays like, kind of, vacations. The day off. On Molly's birthday we always went to a fair—hers was in September, see, there was usually a county fair on, and she was like a kid for things like that. And I like the beach. I can't swim but I like to paddle around and watch the ocean." He looked at his empty cup, and Mendoza poured him a cautious two fingers more. "God, I'm tired," said Killeen suddenly, and drank. "It doesn't matter any more. 'All the harm that I've ever done,' like it says. Haven't been sleeping much lately. Anybody that knows Frankie the way I do 'd know he couldn't any more kill anybody than—than I could."

"The beach," said Mendoza.

"That's right. We went to the beach. Frankie picked me up about one o'clock and we went to Redondo Beach. Even if it was a holiday it wasn't so crowded, what with the Rose Parade and the big game. That afternoon hardly anybody at the beach. And it was nice—nice warm day, like New Year's can be out here. And about five-thirty, a little later, we got dressed again and started uptown. Frankie said we'd go to a real swank place for dinner, expense no object. We stopped to get gas—God, that was another rough break, that kid remembering—but how could Frankie know then? He'd told Bella that he was going out for dinner with an old friend, see, she didn't mind. Well, we did. We ate at a place in Hollywood called the Madison House— Frankie was worried since then that the waiter or somebody there'd remember, and go to tell you—but it was damn dark, you know how these expensive society places are, and I guess nobody saw either of us plain enough to——"

"And I think he dropped you back here at about eight-twenty?" said Mendoza.

"About eight-twenty," said Killeen, nodding; he was

talking now as if under hypnosis, unemphatic. "I was tired—all that hot sun. I got undressed, and I had a magazine to read in bed, the latest *Saturday Evening Post* it was—when Frankie——"

"Just one moment, Mr. Killeen," said Mendoza. He looked over at Palliser. "John, I don't want a witness to this. You're an honest upright officer"—his tone was only half humorous—"and I won't ask you to have to decide between loyalty to me and the oath you took with the uniform. Go out and take a walk for half an hour."

Palliser was surprised, but he saw that Mendoza was serious. He went out, and down to the street, and paced around the block. He wondered what was in Mendoza's mind. It was a fine night, cool now.

He stopped at an all-night drugstore and had a cup of coffee. He thought about Roberta Silverman. It would be a little squeeze, because he had his widowed mother to support too; but she and Roberta got on fine, and Roberta could keep on teaching for a couple of years anyway. . . .

It was twelve-thirty when he tapped hesitantly at the hotel-room door. Mendoza opened it to him.

Killeen was asleep, stretched out full length on the bed.

"O.K., John," said Mendoza. He dropped the key on the chest, took up his hat, and came out, switching off the light. He looked a little excited.

"Get what you wanted, sir?"

"I think so. We're getting there—step by step." Mendoza laughed. "I needn't have banished you. Thought

I might be on the way to acting as accessory—this precious old pair, I'd hate to see them tucked away for any reason—but it turns out better than I hoped. Now for Ingram—and, at that, I think I'll keep this under wraps until I get something more definite. . . ."

CHAPTER EIGHTEEN

"WE HAVE simply got to come to some decision," said Alison on Sunday evening. "Of course, if you want to leave it entirely up to me——"

"*¡Dios me libre!* The minute my back was turned you'd have the poor infant named Adolphus or Hector. All right, all right." Mendoza was lying full length on the sectional with Bast curled up on his stomach. "We have agreed on Teresa. Now I suggest——" He uttered a pained yell as Sheba, making passes at Bast, got all ten claws through his trousers and dug into his thigh. "*¡Porvida! ¿Qué puede uno hacer?* Get off me, you little monster!" Sheba clung like a limpet, then swarmed up his legs and invited her mother to a game of rough-and-tumble by pouncing on top of her. Alison laughed and Mendoza sat up as the cats thumped to the floor, rolling over each other. "You're an unfeeling woman. I'm bleeding. Why do we keep cats?"

"As a matter of fact, *mi marido honorable,* we're breaking the law by keeping four. It's illegal to have more than three permanently."

"No, we're not. The house is built on two lots, so technically we're entitled to six, God forbid." Mendoza was still feeling his thigh. "I'll give you Anne for Michael. . . . I need a drink after that." He started for the kitchen.

"What do you m—— Oh. But why Michael, of all——" She followed him, book in hand.

"I like it," said Mendoza simply.

Alison leaned on the doorpost and said maliciously, "Oh, you do? It means 'Who is like unto the Lord?'"

"Oh," said Mendoza the agnostic. "Well, I don't mind Matthew."

"I do," said Alison. "And that means 'gift of Jehovah.' I——¡*Cuidado!*"

Mendoza froze with the bottle of rye in one hand and a glass in the other, and braced himself. El Señor landed heavily on his shoulder and spoke in a loud, bitter voice.

"There you are," said Alison. "You've corrupted him for life, Luis. He'll get to be an alcoholic."

"Well, how in hell could I have known he'd like the taste of it?" Ever since the evening when Mendoza had upset a half glass of rye on the kitchen drainboard, and in idle curiosity lifted El Señor up to sniff at it, El Señor had to have his share when the bottle was brought out. "¡*Señor Borrachón!* All right, all right." He poured an ounce of rye into a saucer, and El Señor crouched over it pleasedly, eyes shut, lapping steadily. Mendoza poured his own drink.

"I don't mind Anne," he repeated, "if there's two females. Will you give me Nicholas for that?"

"*Nicholas.*" said Alison with loathing. "I will not.

All right, I've agreed to John, but—— Have you any other offers?"

"Thomas," said Mendoza, tripping over Nefertite and recovering himself to make the sectional safely. "Don't tell me what it means. I know. It means 'twin.' "

"Well, that *is* a thought," said Alison. "Thomas. Thomas. If it stayed Thomas and didn't turn into Tommy."

"Of course I don't suppose for a minute," said Mendoza, "that we'll need four possibles to choose from. It's a perfectly ordinary single infant, and will turn out to be either John or Teresa."

"But *look* at me!" said Alison. "I still think the doctor should put me on a diet."

Mendoza looked at her. "You're very agreeable to look at, *querida*. I've always thought so. I like the new shade of lipstick."

Alison poised the Oxford Dictionary of Christian Names, and then relented. "It's not heavy enough to do you much damage. . . . Just look at that. A disgusting sight, I call it." El Señor stalked in, weaving slightly and still licking his chops. He made directly for Nefertite and cuffed her across the jaw.

"It seems to affect him the way it does me."

"But I must say you're much better company tonight than you have been lately. Making unfunny jokes and—— Is something coming unstuck?"

"I really think so," said Mendoza. "And in an unexpected way, too. . . . Damn it, marriage has dulled my reading of nuances—in that direction, anyway. And there are a few details I haven't unraveled, but—— What was that you just said?"

"When?"

"I don't know——" He considered. "I just suddenly had a feeling you'd said something important— I mean, relevant to this thing. But it's escaped me now. . . ."

"I tell you it must be twins, Luis, the way I'm gaining. And five months more! You can't imagine how annoying the most ordinary things are, like getting out of the bathtub. I——"

"Well, it was your idea," said Mendoza reasonably. "You needn't glare at me, *chica*."

Alison glared at him and said coldly that it was easy for *him* to be so cheerful about it.

The first little thing of interest that had turned up from Landers' sporadic tailing of Lauderdale was that Lauderdale had quit his job. The night before last, Landers, hanging about the third-floor landing of the apartment house where Lauderdale shared three rooms with his older brother, had overheard quite a slanging match between them. He hadn't been able to hear every word, but the brother, who was a sober, hard-working skilled carpenter, had been calling Bruce down for quitting a good job and hanging around with "them beatnik types." Finally, after a lot of swearing, Bruce had shouted something about "getting out of this crummy dump, anyway" and added, "I've got the dough to live in a classier joint!" And fifteen minutes later he'd come out with a couple of bags; Landers had followed him to the Hotel Franklin downtown where he'd taken a room.

Mendoza was (though he'd have denied it vigorously) essentially superstitious. In his experience, there always came a time in a tough case like this when things started to move. From a static position, the people involved began to shift around, this direction or that, and that was the time you often began to find out more about them. In this instance there was also the fact that, while the Ingram case was in the headlines, these people had been more or less in the limelight; if any of them had any reason to walk carefully and put up an innocent front, they had then—but now the heat was off. So . . . Anyway, he had a hunch that this was the time to look.

So he took the gamble—and it was a big one; if Holmes should find out what he was doing——! He pulled a man off this case, a man off that (and Hackett, Galeano, and Rolf called down curses on him for being left shorthanded), and he set up a full-time tail on Bruce Lauderdale.

What had come in so far was interesting. Lauderdale had quit his job on last Wednesday. He wasn't making any effort to find another. He had rented an apartment (at a hundred a month) on Cahuenga Boulevard; he had bought some new clothes at an expensive men's store. That evening he had gone to the Hotel Knickerbocker in Hollywood, alone, and spent about an hour there, having a few drinks in the bar, wandering around the several rooms of the lobby. The tail had reported that it hadn't been hard to keep out of his sight; the hotel was currently entertaining a convention of the V.F.W., and the lobby had been crowded. Lauderdale, that genial fellow, had got into conversation with quite a few of the veterans.

Then on Saturday morning Winthrop had come in

to Mendoza's office. That entire little scene had surprised Mendoza considerably. The first thing he noticed was the great change in the man himself. Winthrop looked gray and ill, and at times his voice shook uncontrollably. Overnight he seemed to have aged ten years. And what he came for was to protest the police retention of his sister's jewelry. "Most highhanded—most highhanded," he said, sounding merely fretful; all the man's old vigor was gone.

Mendoza had eyed him, somewhat incredulous; after all, Winthrop had been a businessman, was reasonably educated. "But surely, Mr. Winthrop, you know enough about the law to realize that it's only impounded as evidence. Once Honeywell has been tried, the jewelry will be released to Mrs. Ingram's executor, as part of her estate."

"Oh—ah—but it is highhanded," Winthrop quavered. "My sister Janet spoke to me—— You—ah—assure me of this? Yes, I see, that—ah—technicality had slipped my—— Well, in that case——"

Had the man had a stroke? Mendoza wondered.

Hackett, swearing about it but adding that he'd at least get a night's sleep for once, had gone up to San Francisco to collect a wanted man and escort him home. Mendoza went out to lunch alone.

Strolling into Federico's, he spotted Andrews sitting alone at a table, and went over to join him. "Hello, Perce. They keeping you busy?"

"Come outside and say that," said Andrews. "Brother." They ordered, and joined desultory conversation; Andrews kept yawning. "Sorry," he apologized. "I didn't get to bed until three. Martha says she's going to have my portrait taken and put it up somewhere so she'll remember what I look like."

"Out on a raid?" asked Mendoza idly. Andrews was an old colleague of his, still down in Vice.

"Oh, not exactly. Laying in wait for some call girls. There's been the hell of a lot of it lately, the graph's way up. And the damnedest thing——"

"I noticed that article in the *Times*. More of it than usual?"

"I'll tell you what gets me," said Andrews. "It's the damnedest thing, Luis. A good half of the ones we pick up—well, they're a new type. Girls from respectable backgrounds, even educated girls. Take the ones we brought in last night. Four of 'em, operating in two different apartments, *and* respectable places, too. Of course the high-class ones never are the type you get in regular cat houses, but, my God, it used to be you could spot them! I mean, even when the pimp locating clients bragged them up as refined society dames out for a thrill. You know what I mean. They turned out to be about as refined as—— Well, sure, better types, disappointed actresses who hadn't made the grade, and so on. But only a few steps up from the house girls. Now it's different. I swear to God I don't know what's happening to people, I don't like it. . . . What kind of pie today, Adam? O.K., make it apple. . . . This bunch we dropped on last night. The fellow contacting clients—at fifty bucks a lay, I ask you!—he'd been a bank teller. And the girls—one of 'em had a degree from U.S.C., and another one used to be a legal secretary. I can't figure it. You'd never spot them."

"It's a convenient idea," said Mendoza, "that you

can put labels on people according to whether they use proper grammar or eat with a knife. . . . No dessert, just more coffee. . . . It may be a sad commentary on human nature, Perce, but some women just like being prostitutes. If you happen to be built that way, and of course it's essentially a sexless way, it's an easy living."

"Oh, well, I know, but what I can't get over is the *types* we keep getting now. Like I say. One of this last batch, her father's a lawyer, and she had three years of college." Andrews shook his head mournfully.

Mendoza went back to his office and got through some tiresome paper work. Just before six o'clock Dwyer came in and said he'd handed Lauderdale over to Higgins for the evening shift.

"Where's he been today?"

"Well, he got around," said Dwyer, yawning. "Some funny places, too. Unexpected, I mean. And I had a kind of funny idea about it, but on second thoughts it doesn't seem—— Well, he must've made a few new buddies at that Hotel Knickerbocker convention, because he went back there for a while and talked to some of 'em in the bar. Then he went to this apartment house on Beverly. The Old English Arms. Respectable middle-class. I couldn't see which apartment he went to, but he didn't stay long, about forty minutes. After that he had lunch, and three or four drinks, and then he went downtown to the Hotel Garner, and into the bar there. It was damn crowded—there's a state convention of barbers or something. After a while he took a little cab ride. I couldn't figure that, he'd left his car in a lot not a block away, and he had the cabby bring him back there. About then I had this funny idea, you can see what it looks like, Lieutenant, but it doesn't seem possible. I mean we haven't had a hint of anything like——"

"*¡Largo de aquí! ¡Frene! ¿Y qué es esto?* Wait a minute, wait a minute! Do I believe what this says to me? My God—if it *was,* could it be that—— Yes, I see—— But if Carnahy tried blackmail, he wouldn't have—— Of course he might have made a report first——" Mendoza shut his eyes, concentrating, fitting pieces together.

Dwyer stared at him. "You think it's so, Lieutenant? But what the hell connection——"

"But they don't as a rule go so far as murder, you know," said Mendoza to himself, reasonably. "They really don't. There's something here I don't quite—— But we're going into this a lot deeper, by God! O.K., Bert, thanks."

"Something's struck you all of a sudden about this rigmarole?" said Dwyer curiously.

Mendoza smiled. "Something's struck me. I've just remembered that Ingram told me she was a literal-minded woman."

And it was very convenient that, technically speaking, this new development wasn't his business. He called Andrews and passed on the information; Andrews let out a groan. "As if we weren't busy enough! All right— I've got that. Yes. Thanks very much for the tip."

"You understand that I want to know what happens *inmediatamente?* This ties up to something the hell of a lot more important."

"O.K., O.K.," said Andrews. "I'll keep you briefed."

236

Mendoza sat back and for five minutes contemplated an entirely new and different picture within the framework of the Ingram case. It was a picture drawn, so to speak, from an unexpected angle. All through this business, interest had been focused on the money; all that nice money. And the will. If the new picture had any truth in it at all, the money hadn't had a damned thing to do with the murder.

Not Bella Ingram's money.

And yet he couldn't quite see those two doing a murder. . . .

But if—— Considering what Killeen had said—— Yes. *And* that fingerprint. . . . The frame. The frame, and that *had* been on account of the money, of course. Also——

Kay Webster. Pretty, thrilled, young Kay Webster. Probably a very good pair of eyes and a good memory. And it hadn't, after all, been very dark. A medium-sized car, like a Dodge. A light-colored car.

Facts, nice solid evidence to produce to a judge (or to Holmes), were what he needed.

He picked up the inside phone and told Sergeant Lake he wanted a search warrant for the apartment shared by Janet and Linda Barron. Andrews would be looking at the apartment rented in the name of E. Smith in the Old English Arms on Beverly Boulevard.

Pending the arrival of the warrant, he went downstairs for the Ferrari and drove up to Wilshire Boulevard, to Winthrop's apartment. Not to talk to Winthrop. . . .

"It is easier to speak in my own tongue," said Giorgio

Copas, "if I am to be questioned again. But I do not know what more I can tell you, sir. I have told before——"

Mendoza said, "Yes, but I have a few more questions for you now." Copas was an elderly man, small and very dark, with intelligent eyes. He had made a statement, and he had been questioned twice; all the police had wanted from him then was corroboration that Winthrop had come home at a certain time and stayed home. He hadn't looked like a very important witness; all attention had been focused on Ingram. Mendoza suddenly remembered something else: "How was it that you hadn't had the day off? It was a holiday."

"Yes, sir, but I have no family living here, and few friends. Mr. Winthrop had said I might go out, and in the afternoon I did go into the park for a little, but there is not much of amusement for an old man"—he smiled—"and I came back to cook Mr. Winthrop's dinner for him. It was not a night when guests were expected, you see. Sometimes Mr. Winthrop gives dinner parties. It is nearly always for these friends of his who are also interested in cookery, Mr. Godwin and Mr. Russell and others. Then he will cook the dinner himself. Very difficult, exotic things—he is a gourmet, you see. Of course," and Copas smiled again, "it is I who washes up all the pots and pans!"

"I see. Well, now, what I want to ask you is this. When Mr. Winthrop came home that evening, what was his manner? Was he the same as usual?"

Copas hesitated. "I—I do not want to say too much, sir. Of course it means nothing, because we know that

238

this other man is the guilty one, him you have in jail. That, it presented itself at once, did it not? Mr. Winthrop is often"—he shrugged—"a little put out over this and that. If something goes a little wrong, he is immediately angry."

"Did he seem put out about something?"

"It was not exactly that, no. He was, I remember, very silent, and twice did not hear what I said to him. He said almost nothing. He did not ask about dinner. He sat down over there in the big chair by the hearth, with his book." Fortunately Winthrop was not in; they were talking in the living room of the apartment. "He looked very pale and perhaps worried over something. I remember that I asked him if he felt well, he was so pale, and he said angrily he was quite all right, he had walked too far was all, there had been no parking place near Mr. Godwin's house. . . . Why do you want to hear all this? I do not understand, it is nothing to do with this murder."

"Detectives always like to hear all about the details," said Mendoza. "Please go on, Mr. Copas. Tell me everything you remember."

"Well!" said Copas, shrugging. "I said to myself, he is anxious to go on reading in his precious big book. He had taken it to show to Mr. Godwin, who is also interested in cookery, you see. It was only the day before he had taken it from the library, and when he came home from visiting Mr. Godwin, he read it for a long time. He had been waiting to take it from the library, he had, what is it, a reservation for it. He told me all about it that evening."

239

"It was a book he was anxious to read. Why didn't he buy a copy?"

Copas smiled. "He told me he would not do that until he had seen it and knew it was worth the cost. It is very expensive. And no wonder, it is a big, big book, very heavy. It is"—he groped for the word—"an encyclopedia of cookery. It has in it all the recipes for food known to man, and a queer name, a French name, I think."

"Yes, well, never mind the book. **Mr. Winthrop** sat here reading, and you cooked his dinner. Was he hungry that night?"

Copas looked at him strangely. "What is all this about? How did you know to ask this? No, sir, he was not, he ate hardly any of the dinner. I think he was not feeling well."

"He isn't looking well now, is he? I saw him recently. He looks as if he's been ill."

"He has—changed, yes, sir. He is not well, I think, but he does not go to the doctor. It is this murder, his sister, and all the trouble over it in the newspapers."

"Perhaps so. He sat here all evening, reading this book?"

Again Copas hesitated. "I was in and out several times. He had his coffee in here, you see. And I came for his cup. Then, later on, to ask if he would take hot milk before he went to bed, as he sometimes does. Once when I came he was reading, but the other times he was just sitting there looking at the hearth. You comprehend, as one might stare into a fire, but there was no fire—it was too warm. He was—what is the word?—abstracted. And I remember, too, I thought he had perhaps spilled some coffee on his book, for he was wiping it with his handkerchief."

"Oh?" said Mendoza gently. "A page of the book?"

"No, sir, the outside of it, the edge—and yet he was also wiping it the last time I came, so it could not——"

"You don't tell me," said Mendoza even more gently. Copas was looking more and more puzzled and fearful.

"That is really all, sir. He went to bed, and I went to bed. The rooms are together, I would have heard if he had got up. And he was up very early the next morning, before I was. I heard him, so I——"

"Perhaps," said Mendoza meditatively, "he had trouble sleeping that night. You're an excellent witness, Mr. Copas. Now, will you search your memory further and try to remember the name of that book?"

Copas opened his mouth and shut it again. "Yes, sir, but—there is that man in jail who did the murder, why——"

"Once in a while," said Mendoza, "even with a force as good as this one, the first man who goes to jail isn't the fellow who belongs there." And he thought to himself, private radar be damned! If he was the psychic a few of the boys seemed to think, he'd have come here six weeks back. But Copas had looked so unimportant!

And what about the rest of it? He'd thought he had that figured out, until Killeen had handed him a little surprise.

Still, if the rest of this hunch worked out . . .

CHAPTER NINETEEN

HE WENT back to the office and asked Sergeant Lake to send somebody to haul in Matthew Carnahy for questioning. As it turned out, Carnahy was absent from both apartment and office and didn't show up again until Monday.

He called Andrews and asked whether they had any plans for action. "Plans, yes, but we're not speed demons, Luis. We'll send somebody out on Lauderdale this evening, probably. Let us know where he is, hah?"

"As soon as his present tail calls in. And then," said Mendoza in satisfaction, "you can take him over. But listen, Perce. As a special favor to me, no matter what you get on him, don't charge him right away. If the luck's with me, we're going to break this thing by Tuesday. I think we'll be having a little showdown in my office. He'll be there and you can have a warrant ready to pick him up then. O.K.?"

"You sound pretty sure we'll get certain evidence."

"Oh, I think you will. Yes. I think you might make that warrants, plural. Motive's such a funny thing. . . . And I don't want them alerted, but if you can possibly manage it, I'd like that apartment searched. When they're out of it, naturally. Early morning would be the best time. What I'm after specifically is a diamond ring. . . . Of course she's probably got it hidden at home, but have a look anyway."

"I'm just as short of men as you are," said Andrews. "Why should I work overtime on your business?"

"I'll give you one good reason, if you're feeling egotistic. You'll get your name in all the papers. This is going to make some very big headlines, *amigo*. Lauderdale is Linda Barron's boy friend. Of the Ingram case."

"For God's sake, you don't say. Another little unpleasant surprise for the family."

"Oh, the headlines'll be bigger than that—I think," said Mendoza. "Go and look, but hands off until I give you the word. These things get so tricky at the last minute, and there's all sorts of little odds and ends I have to fit together. At the moment, a lot depends on the Public Library."

Andrews said he hadn't the time to listen to him making like a book detective with cryptic hints, and hung up. And Mendoza did a little cursing because the next day was Sunday; and—very late—went home. There wasn't much he could do until Monday morning except think about it, and get all the details in their proper places.

Because the Public Libraries were all closed on Sundays.

Andrews got him out of bed at an indecent hour on Sunday. He was almost incoherent with shock and incredulity. "Listen, my God, did you suspect—— I mean, I couldn't believe—but I saw some press cuts of her at the inquest, and I—— My God, what a field day the press is going to have!"

"You got some nice evidence?" asked Mendoza. "*Muy bien.* It's always gratifying to see a hunch work out. I suppose you sent one of your handsome, innocent-looking young men to strike up acquaintance with Lauderdale in a bar and give with some broad hints. And?"

"My *God,*" said Andrews. "I mean, I know what I was just saying to you the other day, a new type, but—— He's contacting for three of 'em, Luis. Believe it or not. We haven't seen the apartment yet, but it's one of those old ones—been kept up—that has a dining room and two bedrooms. I'd guess they'll have the dining room fixed up as—— My God. Yes. Yes, sure. I had four-five men on it. Our contact boy made some excuse for not going up right then, but Lauderdale gave him the address. Said you had to make an appointment. Usual line of talk—high-class girls, guaranteed clean, all the works. The price is fifty bucks. Lauderdale talked to a couple of other guys, and made a phone call. We tailed them all, and two of them went there. We watched the place because you said it'd probably be strictly a business office, and sure enough they came out. About 1:30 A.M. Three of them. One by one. *Three.* I ask you. And the first one—— My God. Are you right about publicity! And look, Luis, I can't drag my heels on this very long, you know——"

"I hope you won't have to," said Mendoza. "I'll let you know as soon as I know myself."

"My God," said Andrews again.

244

The Public Library branch Winthrop would use was about a mile from his apartment. Mendoza was waiting on the doorstep at nine o'clock Monday morning, when the doors were opened. He went in and looked around. At a desk against the right-hand wall, surrounded by telephones, a typewriter, innumerable little file boxes and scattered brochures, sat a fat gray-haired woman in a magenta dress and pink plastic glasses. On the desk was a sign: *Readers' Assistant.*

Mendoza went over to her. "Could you help me, I wonder, to locate a book? I don't know the title"—Copas could not remember it—"but it's a very large book about gourmet cooking, and the title is in a foreign language."

"Well, now, let me *see,*" said the Readers' Assistant briskly, shoving her glasses back in place. "I don't know——"

"It was checked out by Mr. Lawrence Winthrop on December thirty-first," said Mendoza.

"Oh, Mr. Winthrop, yes. He recommended it to you? Would you recognize the title, sir? We can look in the files——"

"Well, I don't think so. Of course you can check all your books on the subject, and see from your files which he'd taken out."

She frowned at him. "I'm afraid we couldn't undertake—perhaps the best thing would be for you to have Mr. Winthrop write out the title for you."

"If you'd just try to identify it, please. I'm told it's an extremely large, heavy book and it's supposed to contain every recipe known to chefs—an encyclopedia of cookery." He gave her a persuasive smile. Another woman had come up behind the desk and was rummaging in a drawer.

"I can hardly identify one book out of thousands just by a physical description," said the Readers' Assistant tartly. "And the fact that Mr. Winthrop once checked it out. I think you had better——"

The other woman looked up. "I—excuse me, Miss English—but I think I know the book you mean, sir. I beg your pardon, I couldn't help hearing." She was a tall, stooped, dowdy young woman with a good deal of untidy drab blonde hair. "I *rather* think it must be that Larousse encyclopedia, *Gastronomique*. I know Mr. Winthrop had a reservation in for it, he asked about it several times when I was on the desk."

"Would you please check and see? And I'd like to see the book if it's in." He nearly crossed his fingers.

"Oh, certainly," said the Readers' Assistant, and bustled away through an archway bearing the sign *Non-Fiction*. Mendoza waited.

Ten minutes later she came back, carrying a book in both hands. "Is this what you wanted?"

"I don't know," said Mendoza, looking at it. "But will you please check in your records to see whether this is the book Mr. Winthrop took out on December thirty-first?"

"Really, sir, I'm afraid we can't go to all that trouble —the records are all on microfilm, and——"

"I'm afraid I'll have to ask you to," said Mendoza, and produced his credentials. "This is official police business, Miss English."

She stared at him, uttered an unladylike squawk, and began to ask questions. "I'm sorry," said Mendoza, "I can't say any more now. But I must ask you to check your records. Will you please go and get that started?"

Dumbly, she went. He considered the book. Outside of Webster's Unabridged Dictionary, it was about the largest book he had ever seen. About eight by ten over all, it was a good three inches thick; he picked it up, and found it was a little effort to do so with one hand. It must weigh twelve or fifteen pounds. The jacket bore a colorful photograph of the ingredients for a salad, a copper pan, a kitchen knife, and the legend: *The World Authority—Larousse Gastronomique,* and in smaller print below the picture, *The first American edition of the Encyclopedia of Food, Wine and Cookery—8500 Recipes—1000 Illustrations.* He opened it. It had been published by Crown Publishers, Inc., in 1961, and was priced at twenty dollars.

Miss English came back and stared at him again. "Really, I don't understand—are you really——"

"Tell me, how many copies of this book has the library got? This branch, that is."

"I can check. I shouldn't think more than one, our allotment isn't very large and this is an expensive book——" She trotted off to *Non-Fiction* again and came back presently to tell him that this was their only copy.

"How nice," said Mendoza, and picked it up to examine it minutely. As per library custom, a second jacket of clear white plastic had been glued over the paper jacket, for extra protection. He peered closely at all four sides, and presently ejaculated under his breath, *"¡Ca! ¿Qué se yo?* I wonder . . . There's a little stain here, on the bottom edge, can you see it? On the cover under the jacket too. Quite enough," he added to himself. The lab boys had done miracles with much less.

"Oh, people are so *terribly* careless," said Miss English. "You wouldn't believe—— They *will* eat while they read, and——"

"I think," said Mendoza, "or rather I hope, that everybody's going to be much surprised at what this stain turns out to be. Miss English, I'll have to requisition this book from you, for laboratory examination. I think it's a very important—mmh—silent witness in a murder case."

Miss English stared at him, mouth open, and uttered another squawk.

He delivered the *Gastronomique* to the lab, with an urgent plea that it should receive instant attention. He went down to his office and found Hackett chatting with Sergeant Lake.

"Have a nice trip north?" he asked.

"I understand you haven't been caught up with yet and slapped on the wrist by I.A." Hackett followed him into his office. "Not bad. Kind of an interesting fellow. He's a specialist on folk songs, it's his hobby. I heard quite a lecture on it on the way down. He's a good talker. Pity he succumbed to impulse and shot his wife."

"Folk songs," said Mendoza, and suddenly laughed. "I wonder, did he happen to know one I heard the other day?" He quoted the words Mr. Killeen had dredged up from nostalgic memory. Hackett leaned back and shut his eyes, smoking lazily.

"No, he didn't mention that one. But funnily enough

I know it. My mother's Irish, you know, and that's an old Irish song. The tune's very damned—melancholy. Funny, considering some of the popular notions about the Irish, but some of their music—there's no sadder music anywhere. I've heard her sing that. It goes on— now wait a minute——

> 'Oh, all the comrades that e'er I had,
> They're sorry for my goin' away—
> And all the sweethearts that e'er I had,
> They'd wish me one more day to stay.
> But since it falls unto my lot
> That I should rise and you should not,
> I'll gently rise and softly call
> Good night, and joy be with you all.' "

There was a little silence, and then Mendoza said, "Yes, very appropriate. They're usually such nice fellows. Aside from the one little unfortunate habit. It's too bad that——"

"You're looking pleased with yourself," said Hackett. "Don't tell me you've really got something, on this Ingram thing."

"Have I got something!" said Mendoza. "Have I! We're going to hit the headlines again, that I can promise you, Arturo. Wait until you hear. And isn't Holmes going to be chewing the carpet! But he can't shout me down now, not when there's nice solid evidence. I hope."

"¿De veras, compadre?" asked Hackett incredulously. "What, for God's sake?"

"De veras, absolutamente." Mendoza was looking pleased with himself. "I was afraid for a while, you know, that Ingram *had* had a little something to do with it. I should have trusted my judgment of the type. As it is, I think I've got quite enough to clear both him and Killeen of any charge but idiocy, and that's scarcely illegal. If it was, we'd have half the population locked up. . . . Yes, give the two old cronies a peaceful old age. . . . It's like this——"

The lab came through with the report on the book late that afternoon, and it was the report that Mendoza had hoped for. He was smiling at it, and arranging all the details again in his mind, when Holmes blew in like a typhoon and demanded, "What the *hell* are you up to, asking for a search warrant on the Barron apartment? If you've been wasting time and the force's money on—— Listen, my friend, there'll come a time you'll go too far! Just because——"

"I was just coming to see you," said Mendoza happily. "I said Ingram wasn't guilty, and now I've got some concrete facts to show he isn't—and that somebody else is, naturally. You'll have to look at them, Holmes —and so will the D.A.'s office."

Holmes stared at him, suddenly deflated. "You mean you've got real solid evidence? I don't believe it!"

"I think you will. And you know, I also think we'd better have somebody from the D.A.'s office listening in when I tell you about it, and give you my ideas on how to wind it up satisfactorily. I always said it was a complicated business, you know, and it is, damn complicated."

"Well, for God's sake!" said Holmes blankly. And

then he said, "You'd better come into my office and bring whatever you've got." He turned on his heel. "I'll phone the D.A."

Nothing brings such panic to the heart of a district attorney as the hint that proof is available of wrongful arrest; after all, he has to think of election year. And on Ingram—a case that had had such wide press coverage! DeVries was dispatched to Headquarters within thirty seconds of Holmes's call, and arrived within fifteen minutes looking pale.

"Now what the hell is this all about?" growled Holmes.

Mendoza told them, in precise detail. He took them through all the intricacies—he mentioned Andrews' evidence, at which DeVries turned even paler and shut his eyes (probably visualizing the headlines), and Holmes came out with several incredulous obscenities. He introduced Mr. Killeen into the plot; he mentioned the Public Library; and the link between Reilly and Lauderdale, and between Reilly and the fence Honeywell. He described what Kay Webster had seen, what Copas had said about Winthrop's demeanor, and what had happened to the small scruffy Mr. Carnahy. He told them about *Gastronomique,* on the bottom edge of which was a stain of human blood, type O, and showed that it was indisputably the same *Gastronomique* which had been in Winthrop's possession the day of the murder.

"But he's got an alibi!"

Mendoza explained that.

"There's no *proof,*" said Holmes. "I don't see——"

"D'you mean that idiot of a maid was lying about the car after all? Well, we always thought—— But, my God, why would anybody go to the trouble——"

Mendoza explained that too.

He also made suggestions. "Always playing to the grandstand!" muttered Holmes; but it was an automatic retort. He looked at DeVries.

"It is certainly impossible to—er—ignore all this," said the D.A.'s man. "Really, I can't help but feel that more thorough investigation at the *time*—— I realize that Ingram's guilt seemed obvious, but—— Well, really, I do feel, Captain, that the Lieutenant's suggestion might—er—clear up the matter most economically, one way or the other. If, as he says, the man is taken by surprise, and the—ah—others also, of course, some useful admissions may come out. I must speak with my superiors, of course——"

In the end, they agreed to do what Mendoza wanted. He was late home; and after dinner, not trusting to a phone call which would go through a switchboard, he drove down to Gardena, found Mr. Killeen, and had a long earnest conversation with him. Because there was really no point in introducing all the pro-gambler background; little white lies . . .

When he got back Alison demanded full details. "You are maddening, just saying you've cleared up the Ingram case and then going into a long silence."

"I was thinking. It's so complicated, and I've got to remember every little detail, you see. . . . But I expect by the time the press gets through trying to explain the plot everybody'll be so confused that a couple of discrepancies won't matter—because why should poor Sylvia get lectured to by a judge about that rug? And why does the D.A. need to know that Ingram and Killeen are sharps? No evidence to hold them on, on that. There'll be enough dirty linen flaunted around as it is, on this one."

The crowd he faced at ten o'clock on Tuesday morning was so numerous that they were accommodated in the sergeants' room instead of his office.

Holmes and the D.A.'s man were there, Hackett and Palliser, and Sergeant Lake and a policewoman. Killeen huddled in his chair, looking uneasy and hopeful by turns. Matthew Carnahy had been brought in; and Linda and Janet Barron, protesting loudly, had been persuaded to come. Winthrop sat alone, looking gray and very old; he had not protested the summons or asked any questions; he seemed sunk in a bad dream, muttering to himself. But he had looked up when a uniformed man escorted Carnahy in and, startling everyone in the room, uttered a single loud obscenity. His sister spoke to him, ostentatiously ignoring the police officers present, inviting him to join her contempt for police stupidity, but he did not answer her. Lauderdale was also there, seeming to swagger even as he sat; and Hugh Barron.

Mendoza was sitting at Hackett's desk, and centered on the blotter before him was *Gastronomique*. He looked around at them, smiling, and said briskly, "I've asked you all to come here this morning to hear the true story of how Mrs. Ingram died. I told you that we weren't satisfied and were going on with the investigation. Well, we now have a great deal more evidence, and Mr. Ingram will shortly be released from jail." Janet Barron broke out into loud incoherent protest, and was tactfully quieted by the policewoman. "He's not guilty, you know, and three of you in this room have known that ever since the murder. Three of you helped to build the frame on Ingram, but oddly enough not in conspiracy. Of course"—he looked around at them again, one by one—"we want two of those three people on another charge, and we may as well clear up that matter now." He nodded at Palliser, who was nearest the door. Palliser opened it and Andrews came in. He walked over to Linda Barron and Lauderdale, who were sitting together, and read out the charge in an impersonal tone: conspiring for purposes of prostitution, soliciting; and on Lauderdale's part, procuring. Both looked at him with blank, stupefied expressions; they had, of course, no idea that they'd been dropped on. Janet Barron shut her eyes and began to scream at the top of her voice; the policewoman hastened to her.

And Winthrop, raising his ravaged face from his hands, snarled and sprang at Carnahy. "You little—— You said you wouldn't tell, you swine! You took my money and——"

Hackett and Palliser separated them; Winthrop struggled in Hackett's grasp and then went limp. "Oh, what's the use? What's the use now? It's out, everyone knows." He sank into his chair again and buried his face in his hands.

"No, it's a lie," Lauderdale got out at last. "I don't know what you're talking about!"

"You're the one got me into this!" shrieked Linda.

"You said it was easy, nobody'd ever find out!" She went for him like a cat and raked his face bloodily before Sergeant Lake pulled her off.

With an amiable smile, Mendoza surveyed the sudden havoc he'd created.

Janet Barron was in screaming hysterics now. "I'm sorry, sir, I can't control her," panted the policewoman.

"You'd better get her out." Holmes had to raise his voice over her screams. Palliser and Sergeant Lake half carried her out to be dealt with elsewhere.

"We don't really need Mrs. Barron anyway," Mendoza went on. "Miss Barron, it'll do you no good to make a scene. We have the evidence and the whole story is coming out." Killeen had shut his eyes mutely; Carnahy tried to squeeze farther back in his chair. "We know now that it was Mr. Winthrop who killed Mrs. Ingram. Wasn't it, Mr. Winthrop? We've found the blood on the book, you know."

After a long moment Winthrop raised his head. "Oh yes," he said in a dull voice; he did not sound surprised, or shocked. "Yes, I did. I didn't mean to, but I did. It doesn't seem to matter any more."

CHAPTER TWENTY

THERE was less sensation than might have been expected; Linda and Lauderdale were too busy thinking of themselves. Hugh Barron let out a soft, incredulous expletive.

"But that was only the start," said Mendoza. "This whole story began when, for some reason, Mrs. Ingram became actively suspicious of Miss Barron's—mmh—social life. Frankly, I don't know why she did. Possibly she just got tired of being told how old-fashioned her ideas were, and decided to find out for herself. At any rate, she went to Mr. Carnahy here, who is a private detective——"

"No," said Carnahy unconvincingly, "I never——"

Mendoza ignored him. "Now I don't think Linda Barron and Lauderdale have been at this racket very long. Lauderdale would only quit his regular job when he found this business was far more lucrative. There are two other girls, Evelyn Smith and Marilyn Cass, shall we say, working at that apartment too—friends of yours, Miss Barron?"

"You go to hell," she said furiously.

"Mr. Carnahy was sniffing around before the murder, of course, and even if he isn't much of a detective, he didn't have to sniff far before he found out what was going on. He had, I think, made a report to Mrs. Ingram to the effect that he was pretty sure of his findings before it occurred to him that it might be more profitable to sell his silence to Miss Barron. He could always tell Mrs. Ingram he'd been wrong."

"No, I never——" said Carnahy.

"Another reason why I think you're new at the game is that at first you didn't see any way out but to pay him his hush money. But at the same time neither of you much liked handing over a substantial piece of change to Carnahy. We know how much it was, by the way—a thousand bucks. He paid it into his bank the Monday before Mrs. Ingram was killed." Carnahy licked his lips and said nothing; Linda glared and Lauderdale looked sullen.

"It was Miss Barron who had the inspiration of getting in before Carnahy, with Aunt Bella. Of claiming that Carnahy was a crook, trying to blackmail them both, in a sense. She knew that Bella would be very reluctant to believe the truth Carnahy had told, and she thought she could tell a nice story to convince her aunt that Carnahy had come to her first, threatened to tell her aunt this dreadful lie if she didn't pay him. And she refused, thinking he'd never dare tell such an obvious lie—what, a nice girl like Linda, mixed up in such a thing? But when, by Aunt Bella's outright use of the word 'prostitute' that New Year's Eve, it dawned on Linda that he *had,* she was horrified. And took the

257

first opportunity to see her aunt in private and explain. She'd have made a good story of it, too—how that apartment belonged to a friend of hers, she'd gone there all innocent a few times to see this other nice girl —and so forth and so on.

"She went to see her aunt at about the time she could figure Bella would be getting home from her bridge party. But she got there before Bella did, and found the house empty. Then Lauderdale arrived. I had," said Mendoza gently, "a nice little chat with Evelyn Smith yesterday. Linda had told her what she intended to do, and Evelyn passed it on to Lauderdale, who thought Linda'd be wasting her time, that she'd just make matters worse by discussing it at all with her aunt. He hurried after her to persuade her just to let the thing lie, if Aunt Bella accused her outright just deny it haughtily and let it go.

"Any attempted defense might've just fixed the idea in Mrs. Ingram's mind more firmly, protesting too much, et cetera. At any rate, whether or not he talked Linda round, he got another little idea while they sat in front of the house arguing. The house was empty— and the family knew all about that jewelry of Bella's. If they could get in quick, now, and stage a fake burglary, it'd be easy money. I think that Linda was against it—though she was as eager as Lauderdale to get back the money they'd paid Carnahy—but he prevailed on her to take the chance. So in they went —Linda terrified that her aunt would walk in any minute—probably got in the bedroom window, I noticed the screen is loose. . . .

"And, of course, Mr. Lauderdale, who has some curious friends, knew Mr. Matthew Reilly, who knew a handy fence. Very convenient, wasn't it, Mr. Lauderdale?"

"You're telling the story," said Lauderdale sullenly.

"Anyway, late as it was, they took the chance. Unfortunately, before they could complete the job by pulling out drawers and so on to make it look like an ordinary burglary, Mrs. Ingram returned home. Just as Linda had feared. There they were, caught in the house. If she noticed the cars she took them for those of someone calling on a neighbor—Linda didn't often come there, Bella wouldn't have recognized her car—or Mr. Lauderdale's. Considering the plan of the house, I think——"

"Damn lie—we never——" Lauderdale blustered automatically.

"Bruce, shut *up!*" said Linda.

"—think you retreated quietly to the kitchen, hoping to get out by the rear door. But before you managed it the doorbell rang. Meanwhile, Bella, all unsuspecting, had changed her clothes and removed her jewelry. She was just about to put it away tidily when the bell rang. The two of you stayed in the kitchen, not daring to move. To get to your cars you'd have had to go around to the front of the house, past windows where you might be seen. You had to stay where you were, and hope that the situation wouldn't, as the saying goes, deteriorate.

"We now come to Mr. Winthrop." Mendoza looked at him. "Mr. Ingram told me that his wife had a literal mind. Mr. Winthrop knew that too, and he'd been greatly upset the evening before when Mrs. Ingram threw that accusation of 'prostitute.' He has always been very fond of his niece, had in fact set her on a pedestal and overlooked all her shortcomings. Hadn't he, Miss Barron?" He smiled at her. "Mr. Winthrop had been visiting a friend, as we know, that afternoon, and he'd taken this book along to show him. They share an interest in gourmet cookery. But he'd been feeling, I think, more and more uneasy about that scene on Monday night. At any rate, he stopped at Sycamore Terrace on his way home, for a private talk with Mrs. Ingram. And he carried this book in with him because it was easier than locking up the car. The book was not his property, and it's worth a little money. I think Mr. Winthrop is careful about things like that—he hasn't always had a lot of money."

"Yes," said Winthrop in a dull, expressionless voice. "Yes, that's right." He looked up again. "I didn't mean to—— I—but she said such things about—— She said *he*"—he nodded at Carnahy—"had told her—proof— I didn't believe it, how could I believe a hellish thing like that? I lost my temper—it was all so incredible, I thought she was mad—and before I knew what I was doing I threw that—it would have been whatever was in my hand—I—I was dumfounded when it hit her and she fell. I couldn't move. Then I—then I——"

"You saw she was dead. This very heavy weapon— and it may be an unusual weapon but what an effective one!—had struck her on the temple, where the bone was thin. Otherwise, it might have knocked her down, bruised her severely, but scarcely killed her. But there she was, dead. You simply walked out, leaving her there, and drove home?"

"No," said Winthrop. "Did I?" He looked vague. "I seem to recall I had some idea—I wanted to make it look as if Ingram—but of course it *would* look that way —— Yes."

"Never mind that for the moment. We know all about it." Winthrop looked very ill; the policewoman, who had come back, moved to his side. "You wiped the blood off the book, but you weren't sure you'd got it all off, you kept working at it. Your servant noticed you. And you weren't—understandably—very hungry for dinner. Is that the way it all was?"

"Yes. Yes," said Winthrop. He felt his heart. "I'm not feeling well. I *couldn't* believe—I thought she was mad! I thought it would be—all right, everyone would think Ingram had done it. I never liked Ingram. But then—her body disappeared—I never understood that. He must have—— So I thought if the police——"

"So we come to the disappearance," said Mendoza, putting out his cigarette. "Let's go back to Lauderdale and Miss Barron, all keyed up, in the kitchen with their loot. The kitchen is a little distance from the living room, and they couldn't hear all that was said but they probably heard enough to know that Winthrop and Mrs. Ingram were quarreling. They may even have heard the thud of her body falling. Then they heard the front door close, and silence. They crept out cautiously to see how the land lay, and discovered Mrs. Ingram's body——"

"No!" shouted Lauderdale. "No, it's a damn lie! We never——"

"And, not unnaturally, they both panicked. They hadn't bargained on being mixed up in a murder.

They gathered up the loot from the jewelry box and made tracks out of there.

"But Linda is a very smart girl," said Mendoza, smiling at her. "What I admire about the whole complex little plan is the way she grasped the dangers of the situation. She knew who had killed her aunt. She could guess why. But that mustn't come out, of course. The obvious suspect is always the husband, and if she and Lauderdale kept quiet about what they knew, the police would look hard at Ingram first of all. On the face of it, as the circumstances were then, he was very obvious. But after she'd thought about it some more, she saw that just possibly that wasn't enough. Because whoever found the body, it was bound to be found soon, and so the police would know within pretty narrow limits what time she died. And suppose, said Linda to Lauderdale, Ingram had an alibi? As indeed he had."

"An *alibi?*" said Hugh Barron. He hadn't, after a first shaken moment, let himself show emotion at the charge on his sister; after one astonished look, he had put his armor of sophistication back in place. "Then why the hell didn't he——"

"All in good time. Linda saw at once that it was likely he would have—he was out somewhere in public, and could probably produce witnesses to say where and when. And it wasn't just affection for her uncle, or desire to keep the scandal out of the family, that she wanted to cover Winthrop and shove the murder onto Ingram, after all—she had a very personal reason, too. If Ingram was in the clear, the police would go looking at everybody else, and when a detective as—mmh—inadequate as Carnahy could ferret out her extracurricular activities—well, you see what I mean. And then too, if Ingram was accused and convicted, that will of Mrs. Ingram's wouldn't hold and the family would get what they felt were their just dues."

Mendoza lit a new cigarette, smiling at her over the lighter flame. "A very smart girl indeed, you are. . . . Sometime between nine and ten you two went back to Sycamore Terrace. Very cautiously, to see whether there were any cops around as yet. What you found out was very encouraging, and set your brain working some more. You saw Ingram leaving. And when you managed to get a look through the front window and saw that the body had been moved——"

"What?" blustered Lauderdale. "If somebody else moved the body—— Look, damn it, we never——"

"I'm telling it from your viewpoint. Or rather Linda's—she did all the brainwork. I think Linda must read detective novels," said Mendoza amusedly. "She had an inspiration then. It looked as if Ingram had panicked too, on finding the body, wasn't going to call the cops. If the time of death could be confused, no matter what alibi he had he might still be framed. When he hadn't called the police, he'd be lying to them later on, and that was a heaven-sent piece of luck for you in building a frame on him. You didn't know where he was going, but you seized the chance to build the frame—and the first thing to do was to get the body away, stage the obviously faked accident. It *was* a double bluff, in a way—because you knew the police would find out it *was* a fake accident. The only reason you set it up like that was to delay the finding of the body until the time of death couldn't be pinned down too close. Lauderdale was the brawn, of course. And what a chance you took, with the maid in the house! In the other wing, of course, but you had the devil's own luck. You got in—the bedroom window again?—and found the body where Ingram, true enough, in panic had hidden it temporarily. . . . No need to go into his movements, we've got statements about that now. You noticed that her denture had fallen out, and you put it in the ashes for later discovery—something else to damn Ingram. You put her glasses on the dressing table, half hidden by her hat, to suggest that Ingram had overlooked them. You noticed the stain on the rug, and knew that the maid would notice, and speak up, if the rug disappeared. You expected, of course, that Ingram would simply say he had no idea what had happened, how or why his wife had vanished. And you didn't intend her to disappear for so long. You wanted the body found, say within two or three days.

"It was a clever enough plan. Lauderdale got the body into the trunk of Mrs. Ingram's Cadillac—quite a little job, rigor had set in by then—rolling the car out down the drive by hand first, not to wake the maid. And drove up the Angeles Crest road to stage the accident. With Linda trailing in his own car. You must have been on tenterhooks when the body wasn't discovered for so long. . . . And sometime next day you met Reilly—we haven't picked him up yet, but there's a call out—to hand over the jewelry. We know he was in touch with Honeywell, and it may be we can get him to tell us all about it. But you kept one of the rings, didn't you, Miss Barron? You couldn't resist it. We found it early this morning when we went over the Beverly Boulevard apartment. Of course you had to be careful when and where you wore it, but . . . So that rather proves out what I've been saying, doesn't it?"

"You ————!" she screamed at him.

"You said afterward you'd been at the Cha-Cha Club. That was clever too, because on a holiday night it'd be crowded, who'd remember if you'd been there or not? It's negative evidence, but no waiter or anybody there does remember you.

"Well, that explains most of it, doesn't it? You weren't involved in the original murder at all—I said from the start this was a complex case. Later on, of course, Carnahy tried to put the bite on you again, threatening to inform the police this time, but by then Lauderdale had got a little smarter and hired a couple of thugs to beat him up."

"Listen, this is all a goddamn lie—you can't prove——"

"I rather thought I had proved it, Mr. Lauderdale," said Mendoza in a bored voice. "The rest of what I have to say is just conjecture." He looked at Winthrop, not without pity. "Since New Year's Day Mr. Winthrop has tried to convince himself that the terrible accusation against Linda couldn't be true. He tried very hard to put off the murder on Ingram—he hated Ingram and Ingram was the obvious suspect. But all the while, every hour since the murder, the poison was eating away at his mind. *Could* it be true? And finally—I don't know exactly when, but I think it was only a week or so ago—he found that for his own peace of mind he had to see this detective Mrs. Ingram had

265

talked about. She had told him Carnahy's name, and——"

Winthrop said, entirely without emphasis, "He told me. He told me all about it—the proof—everything. That she was—— He said he'd have gone to the police——"

"I would have, sure, I was going to——" Carnahy chattered nervously.

"But after he was beaten up he was afraid. But he said now he had made up his mind to—unless I would pay him——"

"The old guy's nuts!" yelled Carnahy in panic. "I never did—I——"

"I gave him five hundred dollars—not to tell." Winthrop turned his head, slowly and painfully, and looked at Linda and Lauderdale. "So it was you—did all that. Not to protect me. No, I know that. . . . For the money. To get the money. . . . To protect yourselves. I wondered. I wondered about it. It was very odd. Sometimes, you know, I thought I must have imagined the whole thing. It was like walking in a dream. But she was gone."

"For God's sake," said Lauderdale, "Linda, for God's sake tell them——"

Her face was like a cold white mask; she said, "They've found out, that's all. No use trying to get out of it now."

"But you said Ingram had an *alibi*," said Barron in a high, wild voice. He kept darting quick glances at his sister as if seeing her for the first time. "An alibi—why didn't——"

"Mr. Killeen here," said Mendoza benevolently,

"was actually with Mr. Ingram from about four o'clock to eight-thirty the evening of the murder. It was understandable that he shouldn't want to get involved——"

"Damn it, you should have come in and you damn well know it!" said Holmes, frowning at Killeen. "In a murder case! All right, so Ingram was just a chance acquaintance and you were afraid to get involved! That's the hell of a reason to——"

"I have been very upset about the whole thing, gentlemen," said Killeen humbly. "I—I know I'd have forced myself to come forward before the trial. My conscience has bothered me dreadfully. Of course the alibi was why Mr. Ingram came to see me that night, after he'd found the body. But I——"

"It seems," continued Mendoza, "that Mr. Killeen and Mr. Ingram both like to play cards occasionally, and they'd met down in Gardena, at a poker palace. After a pleasant little session, they had dinner together. And of course when Mr. Ingram found his wife murdered, and realized that suspicion would be resting on him, he called on Mr. Killeen to back him up, but——"

"It was very weak of me, I know. But I told him I couldn't get involved, I—I moved to another place so he couldn't find—— But I *have* come in to tell you now," said Killeen with dignity, "if a little late. I—I always knew I'd have to."

Mendoza stood up. "So we know all about it now," he said. "Mr. DeVries, I hope you'll set the legal machinery in motion to get Mr. Ingram out of jail."

Winthrop said nothing when Sergeant Lake urged him to his feet; he moved as if in a bad dream. A couple of Andrews' men ushered Linda and Lauderdale out; she slouched toward the door defiantly, head high; he was still calling them all damned liars. Hugh Barron, after a last incredulous look at Mendoza and Killeen, hurried out after his sister, calling her name.

"We'll have your statement for you to sign in a moment, Mr. Killeen," said Mendoza. "If you'd like to wait in the anteroom?" Killeen went out in silence.

Holmes stood and stared past Mendoza at the wall, massaging his jaw and frowning. "It's the hell of a funny business all round," he said, "and I still don't understand some of it. I can see Ingram—in a *way*—after finding out that Killeen wouldn't back him up, making up some story. But why the hell didn't he tell us about Killeen? You say he thought we'd just say it was a lie, and either wouldn't look for Killeen or, if we did, we wouldn't find him."

"Well, you know," said Mendoza, "a lot of people don't realize just how efficient we are. It all looked so hopeless to him—everything against him—which was why he ran in the end, of course."

"Y-e-s," said Holmes reluctantly. "Like you say, it's human—— People do act like damn fools, don't we know. . . . You say he told the story on the spur of the moment, sort of, because he was a little ashamed of having been in a gambling dive, and then later on he was afraid it'd just look worse if he changed his story, when he knew Killeen wouldn't back him up. Which it would have, especially if we couldn't find Killeen. I'm bound to say that's reasonable, though I still think——"

"That's my reading of it," agreed Mendoza. "After

all, he had some reason to panic—finding a frame set up on him, as we know now from his new statement."

"And the maid was just mistaken, sure. And as to who actually fooled around with that throw rug— Well, of course it did help to incriminate Ingram—and they all make mistakes somewhere, even the smart ones. I never realized that the fake accident had to be staged to confuse the time of death, but when you think it out, it's obvious, sure. Well——" Holmes looked at his Lieutenant. "More publicity for our glamour boy over this! The press'll go to town on it. But I've got to admit it—you were right and I was wrong. I guess you've got it tied up now, and with a confession and all——"

Hackett and Palliser were waiting to catch Mendoza as he strolled out of his office half an hour later, having seen the final paper work on the case started. They fell into step beside him, turning toward the elevator.

"I thought I deserved an early lunch," said Mendoza, "after being up at the crack of dawn to look at that apartment with the Vice boys. Am I going to have company? How nice."

They were looking at him curiously, Hackett a little amused, Palliser a little troubled. They all got into the elevator; it was empty.

"I heard about Killeen from Palliser, you know," said Hackett.

"So you would," said Mendoza. "Anybody else hear about him, John?" Palliser shook his head. "Just as well." The elevator landed and they stepped out into the lobby. "So my faithful cohorts think I've been suppressing a little truth?"

"Why didn't the maid see the body?" asked Hackett. "Unless it was Ingram who started to cover up?"

"Started is right," said Mendoza. "That'll all have to come out at the trial, of course, we've got a full statement from him now, but it doesn't amount to much legally. . . . Come along, I'll buy you lunch—not at Federico's for a change—we'll have a leisurely drink and I'll tell you all about it." In silence they went out to the lot and got into the Ferrari. Mendoza took them up the freeway to Hollywood, to the very quiet and conservative restaurant called the Madison House. They were early; the waiter gave them an isolated table.

"Something to drink before lunch, gentlemen?"

"I think," said Mendoza, "I'll change my habits for once—one shouldn't get hidebound, and it's a warm day. Say three very cold, very dry martinis. O.K.?" He lit a cigarette and lazily watched the smoke rise. "No," he added, "neither Ingram nor Killeen have the guts for a major effort like that staged accident. Ingram just panicked when he came in and found the body, and a frame set up for him. Yes, there were two frames —I got it out of him finally, after Killeen told me the truth." He smoked in silence until the waiter came back with the drinks.

"So?" said Hackett.

"Very nice," said Mendoza, sampling the martini. "I should try these more often. . . . That precious pair of innocent sharps had had their nice little birthday outing here, and Ingram drove Killeen back to his hotel and then went home. He had—depending on how you look at it—a stroke of luck there, because he got in ten minutes or so before the maid. And he found a setup obviously framing him for murder.

"The doctor says he thinks Winthrop's had a stroke. Anyway, we can see he isn't normal. You remember what he said when I asked him whether he didn't just walk out. Maybe he's forgotten what he did do, after the murder. It was a fairly crude frame but you can see how it must have looked to Ingram. Winthrop left the body where it had fallen. He knew Ingram had been a golfer, and he found his set of clubs, and dabbled the putter in the wound and left it there beside her. Ingram described the setup to Killeen. He overturned some furniture, to make it look as if there'd been a struggle. He could hope that Ingram's prints would still be on the putter.

"Of course, Ingram was a fool. What he should have done was to call the police at once, tell his story, and produce Killeen. At that time an autopsy would have told us that she died about six o'clock, and Ingram had an alibi for that time. Killeen would have been introduced as a respectable old pal, et cetera. But that's reckoning without the temperament of these fellows. All Ingram saw was cops coming down on him, a thousand questions asked, and quite probably his whole past history and Killeen's coming out—so then they wouldn't believe Killeen, of all people, on the alibi. And it was apparently his golf club that had killed her.

"He just panicked. It's a wonder he didn't have a heart attack right then and there. He did take one of his tablets, and then it occurred to him, if he could make it look like an accident, somehow—— He knew the maid would be coming in soon, so to give himself

271

time to think he dragged the body into the bedroom where the maid never came, and hurriedly straightened up the room. He only just managed to put up a good front for the maid. He noticed the rug was gone, and made up a hasty story to account for that. And that's about all he did. As I say, all these details will come out at the trial, the D.A.'s got them now and people are making statements. Ingram will get a little lecture from the judge on destroying evidence. But it was a very human sort of thing to do, especially for somebody like Ingram.

"He was scared as hell—he couldn't plan out any way to get himself off the hook. He just realized dimly that somebody—probably one of the family—had killed her and framed him. After the maid went to her room, he made a beeline for Killeen, to tell him and see if he had any bright ideas. Killeen is a little bit smarter, even if he's the weaker character other ways, and told him he was a damn fool—he should have called us, all righteous. They'd probably been together when she was killed, and we'd be able to pinpoint the time of death within an hour or so, so Killeen could provide an alibi. But of course they're both cop-shy, and Ingram didn't want to get Killeen in trouble. They argued about it, but finally Ingram agreed to go back home, ostensibly discover the body for the first time, and try to bluff it out. He'd already told the maid that his wife had gone away for a few days—that was his first mistake, that and concealing the body. But he thought he might get away with it, by claiming she must have changed her mind or come back for something she'd forgotten.

272

"Then, of course, when he got home the body was gone. That panicked him all over again. I might add here that we know Sylvia did hear a little something when Linda and her boy friend were dealing with the body, but thought it was Ingram. I also think—I don't know, but it's a minor point—that it was Sylvia who disposed of that rug. Linda had just put it in the refuse can, in plain sight. I think Sylvia found it before Ingram, and quietly got rid of it. And then when the police first questioned her, she got nervous and, without meaning to, mentioned it, so they prodded it all out of her.

"Anyway, there was Ingram ready to discover the body and call the cops, and there wasn't any body. What the hell was going on? He didn't know what to do, what to think. He didn't dare phone Killeen—the call would go through a switchboard. Well, you can see his position. He could hardly call us then, or so he thought. It'd just look all the funnier, and all the worse for him. That would have been asking for it, and he may not be a master mind but he's not a fool. In the end, after poking around and finding his wife's overnight case gone, as well as her car, he decided to stick to the story that she'd left voluntarily. Nobody but X could disprove his story and X wouldn't dare speak up. He says he had a vague idea that X might be setting up a fake accident of some kind. He didn't, of course, know about the dentures, and he never noticed the glasses which Linda had tucked away half underneath the hat, all very crafty. He never suspected anything so complex as that double bluff. . . . That girl is a damn sight too shrewd, let's hope she gets a stiff sentence.

. . . And having told the story, he was stuck with it."

"Another drink, gentlemen?"

"Oh, I think so, thanks. . . . The first thing he did next day, after he got rid of Winthrop, was to smuggle that golf putter out and throw it into the Pacific. And to a great extent, you know, he was thinking of keeping Killeen out of it, his old pal. But when we'd found her teeth and glasses, he got scared all over again—and finally when the evidence piled up on him, he didn't see anything else to do but run. . . . Of course he was a fool, but that's about the worst you can say. He'll get a lecture—and so will Sylvia, but I don't think she'll be charged on perjury because of that lie about the cars. She'll just say she got confused, which God knows is true, and as long as he isn't guilty, she'll get the benefit of the doubt."

The new drinks came. They all sampled them thoughtfully. "Um," said Hackett. "Well, I agree there's no point in being vindictive. You can see how his mind worked. Taking into account the kind he is. And not much point in bringing that up either, no evidence."

"I was afraid for a while," said Mendoza meditatively, "that Ingram and Killeen had dealt with the body. I should have known they'd never go in for such a risky operation. Don't think they could have either. There's Ingram's weak heart, and Killeen's too fat and neither of them as young as they were."

"Yeah, and if they had faked the accident," said Hackett, "I'd take a bet you'd have found some ingenious way to cover up for them."

"Don't miscall me, Art. I'm sworn to uphold the law

of the land. Though it would have been a pity, those two rabbit-hearted gentlemanly old idiots. . . . As it is, they'll get a little lecture, that's all."

"Yes, well," said Hackett with a grin, "I still think, you twister, that the reason you're so damn pleased is simply a natural sympathy for pro gamblers. A sort of kinship for fellows in the line you might've been in, but for the grace of God."

"It's such hard work, Arturo," said Mendoza amusedly. "They deserve a peaceful old age. . . . Well, here's to crime!" And he finished his drink.

POSTSCRIPT

MENDOZA didn't see Ingram again, when he was re-leased and the press uproar started. He had a note from him, expressing warm thanks and enclosing cash—cautious cash—in repayment of the lawyer's retainer.

Other cases came along, and new press uproars re-placed that one.

The last time Mendoza saw Francis Ingram was about noon of a hot, late August Sunday. Mendoza was just up—he hadn't got home until 7 A.M.—and was still unshaven, pottering around feeding the cats and waiting for the coffee maker to signal that its job was done, when the doorbell rang.

El Señor, ever curious, accompanied him to the front door.

"Hello, Lieutenant," said Ingram. He looked fine, his old distinguished senatorial self; he was beautifully dressed in a light gray suit, discreet tie. "I just dropped by to thank you again and say good-bye."

"Come in, won't you? You're going away?"

"Oh no, thanks, I've just got a minute, I won't disturb you. Well, there was a little hassle, you probably saw something in the papers, about the will—after the trial. Mrs. Barron and Hugh tried to contest it, but it's just settled now that it's absolutely tight, see. It's still in probate, will be for some time, but I've been able to get an advance on it, which came in very handy. So Dan and I are taking off for Florida."

"Base ingratitude to California," smiled Mendoza.

Ingram laughed. "Oh, well, you see, we always said if we could—you know—retire and settle down, we'd go there. It's a little place called Stuart, on the east coast. Nice town. And it was there—well, Molly's buried there, you see. We're going to buy a little place right on the coast."

"And retire and settle down."

"That's right." Ingram looked interestedly at El Señor, who had taken off from the hall table to land on Mendoza's shoulder and was returning the stare. "Nice cat. Well, I just thought I'd stop by and thank you again. Damned hard to find the right words. If it hadn't been for you—— I hope I didn't interrupt you or—— Are you feeling O.K.? You look——"

"Fine," said Mendoza, yawning. "I just got up— after four hours' sleep. Just about to get dressed and go back to the hospital to see my wife."

"Oh," said Ingram concernedly, "I hope nothing serious?"

"Well, it depends if you'd call twins serious. Just as she kept threatening me. First thing she said when she came to—'I told you so.' At least, praise heaven for small mercies, they haven't got red hair. . . . One of each."

277

"Well, congratulations!" said Ingram, laughing. "That sounds kind of like fun—raising twins."

Mendoza grinned at him. "Have a look around down there for a nice young divorcée—you never can tell what'll happen!"

"No, thank you, brother!" said Ingram emphatically, and laughed again. "A second marriage was dangerous enough for me! Well, thanks again, and so long." He offered his hand.

Mendoza waited until he was ten steps away, and then said, "Oh, Ingram!" Ingram turned inquiringly. "When you said 'retire,' that's what you meant, I hope. After all, you've got plenty of money now. You won't have to—mmh—keep up the practice at overhand stacks and two-handed shifts."

Ingram's mouth twitched, and then suddenly he gave Mendoza his delightfully charming, shy smile. "Well, you know yourself, Lieutenant," he said apologetically, "habits can be awful hard to break. . . ."

M

Shannon, D.

64- 066484

Double bluff.